POSTLUDE

EVE NOT ADAM

Tego Arcana Dei Series

Andrew Man

Book V1

POSTLUDE EVE NOT ADAM

Copyright © 2022 by Andrew Man

Dedicated to those who have experienced a
"Close Encounter of the Third Kind"

In the Tego Arcana Dei Series
The complete trilogy
The Man who Played with Time

Book 5
EVE NOT ADAM

Contents

PROLOGUE

The noise in the observation chamber was becoming unbearable as the huge screens of the two members of the four eyes saw the problem emerging before their eyes.

"We need a precise confirmation of that incoming object entering our airspace over the island," demanded the director.

"Coming online now. Target is acquired and falling fast. Re-entry now expected on the northern coastline, most likely close to shore."

"We now see four other craft coming into view from the south, moving at high speed."

"US fighter planes on the runway waiting instructions, do you want us to launch?"

"No, do not take any further action. We now see a strong magnetic field interfering with our communications."

"Our satellite has lost contact with the object, presumed lost and has crashed into the sea."

"The Governor has been advised of possible land attack and ordered all islanders indoors until further notice."

"Our military is recommending a joint US/UK mission for recon and evaluation of latest situation on the ground."

"POTUS and British PM have been notified and concur with such action," the director replied.

"All communication with Governor has been lost and local phone network has gone down. Until further notice we advise extreme caution. Local airport is closed and no further sailings to island will be allowed."

"Thank you everyone, we are closing down this video link until our satellite is back in position."

"We will remain available if needed," replied the director, as he turned to his number two with a sigh.

"What the hell just happened there? Get onto the navy and find out where's the nearest ship."

"Already done, sir. HMS Medway and her task force are on station near Bermuda, about a thousand miles away, so will take a couple of days sailing to reach Montserrat."

"All right, can you talk to the admiral and ask him if they could reposition his task force close to Montserrat, as a matter of importance. Don't tell him anything about what you may have seen in here. Tell him we think that volcano is going to erupt again, and, er, radio silence."

"Right, understood."

So, what did you make of the other craft we saw from the satellite?"

"Definitely some kind of extra-terrestrial craft. They looked similar to what the US pilots call 'tik- tacs' if I remember correctly."

"Yes, that's what I thought. What I don't like is the interference with the electromagnetic emissions on the island. It's going to take another day to position our satellite over the Caribbean, and in the meantime, we have to wait and see what this joint expeditionary team make of the situation."

****

Three days later, events on the island were being considered a humanitarian disaster, as hundreds of survivors were being helped onto the beach. A complete media blackout was in force in both the US and UK but the airport was open again to US military aircraft, and satellite observation was being done around the clock.

Just as life on the island was returning to normal, the R.N ship arrived on the scene and the UK exploratory team were being sent back home for debriefing, so no one expected anything new. It was only when a house close to the beach belonging to a British expat was destroyed that the intelligence services became involved and started to ask more questions.

As a virus pandemic was spreading fast across the globe, all those who had been involved in the small expedition to the island became suspect. One such person was a Commando by the name of Justin Benbow, who the authorities feared might be infected. In fact, the real purpose for his arrest was to establish what had occurred on the island.

Even more surprising was that most of the other persons involved with the mission had disappeared or were now no longer in the UK, but helping the US military with their enquires.

PART ONE
JULY 2021

1 - TIDMOUTH

It was late evening in the small seaside town of Tidmouth, where Justin, a thirty-three-year-old Marine Lance Corporal, had rented a small attic flat high above the rooftops of the town, with windows facing the sea. He was just opening a bottle of beer after his evening run along the esplanade when he first saw lights out in the bay, hovering over the sea. He could see four bright lights in a triangular-shaped formation lingering in the evening sky above the bay in front of him.

Taking out his mobile phone he managed to snap a quick image before the object moved off to the east and disappeared from view. He had heard about UFO sightings many times, but knew he wasn't losing his marbles just yet. He also wasn't going to report this incident, but was sure someone else would have photographed the lights and would sell the pictures to a tabloid newspaper. Still, after his recent experience after his return from an island in the West Indies, he was being very careful about saying anything to the press at all. Sitting down on his sofa bed he tried to remember the details of his Green Island caper that had gone so wrong.

That all happened back in February 2020, before the pandemic had found its way into the UK. His mood was not friendly, either towards himself or the world at large. Being suspended from active service, albeit on full pay, was not something he was proud of after his last mission that had come to a close some months ago.

After his arrest at Janet's house, close to Windsor outside London, he had been taken by a military car down to a little-known Royal Marine base in Lyme Regis. His identity was logged in at a guard gate and he was taken to a fading accommodation block. There he was met by a sergeant and taken to a single room, with a single bed and wash basin, obviously used more for officers than the lower ranks. On the bed was a pair of uniform trousers and a khaki shirt. Under the bed he saw a pair of black regulation shoes and socks.

"Right, Lance Corporal, you'd better get a good night's rest in here because we'll start the interrogation tomorrow," he said, leaving and locking the door behind him.

Justin was flabbergasted at his treatment, but realised his actions on his last mission must have upset someone, somewhere very high up in the Service. Next morning the sergeant came and took him to an interrogation room in the basement of the accommodation block. There was a large table and two chairs facing each other. On the table was a glass and a bottle of water and the underwater camera he had used on the island. Across the room on the floor was the green rucksack he had stolen from the airport.

After a short delay a young man entered the room, a civilian dressed in a dark suit and a tie, who held in his hand a clipboard, some papers and a pen.

"Hello, my name is Giles Proctor, working for one of the UK's agencies. Thank you for joining us today, Justin. I know it was a long night driving down here, but we need to hear your side of your mission to that island, if you can write a report on this official service paper."

Justin nodded in agreement and reached for a glass of water.

"Take your time, but make sure you list all the people you met on this mission and the dates, if you can remember them. Oh, and one more thing, you need to sign the Official Secrets agreement, here and here, just to keep our records up to date," he said.

Justin smiled, and reaching for the pen, signed in the places indicated with a red sticker.

"Thank you. I will leave you to complete your report. Please seal it in the envelope when you finish and hand it to the sergeant, who will be waiting outside," he advised, then standing up he left the room.

Oh my god, Justin thought. *They really don't want any of this story to be leaked to the press, or anyone else in the service for that matter.*

Now that he had been left on his own to write the report, he glanced at the rucksack lying on the floor that almost certainly contained his personal clothes and belongings. Whether it also contained a torn pair of lady's underwear he couldn't recall, but he remembered she had taken her personal backpack back to the naval frigate. He also remembered taking his on the boat trip back to Antigua.

Anyway, they would have checked the contents by now, so no point in denying that a female RN officer was on the team to Montserrat Island, together with a US army sergeant and a small man – some thought he was a member of the CIA.

How he was going to explain the presence of James Pollack, who he had seen on the island, was going to be more of a problem. He picked up the pen and started to complete the Mission briefing report, keeping the details as brief as possible.

MISSION BRIEFING REPORT

SITUATION

- Loss of communications on a Caribbean Island.
- One way force field preventing communications.

MISSION/EXECUTION

- Joint mission team with US special forces and RN.
- Hire of private boat in St Johns, Antigua.
- No ferry connections or flights to island.
- Remove force field with weather balloon.
- US special forces to secure airport while UK team launch balloon.

COMMUNICATIONS

- Satellite images saw no traffic on the island.
- Head of SIG to report to Commander in Chief in UK.
- Weather balloon used to reopen communications.

SERVICE/SUPPORT

- Two US forces men plus two UK forces teams - one Royal Marine and one RN officer.
- Covert private transport with scuba diving equipment.

RISKS – CONCERNS

- Classified.

COLLABORATE

- The role of the Marine was to ensure a landing and inflate the balloon.

- We may have been dealing with something extra-terrestrial?
- Main concerns were for the island population.

SIGNATURE

-         ----------------------

Justin signed the form, then folded it and sealed it in the envelope as instructed, before knocking on the door to hand the report to the sergeant standing outside. Knowing he must have been observed the whole time he was in the room, he asked if he could be provided with some refreshments and coffee.

"Coming right up," was the reply and a short while later the sergeant returned with a tray of coffee and some English cake. Following in his footsteps was the young man in a suit with a clipboard and a copy of his report.

"Hello, that was quick. Now, about this affair on Montserrat, let's get down to the details," he announced.

Justin thought, *MI5*, and ignoring the introduction he poured his coffee, waiting for the sergeant to leave the room. Then the man produced a small tape recorder and signalling to him, turned it on.

"This recording is made by Lance Corporal Justin Benbow at R.M station in Lyme Regis in July 2020.

"Justin, now we have your Mission Brief Report, can you elaborate a little on the names and rank of the service personnel involved?"

"Not really, I only know the US army sergeant was called Sam, may have been a Navy seal. I have no idea about the second American. He may have been a scientist or CIA, you need to check with the US army or their intelligence services," he replied.

"Right, and don't worry, we know all about the RN officer, Lieutenant Elizabeth K, if we can use that title for this interview."

"Yes, I had arrived a day before her with the US personnel, and at their suggestion had rented a scuba diving boat to sail over to the island of Monserrat. There were no public ferry services and the airport was closed, so it appeared the safest way for such a covert operation at the time."

"And you picked up Elizabeth K at V.C Bird International airport on Antigua on 20th February 2020, didn't you?"

"Yes, that was done to save time and avoid any difficult questions at immigration concerning the reason for her visit."

"But the islanders must have already known there were communication difficulties with Montserrat, without telephones or ferries?"

"Really, I don't know. I just took her straight to the docks and we sailed almost immediately. No one questioned us or filmed us leaving, as far as I'm aware."

"I see, and how did this small team of just four persons co-operate on such a small boat? Did the naval officer try to pull rank over the US forces, or you just got on with the mission in hand."

"We were all professionals with military training, so we got on with the job. At that time, we didn't really know what we were up against and to be honest were a bit scared of what we would find on this island. It was only later on, when we found the cylinder underwater, that we realised we were way out of our depth in understanding what had happened."

"Why did you mark the 'Risks and Concerns' on the briefing form as classified. Because you don't trust UK security?"

"Not entirely, but because we still don't understand what happened on that island…you weren't there on the beach with all the dead fish and no birds, it was just scary," Justin blurted.

"When you say we, did you discuss this with Elizabeth K or any other of the team?"

"Yes, of course I discussed this with the RN officer, and there was another man we met who did some weird things with the underwater cylinder and saved a lot of the islanders."

"So, was this a man called James?"

"Yes, he was apparently known to Elizabeth, from her distant past."

"Thank you, Justin, you have confirmed a lot more than you wrote in the mission brief. Now, did Elizabeth or James introduce you to any other people on the island?" he asked.

"Yes, she took me up to a house on the Old Bluff that was owned by a local British expat called Janet Rumford, where we stayed the night."

"And did you sleep together, because Elizabeth is quite an attractive woman isn't she," he suggested.

"No, we didn't sleep together, because we had an argument about how the virus came to our planet, and a few other things."

"I see, and what happened before you left?"

"Ah! Yes, the US army visited the house and Elizabeth gave her ID as Janet Rumford who owned the house, much to my relief."

"And what did you do, Justin?"

"Well... I went downstairs and found the British passport of James Pollack and said it was mine."

"Really, so you both faked your identity to an official and they didn't notice, such a basic passport check?"

"No, he said they only wanted the passport numbers, that's all."

"So, they weren't really doing a check, were they, Justin."

"No, I suppose not, but Elizabeth said she was Special Forces and always carried other people's passports with her."

"Have you been in contact with Elizabeth since you came back to the UK? Do you know where she is right now?"

"No, I haven't and I don't want to see her again."

"And have you been in contact with James since you came back to the UK?"

"Yes, of course, you know he was at the house in Windsor, where I was stopped, arrested and brought down here."

"Ah yes! And do you know where Mr. James Pollack is now?"

"No, I don't. I hardly ever met the man except once in a scuba diving suit and have no idea where he might be."

"Very well. Thank you, Justin, you have been most helpful with our enquiries. However, you realise your report and the recording of this interview will have to be reviewed by your Commanding Officer in the Royal Marines for a decision. If you can wait a bit longer, he would like to meet you."

Justin sat in the room for another half an hour, eating the cake and drinking several cups of coffee, when the door opened and the sergeant ushered in a young Captain of the Royal Marines.

"Justin, great to meet with you," he announced as Justin rose to his feet and saluted.

"At ease, commando, and sit down. I've read your report and listened to the tape and in the circumstances, we think you behaved in an exemplary fashion serving Queen and country. Is there anything you would like to say?"

"Well, sir, I really need to go to the toilet?"

"Sergeant, escort the man to the loo right away."

"Yes, sir, this way, Lance Corporal," and he led Justin out of the room. Whilst he was waiting, the captain picked up the backpack on the floor and emptied the contents onto the table. It revealed an assortment of men's beach clothing, beach footwear and a torn pair of knickers, just as Justin returned to the room.

"Ah! Justin, I see you had at least had some female company on the beach and were able to relax." Laughing, he stuffed the contents back into the bag and beamed his appreciation.

Postlude

"Now sit down and listen, my man. I see you have signed the official secrets document, so none of this goes any further, do you understand, or you will end up in jail. In recognition of your service, I want you to take a few weeks leave on full pay. Go for a long walk along the Jurassic Devon coast and keep in touch with us on your mobile phone. There will be a formal inquiry, where in the circumstances, we would not want you to appear."

Justin was dumfounded at the news and finally smiled back.

"Sergeant, take this man with his personal belongings to any destination on the coast he needs, and we both wish you all the best for the future," he said, and Justin stood up to shake his hand.

When he got outside with his belongings, he found an Uber waiting outside the guard room and the driver asked him the destination.

"I think I want to go to Sidmouth on the Devon coast for a holiday," he told the driver and the car left, driving west along the coast.

2 – JANET

When the young Captain returned to his office, he found Giles sitting in front of his desk with a cup of coffee.

"So, you let him go, just like that?"

"No, he's on a very short leash. I made it clear that we had the evidence that he had an affair with a female naval officer on the mission. He knows that's a court martial offence, end of career etc.," the captain replied.

"Very well, so can I ask you a few questions. We need your military advice on these satellite images we received from that island," he said pulling a large brown envelope from a briefcase. "The first here shows the crater where the expat Janet Romford had built a house up on the Old Bluff; it's above Lime Kiln beach. What we don't know is if this crater was made by an explosion from above the house. If you look below there's just a pool of water."

"Let me take a close look," replied the captain, taking his seat at the desk. "Hm… no, the crater is definitely not made by a missile or a shell from above, if you look closely no earth has been thrown up around the crater. Anything else?" he asked.

"We know that Elizabeth K ordered a drone strike on the house, but that was aborted because by the time the drone reached the house, it had already been destroyed."

"Do you know where this officer is now?"

"Oh yes, she's a Captain in the US army based in Dallas. But with this new US president, there's no way we can get more cooperation from the Yanks, at present," Giles explained.

"And the owner of the house, do you know where she is?"

"Mrs Janet Romford was ordered to return to the States with her private jet provided, we think, by NASA. She has not been heard of since. We think it's a case of her helping with their enquiries."

"Anything else I can help you with?" he asked.

"There's one more image we can't understand. But this is strictly confidential, even for the military, you understand," Giles said as he placed a second photo on the desk. It was a close-up of the edge of a crater, and a naked girl covered in mud was being helped out of the rim of the crater by two local black women holding a blanket.

"What! That's impossible for anyone to have survived such a huge explosion and still able to walk, let alone climb out."

"We know that, and the local police are making enquiries on the island, but the image is not good enough to identify the people."

"So, this would collaborate Justin's report? He was most concerned, or frightened even, that we were dealing with something extra-terrestrial, people if you remember. So where is this person now, and the house? How does a few thousand tonnes of concrete just disappear like that," the captain exclaimed. "Come on, man, you must have found more evidence?"

"We did. We had a forensic team comb the site last week. But there was no debris at all, the gravel of the driveway went right up to the edge of the crater, hardly a stone disturbed. It was as if the house had de-materialised. But what they found was this tin box that had been stamped into the ground by a size 12 US army boot, with a lot more boot prints around." Giles produced a photo of a small metal box that had been crushed flat.

"Is there anything more I should know?"

"Yes, but that's strictly above your pay grade. Still, for a drop of scotch, I might be able to tell you more," Giles replied.

The captain rose, and opening a cupboard beside his desk came back with two glasses and the bottle of whiskey. They now sat facing each other, as he poured them both a generous amount.

"In fact, it is a military matter, because scattered around the tin box they found a number of used cases from US military small arms," Giles explained.

"So, there must have been some sort of fire fight outside the house, before it disappeared?"

"Yes, that's what we think, but what's of more interest was the contents of the tin. It had contained some liquid, so forensics were very careful in case it was something toxic. They sent it over on the next military flight back to the UK, where it's under investigation at Portland Down.

"Meanwhile, we are still waiting to receive the original plans of the house, to see how it fits onto the crater that's left behind. From the layout of the driveway, we think that someone walked out of the entrance into a squad of trigger-happy US marines and was shot at."

"James sounds like the most likely person?"

"Yes, but we never found a body and he`s not been seen since."

"The one person who knows about the layout of the house is Justin, if you need to contact him again?"

"Good point, but I don´t want him to get involved in the details just yet," Giles replied. "I'll let you know if anything comes up in the next couple of weeks, providing you know where he's staying," Giles added, returning the photos to his briefcase.

The captain stood up, and shaking hands, thanked Giles for his assistance and led him out of the building and back to the gate-house where a car was waiting.

What a strange story, the captain thought, *and all this happened on a Caribbean island, on a British Overseas territory*, and he slowly walked back to his office, where he knew, he would have to make a report to his senior officer, with at least some of the details they had discussed.

3 - KIYA

Meanwhile back on Montserrat in 2020, Kiya had been thrown into the pool at Janet's house where the water was reviving her. She heard an aggressive woman officer shouting at James to go outside, after which there was the sound of gunfire. Lying face down in the water appeared to be the best solution to the chaos outside, as she heard another voice.

"We couldn't kill him, ma'am, he just disappeared," shouted one of the soldiers, and she smiled to herself in the knowledge that her mentor James had survived.

As soon as the people left the house, Kiya knew that James would take more evasive action and the house was going to be moved. When the water in the pool started to go down, she took a deep breath and swam down to the bottom of the pool and waited. In one huge explosion, she was left sitting in a pool of mud and the house was gone.

Looking up she saw two smiling faces waving at her sitting in the mud.

"Come on, my dear, you have to climb up out of there," they shouted down to her and she could see it was going to be quite difficult. Without saying a word, she picked up her naked body and started to climb out of the crater. The old lady dropped the end of a blanket down for her to hold onto, and they helped pull her up the last few feet. When she reached the rim of the crater four hands pulled her onto dry land at the top.

"Hello, my name's Lucy, and this is my grandma. We came to find James and heard shooting. Is he dead?"

"What a dreadful experience you had, my dear," said the grandma.

Kiya looked at them and collapsed on the ground, shivering from her painful climb. They wrapped the blanket around her naked body and helped her walk down the side of the hill back towards the road. When they reached the car, they laid Kiya on the back seat and waited for her to talk.

"James is not dead, he just moved to another dimension," she said, with tears running down her cheeks.

"Yes well, we've had a lot of odd things happening around here. Let's get you home to a nice bath and we'll find you some clothes to wear, isn't that right, Lucy. She always sees a lot more than me and things have been most strange lately."

"Your name is Kiya, isn't it, and you arrived here on that cylinder in the sea, didn't you," Lucy asked.

"Yes, so you can read my mind?"

"Something about another dimension on a boat or a submarine, but how did you know James," she asked.

"You are right, there was someone on the boat called Nathalie, who taught me about the matrix and the golden ratio. I think she sent me back with something important for James," Kiya replied, as the grandma started the engine and they drove back down the Old Bluff Road back to their house near Woodlands.

After Kiya had a bath to clean up, she put on a dressing gown and joined the family in the front room.

"Here you are, my dear, a nice cup of tea to warm you up," said the grandma, sitting back in her chair in the kitchen of the cottage.

"So, you're a British family, living where exactly?"

"Montserrat," replied Lucy sounding a bit bewildered. "It's a tropical island in the Caribbean. Well, it's still a British Overseas

Territory, so we speak English and have picked up many of their customs and habits. We also have a volcano, isn't it, Gran?"

"Twenty years ago, we had awful eruptions on the island and the south is still covered in dust and ash, dreadful times, but we survived. And where exactly are you from my dear?" she asked.

"Yes well… it's a bit difficult to explain. Originally, I was from a city called Armana. It was similar to yours in Egypt, but it was far away in another dimension," Kiya replied to the others who looked at her, a bit confused.

"I see, that's most interesting," Lucy replied. "And did you have a queen," she asked, pointing to the picture on the wall.

"Oh yes, ours was called Queen Susana. In fact, she may have come from this planet," Kiya replied.

Lucy tried to cover up her suspicions from her grandma. "Still, you must be pleased to find it's nice and warm here in the tropics," she said, wanting to change the subject. "Come on, Kiya, let's go and find you some clothes to wear and maybe you would like to sleep with me as there are only two bedrooms."

"Yes, I would like that very much and I would like to go and see this volcano tomorrow," Kiya replied as she got up to leave the room.

"I'm afraid no one is allowed to visit that part of the island; it's called the Exclusion Zone."

"Oh, I see, maybe we can go somewhere else then. Like down on the beach?" Kiya replied.

4 - LATER

The next day, having found shorts and a tee-shirt for Kiya, the two girls set off on bikes to explore the coast down by the sea. Kiya, never having ridden a bicycle before, found the going difficult as they had to pedal up the hill along Woodlands Road. After that Kiya was going at breakneck speed down Salem Road towards the National gardens, where she left the road and went into a ditch.

"I'm never going on that machine again," she exclaimed as Lucy went to help her put the bike back on the road. Both girls stood back as a big truck thundered down the road carrying concrete posts, with a gang of local men who all waved and laughed at them.

"You know, that's the second truck we've seen today going down to the beach, and the first was full of army men which is strange," Lucy remarked. "All right, let's leave our bikes at the Botanical gardens as I know a perfect walk for you. It's a back way down to the Kiln beach and we shouldn't be seen by anyone, if that's okay with you."

"Yes, I don't mind walking at all. Is it very far?" replied Kiya.

"No, it shouldn't take more than half an hour and you can tell me about your time travelling experiences on that cylinder thing," Lucy said.

"Okay, but I don't remember very much at all. I know Nathalie thought it was very important as she wanted to give something to James. But exactly what, I don't know. All I remember was seeing James at that house. I think there was a kind of temple in front of the pool, but on hearing an argument and gunfire I swam down to the bottom of the water and waited. The next moment I was sitting in mud and the house had disappeared. You know, places with volcanoes are very powerful and can interfere with reality."

"So, you think that James never died, but moved on with the house?"

"Yes, I'm certain, there was a temple beside the pool like we had in the past in Armana. Our priests could levitate people and even move huge blocks of stone as if by magic. Have you ever seen that done here on this island?"

"Oh yes, we've seen all kinds of things here, fields of force and people flying through the air, that all started when that cylinder thing arrived on Kiln beach," Lucy explained.

"Yes, that's why we have to get onto the beach and see if it's still there," Kiya replied.

"So, here we are on Lime Kiln Beach Road, but keep to the side as we don't want to be seen," Lucy said as they could see the trucks parked ahead, with a lot of construction noise. "Come on, this way, Kiya. We need to cross the road and get down onto the beach, where there's cover from some rocks," she explained. Taking her hand, they ran across the road and disappeared down another path.

"It looks like they've started work on the north end of the beach so we should be able to see the cylinder from here."

"Oh my goodness, Lucy. The cylinder had been pulled back up the beach by a system of pulleys with soldiers doing the work."

"Yes, they look like Royal Engineers with their white faces and uniforms, and must have come here from England. But what are those locals doing working on the far end of the beach," Lucy asked.

"I think they're starting to build a fence, so it looks as if the whole beach will be shut off in the next few days," Kiya replied.

"Let's stay here behind these rocks and wait for the soldiers to take a break. It's nearly midday so can't be long," Lucy said, looking at her watch. While they waited Kiya looked at the seaweed growing in the rockpools with interest, until Lucy whispered to her.

"I think they're leaving, probably going to lunch at the Lodge close by and we can check out the cylinder, if you still want to go, Kiya?"

"Yes of course, but it's going to be scary for you, so let's go together."

With the soldiers gone, they walked some 500 yards across the empty sand and looked up at a rusting cylinder, towering above them.

"What do you think, Kiya, this thing is enormous, much bigger than I thought, can you see a way to get inside," Lucy said, but Kiya was already digging away in the sand with her hands.

"Can you give me some help here? I think there's a way in below here where I can crawl inside," she said.

"All right, but you will have to be quick because when the tide comes back in you will be trapped."

"Don't worry, I know what this thing is now, as we often saw them on our planet," Kiya said, panting hard from digging the hole.

"So Kiya, please tell me what it is."

"I don't know what you call this machine, but it looks to me like a 'tic-tac.' It's a spaceship that can move people and fly through space, but I never saw one that had crashed before," Kiya replied.

"But why would it have crashed here on Montserrat?"

"I told you before, it may have been done by that volcano of yours. It must have interfered with their magnetic fields, but I need to get inside to see what really happened. You stay here and watch in case the water comes back, as I think I can squeeze through this entrance and get onboard."

"All right, but if you're not back by the time the soldiers return, I'm going to tell them someone may be trapped inside."

"That's a deal, now wish me luck," Kiya said as she wriggled her way inside, leaving Lucy alone on the deserted beach.

'We really should have brought mobile phones,' she thought, looking at the sea, and as the tide turned the water started to come towards the cylinder.

Half an hour later, Lucy was in a panic as none of the soldiers had returned from lunch and the water was getting closer. Suddenly, the whole cylinder started to glow and the entrance was closed shut.

"Oh my God, this thing is moving," Lucy shouted, thrown into the shallow water of the incoming tide as the cylinder kept moving up the beach. It stopped above the high tide mark as Lucy followed it up the beach and a small door opened close to the sand.

"Hello, Lucy, did you see that! I managed to move this thing to somewhere safe, without all those silly men running around with wires and pulleys," Kiya announced.

"Kiya, that was amazing. But I think it's time we disappeared before the soldiers arrive and we get asked a lot of questions," Lucy replied.

Kiya jumped down onto the sand, and holding hands they ran up into the trees above the beach, where Kiya stopped.

"I did get some training from my first husband in Armana who taught me how to control these things, if ever needed."

"Oh, look, the soldiers have returned from a long lunch only to find their cylinder has moved further up the beach. That's really funny isn't it," Lucy replied. "Wait, Kiya, you left that small door open, that's not good."

"Actually, I stole the control panel so let's close it before anyone decides they might get inside," Kiya said, and pushing a button the door closed. In an instant, the sergeant of the engineers ordered his men to search for the people who might be controlling the cylinder.

"Come on, Kiya, we should leave quickly on the back roads before they set up a road block," Lucy warned as they ran up Lime Kiln Road towards Hibiscus Drive and they talked again.

"Did you find out any more about why this cylinder might have crashed on our island?" Lucy asked.

"Sorry, no, it was very dark inside and it took me a while to find the room that had the controls. Remember, there are no windows so until I put the power on there wasn't much to see at all."

"But you must have had an idea of where you were going, so tell me what these things were used for on your planet?"

"Our planet was most unstable, with a big moon that came back every ten thousand years, so our kings and queens needed help to move a lot of people to safe places, often on other planets. Doesn't your queen here see that need at all?"

"No, it's not quite the same here. It's our governments that make such decisions and until recently they refused to allow us to believe in extra-terrestrial visitors. They said they aren't real, can you believe."

"That's most strange, because we met some of your people on the boat who helped us escape. It was as big as the cylinder thing we found on the beach, so someone must believe it's real."

"That's interesting, you have to tell me more of your past experiences on that boat, you haven't said anything."

"That was after our escape from Armana, before it was flooded. What I don't understand is your people's requirement for uniforms. We had to sew our uniforms to work and it was quite a new experience for me."

"So, you were working with these people from our planet at that time?"

"Yes. You know the good thing with this control panel I stole is that we can get inside again and perhaps fly away to look for James," Kiya replied.

"But we don't even know which dimension James is in now."

"Yes, and we don't know how to get back to the planet where that boat is now. The captain was my lover and now I've lost him forever," Kiya said, with tears in her eyes.

"I'm so sorry, but for us women that's often how men come and go in our lives. Look, we are nearly at Mary's clothing shop, let's go inside and buy you some proper clothes that fit you."

"Thanks, that's most kind. If we get stopped by the army patrols, we're just two girls who have been out buying clothes," she said smiling.

"And after that we pick up our bikes at the garden place and cycle home," Lucy replied.

"Right, just in time for a cup of your English tea with Grandma. I'm really starting to like your way of life," Kiya replied.

PART TWO
NOVEMBER 2030

5 - ISLAND

James finally saw daylight again as he woke up in a place he had never seen before. It was not just the light that was uncomfortable but he was hot. Turning his head to look around he could see only a concrete room with sunlight streaming onto his face from outside. He was wearing his usual travel pants, a shirt, and trainers on his feet.

He tried to remember what he had been doing before he woke but his memory was a blank. Something seemed familiar about the place, with a white wall of limestone on one side of the room, and dark concrete on the rest with only the sound of the wind blowing outside. Slowly, very slowly he raised his body and tried to stand up, eventually able to reach a sitting position to look outside. There was a lot of sand and a few tufts of grass or some green plants that looked like more of a desert. Turning back, he went into the concrete house to see what he could find there. Across the room was a flight of stairs leading to darkness below and he went no further.

My god, what is this place and where am I in reality? Perhaps I died and have now come back in a dream, James thought as he turned to look at the white stone on the wall that was pulling him towards it. Feeling the smooth stone, his fingers began to descend into the stone as he remembered where he was at last. This was the house on the island of Monserrat, where he had been staying with Janet and her family. As images flooded back into his memory, he saw the dangers of a global pandemic after a virus arrived on the planet, but nothing more. That must have been some time ago, as he remembered nothing since.

He withdrew his hand and sat on the sandy floor to start to think. So, if this was Janet's house in a different time and space, where was he in time today? His mind moved back to all the problems at that time as he walked across the house to the open entrance to see what was outside.

Standing at the doorway, he could see nothing but sand and grasses all pushed down in the hot wind. "This is definitely not a Caribbean island," he said. *So, let's see where we are on this planet,* he thought as he started to walk towards the setting sun.

He set off walking west across the flat sand and small plants that made him realise he was not in a desert, but somewhere much further north in temperate climates. After half an hour he reached a deep gulley in the sand where everything had been removed as if by a great force of water. Whatever had happened here had been sudden and violent.

He had an impulse to follow the path of destruction and see where it led. Climbing down into the gulley he followed the path north towards where he had no idea, until it opened up to a view of the sea and he could see the coastline of the island.

"That explains a lot," he said, looking at the scene below, an entrance to a small port. It looked to be demolished by some force that he could only assume was a huge tsunami wave of some kind that had rolled over the island, destroying all in its path. Looking across the water he could make out some tall buildings that still appeared intact and knew that was the best way to go. When he walked down to the water, he only found twisted metal from an old landing stage, sticking up out of the water. What he really needed was a boat to travel across to the mainland in front of him, but everything appeared to have been washed away.

He retraced his footsteps onto higher land, looking for something that might be useful to float in the water. It was then that he heard a dog barking in the distance and looked to see where it was coming from. Walking back up the hill towards what was left of the village, he saw the dog was trapped by a fallen block of wood and ran forward to release it. Once done, the dog stopped to look at him and then ran off to find his old home. Underneath the rubble was something that looked like a plastic paddle board and seeing a metal rod, he placed it under the board to lever it free. The paddle board was damaged in places with the end missing, but might just keep him afloat. He knew he had to cross what looked like a huge lagoon of water, perhaps three miles across, back to the mainland.

Carrying the paddle board back to the water's edge, he found a short piece of wood that could be used to paddle. Turning back for one last look at the damaged shoreline, he launched the board on the water to check it would take his weight. Then sitting astride the board, he started to paddle, just as the sun was going down to the west of the island. He knew it was going to be a long night of cold on the water, but there appeared no other way to reach the mainland and find other people alive. Setting up a steady rhythm of paddling, the island was soon far behind him as the sun set in a ball of yellow and a toe-nail moon appeared above him in the clear night air. He could see gulls and other birds flying above the water in the fading light, but no other boats came into view, only wood and other debris floating on the surface of the sea.

About halfway across he noticed that the board was sinking lower in the water and realised that he wasn't going to make it to the shore without swimming. From his position sitting up, he could make out a red light flashing on the shore that was most likely coming from a jetty or harbor light that he would have to swim towards. There were no other lights shining in the darkness, so whatever hit the island must have continued inland to damage the coast. Finally launching himself off the board he started to swim in the cold water.

He had done long distance swimming as a boy, gaining his half mile certificate in a pool, but this was different, swimming in the open sea. As his arms circled into the breast stroke his mind wandered as he drifted into a new feeling of freedom and a shift in perception that was awe, keeping his eyes fixed on the red light ahead of him. As his feeling of panic receded, he felt an unusual concept of time slowing down as his legs pushed him slowly towards the shore. In front of him was a mountain of debris that must have washed back into the sea and he was on the point of giving up when a school of dolphins appeared around him, pushing the debris out of his way.

It was at that point he realised he was not alone on his swim and he knew he would make the final distance to the red light or whatever was waiting for him on the shore. It was no surprise when after another hour he found himself at the bottom of stone steps leading up to the quay. Pulling his tired body out of the water, he sat on the lower step feeling cold and very wet but in awe of what he had done, when a voice called out to him from above.

"Hello James, you're late, almost ten years late," a familiar voice said from above. He knew it was Ben, Janet's oldest son.

"Really? Sorry, I don't remember much, except I think I left Janet's house on that island across there," James replied laughing, "…and swam most of the way back here. So, if I'm late, what year is it now?"

"You really don't know what's happened to our planet… well the year is 2030, or November 2030 to be precise," Ben explained and went down to help James climb the steps to the damaged quay above.

"There was a pandemic on this planet, wasn't there," James asked.

"Yes, but that was years ago. They injected people with vaccines that infected everyone with a form of AIDS… so millions more have died. Here, take this blanket before you catch a cold."

"Okay, so how do we get out of this place? Everything looks derelict and swept away by the flood. Can we still get to an airport?"

"No, James, Faro airport was badly damaged and has been under water for months."

"Great, so how did you get here?" James asked.

"We got a note of your pending arrival and I flew down here in Janet's new hover plane."

"Which is where?" James asked.

"Just across there on the open space. It's a lot smaller than before but faster—you will see. Let me just recover the red light as the electricity is still not back on and most of the marina boats are up on the road."

"Where are all the people, there looks to be no one around."

"They will have been evacuated to higher ground, as more waves may come. Come on, James, we must leave as soon as possible."

"Do you know the location of Janet's house now?"

"Yes. of course, it's on an island called Culatra off the coast of the Algarve, but by the time I found out you had already gone swimming."

"Thanks, Ben, for coming to look for me, you may have saved my life."

"No, James, I think the dolphins already did that. Come on, follow me to our plane, we need to get you back to London," Ben replied.

6 – No 22 GROUP

James was standing beside the hover car on an open platform close to a damaged marina in Olhoa, Portugal. It looked more like a military jet until Ben hit the activate button and the flying object lit up.

"What the fuck, where did you get this thing, it looks alien," shouted James.

"It is partially alien, and has room for three persons in the back, James," he replied.

"I'm not sure I want to go anywhere with you. Do you know how to fly this thing?"

"Yes, I've had some preliminary training, but this is only the second flight I've done. The first was coming down here to find you."

"Okay, how do I get onboard?"

"Go under the tail, look for the footsteps in the hull and pull yourself up inside. I`ll open the rear door for you and climb onboard. Just put on a headphone set, so we can talk to each other."

James waited for the entry door to open and climbed up inside. There were two executive seats at the back and a small jump seat in front. Once onboard, the door closed automatically and he put on the headphone set as instructed.

"Wow, this looks really cool, all brand-new technology. Where did Janet find this machine?"

"Eight years ago, after you disappeared, Mum had fallen out with the US authorities and decided to go private for a replacement plane. She met up with a team of designers who wanted to build something from military patents that had been made available to the public. So, some of the design may be reverse engineered stuff. It's only a prototype, but very fast," he explained.

"Okay, so how's it work, Ben?"

"You may have noticed the plane has no air intakes, no blades or turbines, just a lot of power? So, we climb to about 300 feet off the ground with an anti-gravity device and I input the coordinates and we move to our destination."

"What's the speed, Mach 5 or something?"

"No James, it's instant as in time travel. As soon as I input the coordinates we arrive there. A bit like that medallion of yours and just as fast. Now, if you put on your seat belt, I'll start the procedure."

"We're going back to Janet's house in Windsor?"

"No James, London's flooded all the way past Windsor. We have to land at a higher elevation in High Wycombe. Janet has rented a small house for us to stay, while I continue the training for this plane."

"Would this place be a training centre for military-based aircraft?"

"Yes, James, it's called the No 22 Group in the UK."

"What if I don't want to go to a UK military base, Ben."

"That's not possible, as we're already there. You can't go outside the airfield as there may be looters roaming in the woods. We have just received a unit of marines to help with security at the base. Fortunately, Janet's house is inside the perimeter, so it's fairly safe."

"What will I do after arrival?"

"You will almost certainly have to quarantine for some days, and when that's done, we can meet at the house to plan our next move."

When James looked down, he could see the lights of the airfield below as the craft slowly touched down onto a raised landing pad.

He thought he was going to have to go with whatever Ben was planning, as a team of men dressed in white protective clothing and helmets started to spray the plane.

"What's happening now, are we being de-iced?" shouted James.

"No, that's a spray to remove any of the toxic chemicals after our flight through space, although it was only a small jump. When they finish, let me de-board first and explain who you are. After that, I will have to leave you in the hands of the medics," Ben replied.

"Thank you, Ben, that was a most impressive first trip," James said as he watched Janet's young son climb down from the plane and talk to a military arrival team, dressed in RAF uniforms and all wearing face masks.

The plane was then towed inside a small hanger, where steel doors were closed behind them. After a further wait, the plane's rear door was opened and James saw he was looking at a plastic tunnel, with an emergency slide down to the ground.

"Please leave the plane now by the slide, Mr Pollack, and walk along the tunnel to our medical reception area," a voice instructed him.

James did as he was told, and thought that someone was taking no chances with his arrival.

7 – AIR BASE

After ten days of tests, James was finally released from quarantine and contacted Ben to say he was free to come to Janet's house.

"Okay, that's great. I will pass by early this evening when I finish my training here and can pick you up," replied Ben.

James spent most of the afternoon getting to know the layout of the base and chatting to an attractive female orderly who had been helpful to him during his stay.

"It's impossible to leave the airfield after what's happened outside," she confided to him, as James looked for more answers.

"There are several rumours, but what's clear is that our planet must have been hit by a space rock that created tsunamis over most of the English coastal areas. Then, everything electrical stopped and we had several days of darkness before the sun returned, and it was very cold outside. Don't you remember that?"

"Not really, I was living underground at the time, near the Atlantic Ocean, but I saw the destruction in the region before I was rescued," James replied, not wanting to give too much away.

"You were lucky, because there are thousands of homeless people in London and a lot more who didn't survive when the Thames River valley flooded."

"Yes, I know that, but weren't the governments prepared for such an impact?"

"Wow, you have been out of the loop for some time. Who exactly are you and why were you rescued?"

"I'm sorry, but it's a long story, and you know…"

"That's okay, I know it's classified. That's all the people on the base ever tell us. If you ask me, there's a big cover-up going on with the military. Sorry, I shouldn't have said that," she said as she put her hands to her face and started crying.

"No, no don't get upset, I'm not anything to do with the military so I'm not going to report you. In fact, I'm a marine scientist," replied James trying to make up a cover story. "Yes, I was studying underwater earthquakes and they brought me back here to explain the data. I was living underground on an island, so I'm just as lost as you are."

"And your friend coming to pick you up later is living at that old house on the grounds of the airfield?"

"Yes, I think so, but I've never been there before."

"Why don't you ask him what's going on here, because I've got to know Ben quite well and there's a lot more, he can tell you."

"Thanks, will do, and what's your name again?" he asked, but she had already stood up and walked away down the corridor.

James had to wait another hour in the medical waiting room before Ben arrived with a man in Royal Marine uniform.

"Sorry I'm late, my training took longer than expected. Oh, this is my security detail today, who will be escorting us back to the house."

"No problem, I can't wait to get back to real life and find some comfortable clothes again," James replied, and followed Ben outside to the transport. The house was a long drive from the medical centre, set in a hollow at the end of one of the runways and surrounded by a high fence.

"Here we are, the humble home of one of the last Air Chief marshals who refused to allow it to be demolished. Bit out of the way, but that's how I like it after a day like today. Bring your kit inside and I can show you around."

"Ben, I don't have any kit, just the clothes you found me with and a jacket the medics gave me at the centre."

"Right, let me put the code and we can go inside," Ben replied, putting a finger to his lips and looking at James, so he knew their conversations would be monitored.

"It's a lot smaller inside than it looks outside, but they have kept most of the old wooden beams of the house," Ben explained as they walked into a comfortable lounge with sofa, arm chairs and last century furniture to match.

"Wow, this really is a home from home, you must be well appreciated here on the base."

"Would you like a beer and I'll show you around," Ben replied, and James followed him into a small kitchen, where Ben opened a fridge and handed him a cold beer.

"There are two bedrooms in the basement, with a bathroom. I've already taken the master room, so you can take the single room next door. Look, why don't we take our beer on the terrace and you can tell me your story," Ben said, opening a back door to a tiny terrace with two chairs and an old garden table.

"Sorry, James, but I'm sure the house is bugged, so better if we talk outside. Sometimes I wonder what I'm doing here, so it's great to see you again after all those times on Montserrat. Tell me, truthfully, what actually happened with the house and where did you go?"

"Ben, it remains a great mystery to me," James replied, taking a swig from his beer can.

"All I can tell you is that I've lost eight, no ten years of my life, not knowing where I've been. I think my return may be connected with this space rock impact you experienced recently. I spoke to one of the nurses at the medical centre, but she didn't know much either."

"Really, did you tell her where you're from?"

"No, of course not. I said I was a marine scientist living underground and had been rescued. She appeared to know you."

"Wow, you do get around. Yes, that's Michelle, we got to know each other recently, and try to be discreet, but she's cute."

"Come on, Ben, she's really attractive. So, you've hooked up with a good-looking girl, but she told me to ask you about a 'cover up' story going on here."

"Yes, but that's something Janet's working on in the States, so I'd rather she explained to you what we think. It's just an idea after what happened on that island."

"Okay, no problem at all. So, what's with all these military escorts and when did the Royal Marines get into security on a RAF base?"

"You have to understand, James, this country is in a military lock-down after so many died in London. We had a security problem and they sent some Marines to help us with security.

"They come and pick me up at 0800 hrs and bring me back. Remember, it's a bloody long walk to the end of the runway here."

"Sorry, I shouldn't have asked. Let's go inside and see if you can find me some warmer clothes that might fit," James said.

Once back inside James started to consider his position on the air force base and decided he needed to know more about the world outside, when Ben came back with a pile of clothes.

"Have a look through these winter things that I no longer wear, and I found you a spare toothbrush and a razor."

"Thanks, Ben. Would it be possible to come and join you with your training tomorrow? There's really nothing to do here."

"Yes, okay, we leave at eight sharp and I don't usually have any breakfast. See you in the morning. Good night," Ben said and went downstairs to his room.

8 - LATER

The next morning, Ben and James were picked up by an open army jeep and driven to the NAAFI at the main base, where they had coffee.

"Come on James, drink up. We have a meeting this morning with some big wigs of the Air Marshal. They all want to meet you."

"Anything in particular you can think of," James replied, as they stood up and made their way to the exit. Ben led the way to another imposing building with RAF and Union flags flying outside, with a sentry guarding the entrance, who Ben ignored.

"Hey, you. ID and papers first."

"Sorry, but I lost mine and he doesn't have any," Ben replied, until an officer from the military police came out with a check board.

"And you are?"

"Ben Rumford and James Pollack."

"Ah, yes, that appears to be in order, follow me," he said, and they followed the man along a corridor and down two flights of stairs to a basement. This time a Royal Marine with an automatic rifle stood guard, until the heavy door swung open and a Group Captain stood before them.

"Thank you, Captain. That'll be all."

"Sir," he replied with a salute, and Ben and James entered a large conference room full of both RAF service people and some civilians.

Some looked up on seeing the two arrive, but most were engrossed in a recording on a large screen of a strange, small plane making a vertical touchdown on a landing pad at night. James immediately

43

recognized the craft as the one he had flown in with Ben, back from Portugal.

"This, James, is going to be interesting," Ben whispered, as they were directed to a smaller room where two figures sat facing each other at a table; a man still wearing an overcoat, and a woman.

"I'll leave you to your discussion as it's a security matter," the captain said and left the room.

James looked carefully at the woman who appeared to be in her early forties. She had dark brown hair tinged with red and a wide mouth, bright with red lipstick, and didn't look up from a file on the desk.

The man was older, gaunt, with hair that was greasy and starting to grey. His complexion was grey and his shirt collar pinched his neck. He appeared tired and uninterested in their arrival.

"Hello, anyone here," Ben asked in an unfriendly tone, while James slid to the floor with his back against the wall.

"I think you're going to have to bring more chairs if you want us to talk," said James quietly.

"Oh! I'm sorry, I didn't see you come in, of course, more chairs," said the woman, getting to her feet and hammering on the door, demanding more chairs from the orderly outside.

"Yes, and can we have some more coffee," shouted Ben.

Meanwhile, James stood up and approached the man, offering his hand.

"James Pollack, haven't we met before? MI5 about ten years ago in Windsor, wasn't it?"

"Erm, don't remember that."

"You know, I was staying at Janet Rumford's house."

"James, please sit down, we are not playing games here," the woman instructed.

"Now, I'm Ruth London from the Home Office." She did not introduce her colleague as two more chairs appeared along with coffee for four.

"So, Mr. Pollack, it's good to see you again after such a long time. Can you tell us where you've been?"

"As I've already told everyone here, I don't remember what happened after the house was destroyed. I woke up ten years later in the same house on an island off the coast of Portugal. That's all I can tell you," James replied.

"That's true, I questioned him last night and that's all he remembers. When I rescued him, he didn't even know what year it was," Ben added.

"Tell me, Ms. London, what's the current security level at this base today?" James asked.

"You can call me Ruth. I don't know what you mean."

"I've been here for over ten days now and have never seen or heard a military aircraft take off or land. We are transported around in a jeep from the last century, so what's going on."

"You mean you really don't know?" she replied.

"No, ma'am, he really doesn't know what happened after the impact," Ben interrupted, pouring himself a cup of coffee.

"Well, our planet was hit by a strong CME that has taken out most of our electronic systems, surveillance systems, internet and communications. Satellites have been reduced to multimillion dollar ornaments barreling across the sky and only a few undersea cables are still working."

"I see," said James. "So, no electric cars and you now drive around in 1940s jeeps. What about the planes? The fighter jets and helicopters that were all stationed here," James added as the woman threw her hands up into the air.

"They are making some progress to get the planes flying again, but without any guidance systems or ground control they've gone back to the old planes from the past," she explained.

"That's why it's so important for you to have come all this way. Exactly which part of the Home Office are you from," James asked.

"Technically, security. But the inspector and I are not here on security business, we are here to give you a chance to explain to our scientific community how you've travelled in the past and explain how Ben's plane can fly when all the others are grounded."

"Okay, but you had better ask Ben, or better still his mother, Mrs. Rumford. She appears to have invested a great deal of time and money developing the craft," James replied, looking completely lost.

"I'm sure you think our sudden arrival a bit overdramatic, but as you can see, we really want answers and that's more important to us," she replied with a smile.

"What exactly do you want me to do?" asked James.

"Mr. Pollack, as without your time travelling medallion you're also trapped here," she replied with that smile again, "you and Ben can either work with us or face a long term in one of our H.M. prisons," she finished, looking at his personal file on the table.

"We've brought all the documents for you to sign. Official Secrets, that sort of stuff, just in case it doesn't work out as we hoped," her colleague proposed, pulling some documents from his case.

"Forget the administration, do you have any idea what we should do next?" James asked.

"Oh yes. You need to return the craft to the US military. Then find Mrs. Rumford and bring that RN officer back to the UK. We also want to know about the cycle of these events, *the three Unstoppables*."

"Wow, you have read my file after all. Let's start with Ben returning the craft to the US. I assume you must have had a lot of political pressure to request this, but how certain is the pilot that he can do this? Please tell us how that craft arrived here in the UK?" James asked.

"It came over on a civilian cargo flight to the base here before the CME. None except Ben believed it was possible to fly."

"So, the plane has never flown 3,000 miles across the Atlantic and only done a short hop to Portugal and back so far, isn't that correct?" James said and went on, "What does our pilot think?"

"Frankly, I have no idea. Your military people have had the plane for over two months now with scientists crawling all over it and no one has any idea how it works. That's strange, isn't it."

"Of course, there's a risk, that's why we're offering you the chance to help out the nation. Now gentlemen, please sign the documents here with my colleague, as we must be getting back to London." With that, Ruth London of the Home Office stood up and looked impatiently around the room.

"Thank you, Mr. Pollack, Mr. Rumford, for your time and assistance. I'm sure we will be in touch with you again," she said as her colleague offered a pen to James to sign the documents.

After that, the pair left the room for James and Ben to finish the coffee. When they looked at each other they burst out laughing at how ridiculous the situation really was. After another delay, the captain came back and congratulated them.

"Welcome to the Royal Air Force, or perhaps you have signed up for the Space Air Force! Anyway, I have some identity cards for you both," he announced shaking their hands.

"We don't quite know what we've done, but I think someone should give this bird another try," Ben said smiling.

"You should both go and visit the hanger with your plane and tell the boffins how it flies," he replied.

9 - TAURID

"So, what did you think, James? I didn't like that woman, and why does she want you to find my mum?" Ben asked as they walked towards the hanger.

"It's odd that they've opened my file again after ten years. Maybe it was just a coincidence that I reappeared shortly after the plane was shipped over here. It all sounds strange, but may explain why this comet impact is little known to the public here."

"What were the three Unstoppables she was waffling about?" asked Ben.

"You know, multiple fragments of a giant comet impacted the Earth more than 12,000 years ago. They mostly hit the North American ice cap, but the climate disaster was global," James replied, remembering his history.

"Yes, I think governments were expecting something to happen in 2030. They've been launching stuff every day to the moon for years and the first bases on Mars are already started, although it's doubtful they can survive now," Ben replied. "Sounds like it was the same Taurid stream of meteors that impacted Earth again. Much of this was covered up by the media, but Mum told me they had known of a three-mile-wide remnant of rocks from Comet Encke, only this time it was a huge projectile, some nineteen miles wide, like the greatest hazard facing Earth known to man."

"This was the cover-up you were talking about last night?" James asked.

"Yes, partly. It was predicted to hit again in 2030 when the Earth crossed that part of torus that contained the fragments and there was little, they could do to stop it," Ben explained.

"Interesting, and I remember reading that these devastating impacts are often accompanied with gamma ray outbursts, or mass coronal ejections from the sun, so it looks no different this time," replied James as they reached the launch pad.

"Look, James, I really don't want to go through a lot of questions with those boffins again. I know they mean well, so maybe you can help them more with the plane than I can," Ben said, sounding depressed.

"Okay, no problem if you have something better to do."

"Yes, I think I'm going to walk down to the medical centre and catch up with Michelle. Call me at the centre when you're done and we can get a ride back to the house together."

James continued walking straight towards the hangar with his new ID in his hand. The sun was shining and James felt alive and happy to be with Ben. He showed his pass and the guard opened the door to the hangar, only to be met by a technician waving at him.

"Good morning, sir. We were hoping you would come and see us. We would like you to do a short test flight to check the anti-gravity drive. Can you come this way and change?" James was led into a room marked 'pilots' and told to change into a light blue flying suit and was given a pilot's jacket to wear.

"What exactly do you want me to do," James asked.

"Ah! You haven't been in the pilot's seat before, have you. It's all pretty simple, you lift off to exactly 300 feet above the landing pad and descend when we tell you," the instructor said.

"Okay, that sounds easy to me," James replied, eager to get his hands on the actual plane.

"We don't want you to fly off anywhere… anyway the flight mode has been disconnected, but don't worry, we've done it with your colleague lots of times."

James followed the instructor out onto the landing pad, climbed a ladder to the pilot seat and sat down.

"That's good, now in front of you is the control panel and you will see there's no joystick. When we close the cockpit canopy, we want you to engage the startup procedure and wait for our signal," the instructor said looking down from the ladder and explaining how to lift off.

"Got it," replied James seeing how easy it was. While he waited for the canopy to close, he started to look for a screen to input the coordinates for a jump and put on the pilot's earphones.

"Okay, can you push the startup button," he was told, as the control panel lit up and the craft came to life without any noise.

"Please set the altitude to 300 and prepare to lift off," he heard and doing as instructed pushed the lever to rise. Immediately a panel with flight coordinates lit up as James watched the craft rise in a slow hover. It was at that moment that he realised he didn't want to return the plane to the US authorities and looked at a short list of flights that had been programmed. He decided to add the coordinates for the damaged house in Montserrat, in addition to those in the US. Looking further he noticed a dial to input the time of arrival—calculated in years, months and days. That was all he needed for his plan.

Looking around from this height the land was beautiful, with the runways of the airfield all laid out below and a patchwork of fields in brown, greens and yellow descending to a flooded river Thames, blue water all across the valley below. Almost as soon as he had taken in the view, he heard a new instruction.

"Thank you, you can descend onto the landing pad now." James pulled the lever and the craft descended back down again, with no noise and almost no sense of movement. Two men with paddles, and dressed in white protective clothing, waved the craft back onto the ground and James hit the shutdown button.

Shortly after, an access ladder was placed against the cockpit, the canopy opened and James climbed back down onto the pad. He was pleased with himself, having thought of a better escape plan. If he was going to find his time travelling medallion, he would have to go back to February 2020, ten years in the past.

"Thank you, sir, that went well," the instructor remarked.

"What exactly was being measured this time?" James asked.

"We're measuring the electromagnetic waves in the cavity wall that we think gives the craft the lift to hover and rise through the air."

"What happens during a flight?"

"We're not sure, but we think these waves create a vacuum around the plane, allowing it to propel itself at high speeds through the air. If correct, it can be used underwater or even in space."

"Wow, that's interesting. But I hear we are having to return the craft to the US military; do you think it can fly across the Atlantic?"

"Yes, we heard that too, and have been told to have the plane ready from tomorrow."

"Does that need a lot of charge for such a long flight?" James asked.

"Yes, but don't worry, sir, it will be fully charged for you tomorrow," he replied, as James started to walk back to the hangar to change.

James was given a leather flight bag for his jacket and uniform and left to find his way to the medical centre and hopefully some lunch. He followed the signs to a red cross centre and walking inside, found Ben sitting in the reception area talking to Michelle.

"Hello there. I hope I'm not interrupting but I just came back from a short test flight. Anything new here?" he asked.

"Not really. I was just telling Michelle that we are going to have to leave tomorrow to return the plane to the States and she's not very happy about it," Ben replied.

"Oh, that! Don't worry about it as I have a plan. Well, it's more of an idea, but I need some time in a flight simulator this afternoon to see if it works," James explained.

"Really, that's why you're looking so happy," Ben replied.

"No, let James explain what his idea is first," Michelle insisted.

"It's too early for that. Can you get us a few hours in a simulator on the base this afternoon, Ben?"

"Yes, I mean it's possible as it's not being used by anyone else. I already did a couple of hours in there before I came down to rescue you. So, what's new?"

"We need a simulation with a plane where two pilots sit next to each other."

"You mean like a military trainer plane?"

"Yes, that's so I can instruct you on what to do."

"Okay, but on our craft, you sit in the back and I pilot the plane up front. I don't get what you want to do?"

"It's called training. Come on, let's move and see if we can find a better solution," James said smiling at Michelle.

"Great, I'm up for something new, so sorry Michelle, I have to see what this simulator has to offer," Ben replied, as they got up to leave.

"What happened with the training today," Ben asked.

"Just a test flight up to 300 feet and down again, nothing new, but when I spoke to the instructor after, he gave me a few ideas."

"Really, like what?"

"They were measuring the electromagnetic waves that create a vacuum around the plane. This clears a path in space that gives negative mass to the craft so it can propel itself at ever increasing speeds."

"What, up to the speed of light?"

"No, it must move just below the speed of light, but that's already fast enough. Also, they think it can operate at these amazing speeds under water or even in space!" James exclaimed.

"Okay, so what's your interest in us doing a flight simulation together?"

"First, it shows we are serious about a flight tomorrow and second, er, I can show you what to do."

"What do you mean what to do?"

"Ben, I don't think we should hand the plane back to the US military, a craft that your mother heavily invested in. I don't trust them."

"Tell me your plan now, as I'm sure our discussion will be recorded at the flight simulator," Ben said.

"We fly to the middle of the Atlantic Ocean and descend into the sea so we can't be tracked. Then we continue on a new course to your mother's house on Montserrat."

"James, you're clearly mad. Do you know how deep the ocean is? It's about two miles mid Atlantic—that would crush us if the craft didn't work underwater. Remember, it's never been tested."

"Okay, okay. I'm just thinking of how to return to 2020, because there's a time indicator on the control panel that's measured in years. So, time travel is clearly built into this craft. It's not built for just a short hop to Portugal and back," James replied.

"My god, you really have been all over this craft. Come on, let's go inside and see if we can play around with this idea," Ben said, holding the door of the simulator centre open for James.

10 - FLIGHT

Michelle had been in her second year at Oxford, in October 2030, taking a Sustainable Development course, that was required for all first-year students in 2030. When she was at school, she'd started every Monday morning hating her life. Her brother was like the other kids, the ones who simply got on with life. He'd know the latest bands to listen to, or what was cool or what then was not so cool. She'd miss all his nuances. She was always trying too hard and no one likes people who try too hard, but then she passed all the exams and was thrown into a new world of people at Oxford.

She was living in a hall of residence when the impact occurred and she watched in horror as her world was torn apart and fellow students forgot about going to lectures. They only watched what little news of the outside world was available.

Forty-eight hours later, the lights went out and everything electronic no longer worked. Her mobile phone turned into a brick, electric cars would no longer start, and it remained dark outside for days. During this time, they all remained on the college campus, cooking with candles and helping to prepare food on the college BBQ outside. Then, without any sun, it started to get colder. A few students had already left the college, but most stayed to await instructions from someone in authority, that never came.

After only a few days it was becoming clear that the male students were eying up the females whether they liked it or not. In the absence of real authority, social behavior was no longer going to be respected.

Having no boyfriend at the time she felt vulnerable. Indeed, by the end of the week, it was clear that college food was going to run out and she made preparations to leave herself, hiding portions of cheese and other food in a backpack for her journey.

First, she realised she needed to get to high ground and the Chiltern Hills, not far away, looked to be the best option. It was also where her father had been posted at an air station near High Wycombe. She found an old map of the area and measuring the distance found it was only twenty-five miles to High Wycombe, a distance she might be able to cycle in two or three hours, if she could find the way.

Not saying anything to her fellow students, she waited for daylight and the sun to reappear. Early one morning, when the light outside improved, she dressed in her warmest clothing, and taking her backpack left her room to walk down to the bicycle shed. Although it was early morning it was still dark, and she saw a group of boys most likely drunk on college wine kissing several girls. She tried to hide in the shadows but had been seen.

"Oh! what do we have here? Michelle is leaving us, without saying goodbye?" he said, taunting her.

"No, don't you touch her, or we'll have more trouble on our hands," another student shouted.

"Come on, don't screw around, it's time we got these girls to bed," said another, as slowly the group moved away back towards the main college and Michelle breathed a sigh of relief.

She quickly undid the lock on her bike, wheeled it out of the shed and cycled as fast as she could out of the college. She already knew the way east out of Oxford and made good progress on almost deserted roads. The only cars she saw were those that had been pushed onto the road and now refused to start.

Cycling in the past had been one of her passions, but on dark, deserted roads it was not so easy, having to stop and check the map with her torch. She passed through Wheatley, Waterperry and Worminghall before reaching the town of Thame, when some dim daylight returned. She knew that after this was a long straight stretch of road to Princes Risborough and the start of the climb up the Chiltern Hills.

People were about in the village of Thame, but no one tried to stop her, so she pressed ahead on her journey until she started to climb the hill and wheeled the bicycle beside her. Finally, after the village of Loosley Row, she saw signs to High Wycombe and ten minutes later arrived outside the green gates with a warning to unauthorised persons entering the site being subject to the Official Secrets Act.

Not wasting any time, she dismounted and walked up to the gates that were topped with barbed wire, looking for a guard or someone to approach.

"There's no one there, my dear. The gates have been closed for days," shouted a woman from across the road. "Have you come far on that bike of yours?"

"Yes, I've bicycled from Oxford, come to find my dad. He works here," Michelle replied.

"Yes, all of us are looking for family, aren't we, now the phones no longer work. Come over and join me for a cup of tea."

"Thanks, I'm quite tired after all that cycling," she replied but the woman's next comment put Michelle on her guard.

"Do you have any food, my dear, that you could share with me?"

"Sorry, nothing at all. I'll go and look for another way into the base," she said and quickly mounted the bike and rode away. Just around the corner, she found a man standing next to an old motor bike.

"Hello, and who the hell might you be?" he asked.

"My name is Michelle Warwick. I'm looking for my father."

"Warwick, you mean you're Robert's daughter, well I never did. How did you get here, on that old bike?"

"As a matter of fact, yes, all the way from Oxford. Can you help me get into the base? The main gates are closed," she replied.

"Of course, they are, that's for security, see. I knew your father ten years ago and we both know he's retired now. So, what do you want with a Royal Air Force Base?"

"I'm looking for a job, any sort of job that's in a secure place, not like out here."

"I see, well if you told me, you were a medical student, I might be able to help you."

"Yes, only second year, but willing to help."

"All right, follow me. As you're Robert's girl let's see if we can get you inside and work as a nurse, if that's okay?"

"Yes, yes, whatever," she said as she followed the man on her bike down another road where ten-foot-high gates blocked the path. A small door opened in the gate and after a short discussion, he waved her inside.

"We have Ms. Warwick here reporting as the nurse for the medical centre." The man looked at a clipboard and let them pass.

She followed the motor bike down into the airbase, until they came to a building with a Red Cross, where she started work as a nurse.

Her first few days were stressful as she had little or no training, but the doctors and sister guided her new routine, until she met Ben. They quickly swapped stories and he told her he was living in Windsor until the impact and had come to the base, to train as a pilot. The second week she went for a sleep over at his house and became personally involved with him, and became his girlfriend. Still, something at the base didn't feel normal. There were over a hundred airmen working on the airfield but very few flights. An aging fighter plane landed every morning, sometimes bringing a visitor, and an old cargo plane flew in once a week with food and supplies, but no military planes were active.

When she asked Ben, he said that most had been damaged by the CME and his plane was the only military craft that could still fly. She found that unbelievable, so the next day looked on the site's medical records to check on his background. When she was unable to find his name, she looked to see if he was registered as a member of staff and again found nothing, so the next time he came to the medical centre to see her, she tackled him again.

"Look, Ben, if you're training to be a pilot, what kind of plane are you training on?"

"Something very advanced, and you may be needed tonight, as I'm to make the first flight this evening," was the reply that only confused her more. After she finished work that evening, she was about to get changed for dinner when the sister came to see her.

"Please, Ms. Warwick, you must come now in your uniform and coat and follow me as we are needed in one of the hangars."

Michelle followed her outside where two medical orderlies were waiting with a stretcher on wheels, and advanced towards one of the hangers.

Inside, technicians were erecting a white plastic tunnel. After a long wait of watching all the construction work inside, she was sent to bring more medical supplies from the centre. When she went outside, there were bright lights illuminating an area at the end of the hangar and she walked to see what was happening.

Standing with a view of the launch pad, she was able to see a strange craft lit up by the floodlights. The next moment, the plane lifted off into the night sky, hovered for a few seconds and disappeared in a flash, without making a sound. The next thing she knew someone was tapping her on the shoulder.

"Excuse me, miss. You shouldn't be out here, it's a restricted area," an armed marine told her.

"Sorry, I was sent to bring some supplies from the centre. I'm part of the medical team," she replied.

"That's all right, but I will have to escort you," he insisted as they walked back to the centre together.

"Do you what's happening tonight?" she asked.

"That plane you just saw has gone to collect someone. Probably be your next patient," he advised.

"Right so, I'll just go inside and get what's needed, and you can escort me back again," she replied, not knowing what to expect next… and that would be the first time she saw James.

11 - ARRIVAL

It was just before eight in the morning when Ben and James left the house and walked to the army jeep waiting outside.

"Morning, guys," shouted the driver, another young marine. "See you put your uniforms on as well, going somewhere today," he remarked, smiling at them. Both James and Ben were dressed in the RFA's blue jumpsuits, wearing their pilot's jackets, and each carrying a leather flight case.

"Good morning, yes. Today's the big day," replied Ben, as James saw that the day had warmed up with patches of sun and an unbroken stretch of cloudless sky.

"Can you drop us at the NAAFI as usual for a coffee. After that we need to say goodbye to some of our friends here," Ben added, as they drove down the runway straight towards the centre of the air field.

"You know, Ben, I still can't believe how quiet it is here compared to what's happening in the outside world," James said.

"You wouldn't believe some of the chaos outside London. Army running low on people, weapons, food, everything. As soon as one place of civil rioting settles down, another bit of the country goes red."

"But the military jets, why don't any of them fly now?"

"Simple, most electronics in the planes were controlled by military satellites. When the CME hit some were lost and the rest damaged, so no GPS navigation, no controls, no fly," Ben replied.

"So here we are, on an airbase with no planes," said James.

"Yes, but we're just in time for our last cup of English coffee before we meet the big folks and they give us their approval to leave. Come on, let's go inside," Ben said, and after a short stop they made their way to the command centre for the goodbyes.

Ben and James entered the conference room as before, full of both RAF service people and some civilians. This time, a high table had been placed at the end of the room and there were two chairs in front of the long table, where they were asked to sit. Proceedings commenced with the Group Commander welcoming everyone and praising the two pilots sitting in front of him.

My god, why don't they just let us fly away, thought James, as the speech reaffirmed the commitment to the USA and the special craft, they had been able to study for the past months. Special thanks went to the scientists and support crews who had made this possible. After that, the Commander came down and shook their hands as the pilots of the future. When James stood up to leave, he felt a tap on his shoulder and turning around saw it was Ms. London, with a smile.

"Can you come with us, Mr. Pollack, we need to talk," she ordered.

"Delighted," replied James. "But you're not going to stop us leaving here now, are you?" he added, following Ben and the Commander out of the conference hall.

Once outside, Ben said he had to say goodbye to a friend while James accompanied the Commander to the hangar with the plane. Once there, they walked up to the plane that already had the moveable stairs in place for the pilots to board.

"I suppose this is the last time we shall meet for a very long time," he said and shaking his hand again, James mounted the stairs at the rear of the craft to wait for Ben. He settled himself into one of the seats and waited for what seemed like a very long time. Then just as suddenly, another person climbed the stairs and sat down beside him. She was dressed in a light blue jump suit and carried a leather bag.

"Michelle, I was wondering when you would show," James said smiling, and squeezed her hand just as the rear door closed. Then they both put on their earphones to hear instructions from Ben, the pilot.

"Initiating the start sequence now," he reported for the ground crew monitoring the lift off, as the craft lit up without making a sound.

"You have done this before, haven't you James," Michelle asked.

"Yes, twice, first as a passenger and later in the pilot seat."

"So, where exactly are we going to," she asked, as the craft rose in the sky and hovered above the base in the autumn sunshine.

"Everyone ready back there," Ben checked, as he inserted the coordinates in the control panel.

"Yes, let's do it," James replied almost shouting into his microphone. In a flash, the plane left and it went very dark outside.

"What happened, James, where are we?" asked Michelle, waiting to hear Ben's reply.

PART THREE
MARCH 2020

12 - MONTSERRAT

"We're hovering 300 feet above the sea in the mid-Atlantic. Sorry James, I'm not going down into the water. I'm changing to the co-ordinates of Janet's house and a time change to February 2020 is it, James?"

"No, wait, make that beginning of March 2020," James replied.

"March 2020 it is. Here we go," Ben replied and in an instant the plane was hovering in sunshine above palm trees in the tropics.

"Wow, that was quick, I can see the huge crater left by our house but need to maneuver a bit to avoid the palm trees in the garden."

"Looks good to me, Ben," James replied, as the craft slowly descended onto the grass beside the gravel driveway. Then Michelle started to question him.

"James, where the hell are we? You're not a marine scientist, are you, and why does it look like we're in the tropics?" she asked.

"This is what's left of Ben's mother's house on the Island of Montserrat in the West Indies. It's a British Protectorate so you're quite safe here," James explained. When the door opened, James breathed a sigh of relief as fresh sea air filled the plane.

"But why did Ben want to come back here?"

"I think it's better that Ben explains the details," he replied and removing his seat belt, swung onto the steps and jumped down onto the grass, where he faced Ben again.

"That was a great piece of piloting," James said as they hugged each other at the success.

"Do you really think we're in March 2020?" Ben asked.

"I think you have visitors on your property already and it's someone you must remember," James replied, pointing to two people crouched on the other side of the crater.

"Lucy, it's me, James, don't you remember," he shouted at her. Slowly, she stood up and ran towards James with a big smile on her face, followed by another young woman.

"James, so you finally came back, how did you do it this time?"

"With a lot of help from your classmate, remember Ben?"

"But he's a lot older now. Looks like almost a man. How's that possible?" Lucy asked.

Michelle appeared at the door of the plane and tried to climb down, only to miss her footing and fall onto the ground, as Lucy ran across to help her.

"Oh! you poor thing." She shouted at James to come and help her when she vomited on the grass and passed out.

"Ben, Michelle needs water, can you bring your flight bag," said James as they crowded around to help her.

"I think it must have been the time jump. It was the first time for Michelle on the plane," Ben explained as colour returned to her face and she sat up at last.

"I don't think I want to fly on that plane with you ever again, Ben," she said quietly to him and kissed him on the lips, but she knew that her sickness had nothing to do with travelling on the plane.

She realised that her relationship with Ben was going to be different, but it was not until she had taken that pregnancy test that she understood how different. She had been at the hospital and felt the slam of fear as the blue cross emerged. Relationships can always be ended, but having a child with someone was forever.

"You, okay?" Ben asked, and she just nodded to him, smiling.

"Thank goodness for that," James announced, suggesting they gave the couple some private space for a while.

"James, I still don't understand how you got back to Montserrat again in 2020?" Lucy asked.

"It's all thanks to Janet who invested in this new plane, and Ben's piloting that brought it here for safety, away from the US military," James explained.

"It's good you didn't come two weeks ago, we've had forensic and military people crawling all over this site," Lucy added.

"Oh, and look who we found as well," Lucy announced, pulling Kiya forward to meet James.

"Kiya! You survived after they tried to kill you at the house?"

"Yes, James, but that was not a good experience. However, if you came back to find your medallion, I'm afraid it's not at the bottom of the pool over there," Kiya replied, pointing to the hole in the ground. Taking his hand she led James towards the crater, leaving the others to explain to a very confused Michelle.

"James, I survived because of some special water in the pool at the house and only climbed out with the help of Lucy and her grandmother, but since then we have more news."

"What kind of news, Kiya, what are you talking about?"

"The cylinder you found on the beach is still here. You must remember that?"

"Of course, so what's the problem now?"

"Come, follow me. I know you've only just arrived but Lucy and I managed to get down to the thing on the beach the other day and I went onboard," she said, leading James through the gates to the house and looking out onto the Bluff overlooking the beach below.

"Kiya, that sounds most dangerous."

"Not really. These craft were used on our planet in the future to move people around. Remember, that's how I got here, but now the military have fenced off the beach and it would be best if we act tonight, James," Kiya explained.

James and Kiya looked down on the beach with most of the cylinder now above the high-water mark, surrounded by a fence of barbed wire.

"So, when I got onboard, I took the control to open the entrance. No one else, not even your military, have found a way inside and we need to go back inside tonight," she said, smiling at James.

"Okay, so what do you want me to do?" James asked.

"Can you leave Ben and his friend to take care of themselves tonight? Lucy's too young to understand time travelling. It's best if they all go off to celebrate and we go down to the beach later tonight."

"Yes, of course, if you really think it's necessary," replied James.

When they walked back to the others around the plane, Ben had already decided to show Michelle the delights of the island at the best hotel. They had invited Lucy to join them at Olveston House for an English tea, leaving Kiya and James to catch up.

"Don't worry, Ben, Kiya and I will stay up here and keep an eye on the plane. We can even sleep onboard, if necessary," James reassured him.

"I hope so. I've already called my mum in the US and she's flying down to meet us here tomorrow," Ben replied as the three of them left to walk over to the hotel.

"So Kiya, what are we going to do until the sun goes down," James asked as he went back to get his flight bag from the plane. "I need to change into more comfortable clothes, these jump suits are too warm in this heat," he complained. Stripping down to his underpants and putting on a summer tee-shirt and grey pants, he went to sit in the shade under the wing, next to Kiya.

"Can I ask where you have been since we last met here on this island?" Kiya asked.

"Good question, and honestly, I don't remember. All I do know is that Janet's house was moved some 7,000 miles to a barren island on the edge of a land mass we call Europe. It also looked to have been underwater for some of those years. I suppose I may have been trapped inside, but don't remember any of that either."

"Really, so from what I know about time travel that's entirely possible. What triggered your release?"

"That's a good question. But I think it may have occurred when a big comet impacted on our planet, ten years in the future. When I woke up, the island outside had been mostly destroyed by a giant tsunami wave, or that's what it looked like when I swam to the mainland."

"You swam? So you didn't find your medallion at the house."

"No, I was wearing the same clothes as you last saw me in here. What happened to you?" James asked.

"After I was rescued by Lucy we came back and watched some people in white suits search the driveway. They went down into the water below," Kiya explained, pointing to the crater.

"Did you see what they found?"

"Not really, but your medallion was not in the water below here. They found a metal box and some small pieces of brass metal I've never seen before. There were a lot of flashes with a black box."

"Yes, that might be pictures of the footprints of the military people outside the house, who were shooting at me."

"James, why did they want to kill you?" Kiya asked.

"It's a bit complicated. These soldiers had been sent here by another government force. They wanted to cover up the story about the cylinder, so people couldn't see what had happened," said James.

"But don't you think someone was working against us, like that woman who had me thrown in the pool?" asked Kiya. "Why would they do that, when we both know your planet has been invaded by another race of people?"

"Yes, Kiya, but this is an island and they think they can hide why these people came to our planet," James said.

"James, you have no idea how dangerous these alien people can be. There are some who help us but others, like the greys and the reptilians, mostly want to abduct us. We need to do something about this as they might come back to recover the tic-tac," Kiya replied.

" I agree, so what's your plan?"

"We have to go down to the beach tonight, climb under this wire you saw and get inside the cylinder again. After that you can help me find a solution to this problem, or go back and join Ben."

"You know all about this cylinder thing and how it works?"

"Yes, of course, we have used them on our planet to move people away from dangerous places, to better places on other planets. Your military people know them as 'tic-tacs.' They jump around in the sky to scare off your military jets that are so slow."

"What do you think of this plane of Ben's?" James asked, pointing to the plane they were sitting under.

"Oh! That thing is an early model, or what we call a scout ship. It can only carry two or three persons, can't it?"

"Correct, and this has only been developed ten years in the future. So can we expect more visits from these 'tic-tac' cylinders?"

"Yes, of course, they are here all the time. In fact, I'm surprised they haven't come to recover this one. That's why we have to move tonight, before they decide to come back," Kiya replied with some force.

They were interrupted by the return of Lucy. "Hello there. Sorry, I didn't see you sitting under the plane. I came back because after a lovely tea on the lawn at the hotel, Ben and Michelle wanted to check in and stay the night," she blurted. "I either had to walk home, or come and join you guys, I hope that's all right."

"Yes, of course, you're most welcome. Come and sit on the grass. We're waiting for the sun to set and then going down to the beach, if you want to join us," James replied.

"I don't know about that. I already saw that thing and it's scary. Kiya went inside and she moved it up the beach, but I'm not sure I want to do that again."

Kiya quickly replied, "That's not a problem. James and I will go down to the beach. You walk back down the road outside the wire and wait until see our light. Can you signal us with the flashlight on your mobile phone, then jump out of the way? Do you think you can do that?"

"Yeah, I think that sounds all right, as long as I don't have to come on the beach."

"No, no, you stay on the road and we will come to you," Kiya replied, which left James quite confused.

"All right, that's all agreed, now let me find some water for us in my flight bag," James offered, tipping out the contents.

"Listen, James, I think there's something more important. Lucy should call Ben to warn him that we may be away from his plane for a while. Can you do that?"

"Yes, but Ben doesn't have a mobile phone here. Wait, I can call the hotel and see if he's in his room," Lucy replied as they all listened to her call.

"Reception says he's not answering in his room, what can we do?"

"Can you leave an urgent message for Ben to return to his mother's house as soon as possible?" James suggested.

"Right, that's done," Lucy replied.

"I'll leave a message on the pilot's door to say where we have gone. Well done, Lucy, and now I think we should be going," said James.

13 – LIME KILN BEACH

The sun was setting as the three of them set off for their destination. A huge ball of red was going down fast, leaving behind a crimson sunset with an unbroken stretch of blue cloudless heat. When they reached the top of the Bluff, James stopped and turned to Lucy.

"We're going to have to leave you here and take the footpath down to the beach. Follow the road down to the beach road and wait for us there. Nothing's going to happen until it gets dark, so better if you hide in the trees close to the fence and wait," he said, handing her a bottle of water from his bag.

"One more thing, Lucy. When I start up the cylinder it will look brighter in the darkness. Don't be afraid, just jump out of the way if we get close to you. Also, it may attract fast moving lights that are quite scary, so don't walk home on the road. Follow the back path, you know the path we took last time," Kiya advised her.

"Okay, I understand, but will I see you again, James?"

"I don't know. You could take my place on Ben's plane, if you want to," he replied.

After they hugged each other, Lucy walked slowly down the hill, giving a wave to them.

"Poor girl, I think she's terrified of what's going to happen."

"I'm also interested as to why you want to put the cylinder on the road," James said.

"All in good time, James. But are you really coming with me, without your medallion?" Kiya asked as they walked back to the top of the Bluff.

"Don't have much choice. I didn't find it on the island in Portugal and it's not here, so I have to hitch a ride with you… if you'll have me," James replied.

"That's okay, now show me where this footpath is to get down on the beach," Kiya replied as they both looked down at the cylinder on the beach below in the fading sunshine.

"James, do you see what I see, there're guards down on the beach, what does that mean?"

"It means that someone in government wants to stop any outsiders from getting onboard that cylinder, so what do we do?"

"Come on, show me this path, we need to climb down before it gets completely dark," Kiya replied as James led the way.

"Be careful, this path is steep, we need to go slowly as it's a long way down if you fall. From now on, no more talking until we reach the bottom, okay?" James insisted and started the climb down.

It took them thirty minutes to reach the fence at the bottom, where James pulled out another bottle of water from his bag and they rested.

"How does it look, Kiya?" James asked.

"The guards don't look that serious, in fact there are only four and they look bored. The tide's out at present, so when it starts to turn, we can make a move to get onboard."

"Really, why can't we go now?"

"James, have you looked below. There's not only a fence, but lots of barbed wire to cut through. Got any ideas?"

"Yes, if we had wire cutters in my bag it would be possible."

"Come on! What's inside that bag of yours," she whispered.

"Only if you tell me where you want to go next."

"God, you men are impossible. I just want to find my boyfriend."

"Right, and where is he now?"

"He's in a parallel universe, ten light years away, we can reach it in a flash once we get onboard. Like your scout, this craft can jump through time."

"Good, that's what I thought. Now here's something that may help us cut through the wire." James handed Kiya a small object that looked like a gun.

"What's this? It's not for cutting wire, it's a laser for cutting metal."

"Yes, I know. Maybe we can hide the light it emits with my bag."

"My god, you people are hopeless," she replied shaking her head.

"I know. Let's wait for the tide to come in," James replied.

"All right, let me think. We need to make a beam of laser light invisible on a dark night. Do you have anything else in that bag of yours?"

"Yes, some dry rations and that bottle of water."

"I think that might be possible. Can you remove half the liquid in the bottle, and we can fire the laser through it," she announced as James drank the water in the bottle.

"Right, James. Don't worry about the wire outside, we can dig our way under the sand. We just need to cut away some of the wire on this new fence and then squeeze underneath."

"Sounds good. I can hear the tide coming in, if that will help us as well."

"All right, let's wait until both hands on the clock are on the number eight," Kiya announced to the surprise of James.

"What? How do you know that?" James replied in a low voice.

"I was taught your time system on that ship in the other planet by my boyfriend. We had to follow that to survive."

"Well, we have less than an hour to eight o clock, can't we start cutting the fence now?" James asked.

Kiya fired the laser beam through the water and they started to cut the wire in the fence, but it was slow going.

"Let me try and cut some more. I think we only need to cut another two wires and we can squeeze underneath," James said, and taking the laser cut away the last of the wire. When he finished, they both looked at the guards close to the cylinder.

"See, as the water is returning, the men are becoming more distracted in their duties. They have set up a table to play a game," Kiya said as they watched a bright light illumine the top of the cylinder.

"Yes, I think they are playing cards or something."

"James, this is our chance to get onboard. If we can get down to the water and pull ourselves along in the small waves, I think I can access the rear door without us being seen."

"You go first under the fence and I'll follow," James replied.

Kiya eased her way under the fence and started pushing the sand away from under the barbed wire. After ten long minutes she was through to the other side and James followed, pushing his leather bag in front of him, only to find Kiya lying on the beach telling him not to make a sound.

"You will have to crawl on your stomach down to those rocks and wait for the water to reach the cylinder," she whispered in his ear, to which James nodded and followed her down towards the water. Once they were hidden behind the rocks Kiya sat up and told James to relax and do the same.

"As soon as the water reaches the end of the cylinder, we can go for a swim. I know you like swimming, James, but this time you should move along in the shallows and keep your head down, until we reach the cylinder, is that okay?"

"Yes, that's clear, but how do we get onboard from there?"

"Don't worry, I stole the command pad from last time and should be able to open a rear door without us being seen."

"It's very dark now, but the moon will come up soon, so better to be hidden before it rises," James replied, fixing his bag on his back to keep it dry.

"Ready then, let's crawl down to the water and get started."

They entered the water, pulling themselves along the sandy bottom towards the cylinder, hoping their movements would not be heard by the group of soldiers. They had almost reached the cylinder when one of the guards got up and strolled down the beach to the water, while the others shouted at him to return.

"Thought I heard something down here," he shouted back and then walked back to the cylinder and started to pee onto the sand. James and Kiya held their breath until finally he walked back to the group higher up the beach.

After another half an hour, the tide had reached the rear of the cylinder and Kiya felt confident enough to move up the beach and open an entrance. James watched, as at first nothing happened, but then a small door opened and Kiya rose out of the water and approached the cylinder, signalling James to follow.

"I've never used this entrance before, James, but let's get onboard and close the door." She squeezed inside a small compartment with a ladder going up inside. Kiya climbed up to the second rung to give more space for James who climbed inside, and the door closed with a click as they heard voices outside.

"Look, there are footprints in the sand here," the guard shouted.

"Yes, stupid, they're your prints when you came down here for a pee," replied another.

James looked up at Kiya, putting a finger to his mouth.

"Nah, there's nothing down here. Just the tide coming in, that's all, and this cylinder thing that gives me the creeps."

"Come on, let's walk back around the other side and you can look for more of your footprints," one said as the guards moved away.

"Wow, that was close. We made just made it inside."

"James, do you have a light in your bag?"

"Yes, I think so. Do you know where we're going?"

"Roughly, we make our way up this ladder, then walk to the other end of this tube," Kiya explained.

"Is that where we find the main control room to start the engines?"

"Yes, let's start by climbing this ladder and see where it leads," Kiya replied as James followed her. At the top was another small room with a map written with signs James didn't understand.

"Look, we are here and need to get to the other end by this maintenance tunnel, so we're still in the outer casing of the cylinder."

"Yes, James, and between us and the inside is a cavity of gas that we can't get through. How could I have been so stupid, we're trapped inside, but on the outside," Kiya explained, sliding her body down the wall in defeat.

"Whooh, wait a minute, let me look at that diagram again," replied James, coming over to try to understand the layout. "If we crawl along this tunnel to the place above the control room, there may be signs of how to gain access inside. Come on, follow me," he said as they crawled along the narrow tunnel to the end.

"Here we are, anything you can see that might help get us inside?"

"Yes, there's a grill on the floor. Can you open it, James, as that should allow us to get inside," Kiya exclaimed laughing.

"But it's bolted down."

"Can't we use the laser gun to remove the bolts?"

"Worth a try, let's see what happens." James cut away four of the metal bolts, expecting to hear a hiss of gas, but nothing happened.

"Maybe this is another way in. That would make sense for the maintenance guys," James said as he lifted the plate away.

Kiya shone the light and underneath was an access hatch with a lever for opening the door. Sitting on the floor she moved the lever and on pulling the hatch open they saw there was a long drop into the control room.

"I think you should go first, Kiya, and I'll lower you down."

77

"No, James, you have to go first and then I can stand on your shoulders to close the hatch again," she explained.

"All right, give me the torch and I'll try." James lowered himself through the hatch and Kiya helped him, until he fell onto the floor.

"James, are you hurt?" Kiya shouted.

"No, I'm okay, just looking for the light," he said as he shone it up again. "Now lower yourself down and stand on my shoulders to secure the hatch with the lever."

Kiya quickly closed the hatch and locked the lever, then slid back down onto the floor with James.

"So, this is the control room we've been looking for... can you put on some lights?"

"Better than that, I can start up the engines right away, that should scare the guards on the beach," Kiya said with a smile, and a few moments later the cylinder started to hum and glow in the darkness outside.

"Now tell me what you want to do," James said.

"I want to get all those people who came on this machine and return them to the island they came from," she replied.

"Really, you think you can do that?" James asked.

"Yes, once we get the cylinder up on the road outside, we can send out a signal and all those people will walk back to the ship."

"You mean these people have been living... er, like a host in someone else's body, for a few weeks now."

"Yes, James, I think you may be shocked, but that's how things work in our part of the Universe. Unless we return them back to where they came from, these people will only come back with more in the future."

"All right, but let's get the ship onto the road first, if you want to pick up a human cargo," James replied, quite confused.

14 – EVACUATION

These were the migrants. Almost eight hundred of them had walked ashore after the cylinder was pulled up the beach. Another two hundred had perished when it slipped back into the sea, the lost remnants from another world.

The control room was just that, a panel of controls and dials for the pilot to control the ship. There was only one chair for the pilot and a long bench at the back that James was now sitting on, watching Kiya perform a number of technical tasks. He had been here on the island when the cylinder was first found in the bay, deep under the sea.

James and Ben had been with Ben at the school's hurricane shelter on the island when the invasion started. He remembered how the school children were all frightened, not knowing what was going on outside during the night, as he told his story.

I went deeper and deeper into more dangerous places in Europe, where there were a lot of bad men and women, doing hurtful things to the people, but called a Union. It was a soft soviet style union, where some populations were unemployed while the people at the top were undemocratic and well paid. I was imprisoned underground in one country, but managed to escape to Naples in Italy. It was dangerous there as well and I had to leave. Then, turning to my guardian for advice, I travelled to an ancient city in the Middle East to find my friends and lived on an island surrounded by water, just like here, to recover.

In the morning, we found the force field had gone, but still it was dangerous to go outside. One of the boys disappeared up into the sky, while I was talking to Janet about a ship that was anchored in Kiln Bay. Now I think it must have been this cylinder.

When I finally left the school with Ben and the parents came to pick up their children, no one remembered anything of the last night, until one of the dads said, 'They didn't come here to change the past, they came here to change the future,' and then it was raining and the ship had submerged or disappeared.

Unknown to James at that time, the British PM in London was alerted of an invasion on the island, but this was something he didn't want in the press with the current EU negotiations and a pandemic in Asia, back in February 2020, so there was a media blackout and it was all covered up.

James had met with Ms. Kilmister again, on the island and later in London which had been difficult, but it was the cylinder that had his full attention, to pull it back up the beach and release the people inside. That was the first time he heard it described as a people transfer pod, from another planet. Even then he barely thought that these were aliens who might be dangerous.

He knew that Elizabeth was devious but she had betrayed him at the last minute, wanting the soldiers to kill him. She had Kiya thrown in the pool, thinking she was dead. What he still couldn't remember was why Kiya had been sent on the cylinder in the first place and what she had been carrying with her. Then there were the thoughts and ideas of the people in Janet's house near London. Ideas about reducing the human population swirled so violently he couldn't remember his thoughts clearly, until he was swept away to sleep in Janet's house for nearly ten years.

James was brought back from his memories by Kiya shouting at him for help. "James, we are hovering above the beach, can you look for Lucy's light on the road and guide me?"

James jumped up, looking at the control panel in confusion.

"Look on the small screen to your right, and tell me what you see. There are no windows on this ship, just infra-red images of what's outside," Kiya explained.

"Yes, I can see a figure waving, she must be on the road, go straight ahead now and then land," said James with relief. They felt a slight jolt as the ship landed outside on the road.

"James, that was not easy, these craft are not meant to hover like that. So now we can open the front boarding door and start to attract the people back onboard."

"You mean you can really do that, how?"

"It's done by an ultra-sonic signal that radiates across the whole island, and the hosts will walk down here and return to their place on the ship. Any questions?"

"No, of course not, I just didn't think any of this was possible. Tell me how long will it take to load this cargo," James asked.

"Probably most of the night, as many will have to walk from the north of the island."

"Don't you think I should go down and see if Lucy is still on the road, before the people arrive?" James asked.

"Yes, that's an excellent idea, and thank her for the help with the light. I'll only open a part of the door until you say it's safe."

"Sorry, but how do I get down there?"

"Look for the door over there. Press the open button and go down the staircase to the outside. Better take your light, as there are three levels of staircases. It's a really big ship," Kiya replied, and watched as James left the control room.

15 - CYLINDER

James dropped down from the bottom of the last staircase and shone his torch around. When he knelt down to look outside, he felt his heart hammering in his chest. The vertical entrance door appeared to be closed, but in the dark he saw there was a small opening just a foot from the floor. When he looked outside at the trees beside the road, he saw her dark face reflected in the moonlight.

The next moment a revolver was thrust under the gap and fired a round that made a noise like an explosion in the confined space. James put the weight of his foot on the gun and the arm was quickly withdrawn. Then he waved at Lucy to come. Taking advantage of the confusion, she ran out of the trees and dived under the small opening, just before it closed. Tears of fear ran down her face.

"Lucy, don't be frightened. This is the inside of a big spaceship, it's the one you saw on the beach," he said.

"Yes, but what does it do?" Lucy asked.

"You remember that day we went down to the beach and you said that your mother was not vibrating at the right frequency. All those people are coming here tonight and Kiya is going to take them back to their home on another planet," James explained.

"But how can they get inside with the door closed?" she asked.

"I don't know, follow me up this staircase and we can ask Kiya," said James taking her hand as they started to climb to the control room. When they reached the second stairs James stopped to catch his breath and shone the torch around.

"Look how enormous the inside is. Three decks of accommodation, stretching right down to the end," said James flashing his torch into the darkness.

"Hello, hello," he shouted listening to the echo returning his words.

"James, stop it, this place is really scary to me," Lucy complained. They continued the climb to the top level and James opened the door.

"Hello, Lucy, welcome onboard my spaceship, how do you like it?" Kiya asked smiling at her.

"I don't like it all, and there's nowhere for the people to sleep," Lucy replied.

"You know, she's right. Someone has removed all the sleep pods, from what little we could see," said James.

"That must have been done by the friends of your queen," Kiya replied smiling.

"Yes, probably the US military, but why would they want hundreds of sleep pods, makes no sense to me," James replied.

"Anyway, that's not our problem. We will be travelling straight back to the other planet, so we won't need those pods. Now then, Lucy, do you have any idea how many people we can expect tonight?"

"More than two hundred drowned when the cylinder slipped back into the sea. You should be able to calculate the number if you know the total who landed, right."

"Okay so, that's less than eight hundred. We now need to frighten away the guards who were shooting at James and then we can open the door again," she replied.

"By the looks of your screen here, quite a number are already walking down the road towards us," announced James, looking at the screen on the control panel.

"Very good, I can electrify the outer hull. That should keep the guards away until the people reach the entrance, and I will launch some bright lights to fly above the road to keep any locals inside. Until then we just have to wait here."

"There look to be humans outside the front entrance," Lucy said looking at the infra-red screen.

"Yes, and hundreds more walking down the road outside," James confirmed, when an alarm went off.

"Oh no! Everything goes wrong at the same time," Kiya replied.

"What does that mean?" James and Lucy asked at the same time.

"It means that another ship is on its way. Another of the 'tic-tac' machines have found us doing a people transfer. That's not going to be good," Kiya replied. "All right, here's what we need to do avoid detection. First, I'm going to open the front gate and let the people onboard. Lucy, can you go out on the upper staircase and tell me what happens. Take the torch to keep you safe. The people you see are in a trance and will not be violent, as long as the transmission continues. Can you do that?"

"Yes, I suppose so, if you think it's necessary," she replied and James gave her his torch.

"Now James, you are going to learn something new about time travel, if you're ready," Kiya said, waiting until the door to the control chamber had closed. "I'm going to have to move the cylinder back onto the beach to avoid any more detection. Yes, yes, I know what about the humans boarding now, we mustn't stop that at all costs. So I'm going to move the cylinder into another dimension."

"I'm not sure I understand."

"Yes, you do, James. You've been travelling through time for years. This cylinder now is in a four-dimensional world with three dimensions of space and one of time. But I can move this craft into a time-space dimension, with three dimensions of time and one of space that would allow you to time travel again. The problem is that I can only do this for the amount of time we were alone in the control room, that's before Lucy came onboard."

"I don't see why that should be a problem, but go on."

"It's because we are connected in time in the control room, but Lucy only came in later. That would give you just twenty minutes of space time to confront the people who are after Ben's ship and stop them. I will have to stay here in order to return the ship as before and fight off the tic-tacs if necessary. What do you think?" Kiya said smiling at James.

"How do I know where to go without any co-ordinates?"

"Don't worry, once we are in the time-space dimension you will have all the co-ordinates you need. The big craft on the screen looks like a helicopter trying to locate Ben's ship on the screen here. I would start with that if I were you," Kiya explained.

"Yes, I can see the theory of this plan and with the cylinder back on the beach it might fool them for twenty minutes, but not until the morning," James replied.

"That's the best I can think of at the moment."

"Also, I'm concerned that if I should appear on this helicopter, I would be back in space-time again and get immediately arrested!"

"Okay, James, it's not a perfect plan, I know."

"Unless I move straight to Ben's plane and fly around in that and try to scare off the helicopter. Except how might that perform in a time-space dimension?" asked James.

"Really, I don't know. Now, if you're ready I'm going to make the switch to the other dimension."

"All right, let's see what happens," replied James, as the room went dark as if time was now moving backwards, then the control panel re-appeared inverted in front of them, and then nothing. James could see many co-ordinates in his mind, and tried to concentrate. He felt a stronger rushing sound and knew he was being taken somewhere, but he didn't know where.

The rushing of wind was replaced by shooting stars and finally lightning, but this lightning was coming up from the earth, tossing his body around in a maelstrom of light. When it finished, he slowly descended onto a surface of sand and knew exactly where he had arrived. He was back on the island off the coast of Portugal. He was still on the floor inside Janet's house with bright sunshine outside.

OMG, this really isn't working as I hoped. I just hope this isn't a time loop and I have to swim ashore again, James thought and then drifted off to sleep.

PART FOUR
OCTOBER 2030

16 - JANOCA

When James awoke next, jerked from a dream he couldn't remember, it was almost evening. More surprising was his flight bag lying on the ground beside him. He pulled it towards him, sat up and looked inside. There was the bottle of water and some dried biscuits, so he took a drink. Then he stood up and looked around.

It was the same as last time, large empty concrete walls, some limestone remains on one wall and stairs leading down near the opposite wall. This time he walked over to the stairs and looking down could see his reflection in the pool of water. His skin looked pale through tiredness and lack of sleep; one eye unexpectedly reddened. There was no sign of his time travelling medallion anywhere. Nothing much had changed from the last time, he thought.

But why bring me back here, unless it was to meet someone like last time, he thought and started to walk to the open doorway, where sand had drifted into the entrance. Looking outside, the sun had gone down, but in the twilight, he could see the village in the distance and this time there were lights and a faint hum of music.

"Oh my god," he shouted and smiled as he realised, he had returned to an earlier time, before the island was destroyed. Here, he would find help from the local people. Picking up the flight bag from the floor, he set off at a brisk pace towards the lights.

In the distance he could see the dark shape of small houses, probably bungalows or summer houses on an island like this and carried on walking across the soft sand where nothing grew but a few tufts of grass.

After another hundred yards, he reached a concrete pathway that led north towards the centre of the village and the landing stage, he remembered. Turning right he followed the path into the village, but many of the houses were dark inside, so he continued on. Most of the bars and cafes were closed as well as an island store, and that started to look a bit strange. Finally, James reached the port area and could see queues of people waiting with suitcases, standing in a long line.

There was just one restaurant open, its name proudly written under the lights. "Janoca" it announced with music blaring into the night. The next he heard was a woman speaking in Portuguese.

"Oi voce esta bem," she asked.

"I'm a bit lost," replied James, smiling at her.

"Oh, you're English, well you came to the right place tonight, with everyone leaving. Come on inside, I make you the best fish dinner on the island. Come, come this way," she insisted and James followed her inside the restaurant to an empty table.

"I'm sorry, we don't have much on the menu with this evacuation tonight. We can make you a big plate of fried prawns and some wine?"

"Yes, that would be fine," he replied.

"What wine… vinho branco?" she asked. "You look like you've been through some rough times." James nodded. "Okay, if you're staying, you can have it for free."

James realised he had been moved back in time, before the comet would hit in the next few days.

At least, if the islanders were evacuating, they would be taken to higher ground and survive before the tsunami hit the coast, James thought as he waited and watched the line of people outside.

"Here you are, the last plate of fried prawns I probably serve on this island for quite a while," she said, placing a huge serving of prawns in front of him. "And here's a carafe of white wine. Do you mind if I sit with you while you eat, I'm a bit frightened of what's going to happen."

"Tell me, how do you know what's going to happen next?" James asked.

"You don't know, it's the comet. They warned us on the television. Now the Government wants all the islanders to evacuate. Look up in the sky, you can see it tonight quite clearly," she replied, pointing to the north.

James turned in his chair and could see a huge bright star with a long tail passing in the sky above them. "Yes, that's what we were expecting. Can you tell me the month and the year, I'm a bit confused," James replied.

"Holy mother of Jesus, it's October 2030, you really are out of your mind. Where exactly did you come from tonight?" the woman asked.

"I was washed ashore from my boat on the other side of the island and had no contact with the outside world for months," James explained, expanding on his story. "Yes, I would agree, this comet in the sky looks pretty scary, so maybe you should think about leaving as well."

"And what about you. You're not going to make a runner back to the mainland?" she asked.

"No, not immediately, I'm waiting for someone to arrive," James replied.

"You must be a pretty cool guy. How does your contact show up? All the ferries only have passengers going to the mainland. No one's coming back here after tonight, except the military."

"I'm sure he will show, or I'll have to join the queue over there. Please, can you bring me a coffee?" James asked as he noticed a man dressed in a black coat sitting facing the sea.

His heart racing, unable to believe it was true, he had to find out. He stood up and approached the man until he was sure.

"Deepak, it is you? What are you doing here? I really do need your help," James said as he checked out the man again. He was wearing a long black coat, dark trousers and a purple shirt, open at the neck.

He looked slowly at James and replied. "Well, James, what are you doing here on this island, when you should be helping your friends in that other place."

"Yes, well, I tried to time travel to protect my friends, but I failed and ended back here instead," he replied.

"That's because you tried to move into time-space. You should know by now that's impossible. Fortunately, space-time brought you back to Janet's house over in the sand dunes."

"Right, I'm still looking for my medallion, but it's not on either of these islands, and without that I'm stuck here."

"All right James, you've suffered a lot. But I had to stop you following that military woman who tried to have you shot. So I moved you and the house to somewhere safe, where you wouldn't get into trouble," Deepak explained.

"You did what!" James exclaimed, as the woman brought James his coffee.

Deepak spoke to her. "Hello, could you be so kind to bring me a cappuccino?" he asked.

"So Deepak, what do you want me to do now. I had a window of twenty minutes to save my friends and have been stuck on this island for most of the day."

"Oh, I wouldn't worry about that. Time on this island in the future is fast. In fact, you have been away for just over a minute of time on that Caribbean island in the past," Deepak replied.

"Really, can you help me get back there?"

"Not so fast, James. You've been working with that alien woman from the other universe. She wants to return all the people to her planet, most noble of her, but what about you?"

"You seem to know most of what I've been doing."

"Yes, but there are still people on that planet who need to return here, don't you think," he said as the woman set the cappuccino on their table.

"Thank you," Deepak said smiling at her.

"Of course, I haven't forgotten, but without the medallion there was little I could do," James replied.

"All right, I'm happy to give you back your medallion, on condition that you keep your promise on this... agreed?" Deepak replied, pulling the medallion out of his coat pocket and placing it on the table.

"Yes, of course, I will try my best," replied James, taking the medallion and placing his lost personal possession around his neck.

After that James and Deepak talked about the current danger to the planet and Deepak told James to remember the three unstoppable events again. Deepak had some doubts that humans would last the century and how life would be different after the comet impact.

"Remember, you know the co-ordinates for Janet's house, don't you... and a word of advice, James, let the boy fly his plane, not you. It's time you started to take a back seat in these matters," he said.

"Thank you, Deepak, I think I've learnt my lesson. Now if you can excuse me, I think should move away from here right away," James replied, standing up and shaking Deepak's hand. He quickly walked away from the restaurant as he saw a group of national guard soldiers walking up from the dock, and realised he was in even more danger than before.

He walked to the side of the restaurant in the dark, where he wouldn't be seen, and secured his flight bag over his shoulder. Then he set the co-ordinates to Janet's house on Monserrat, and carefully moved the date back to March 2020. He was about to point his medallion at the wall when a dog ran up to him, barking. James, in panic, picked the dog up and pressed the button to open a worm hole. There was a bright flash and James, with the dog, moved back in time to another dimension.

17 - DREAMS

The rushing of wind was replaced by flashing lights, but this time it was different. James was dreaming about his last discussion with his mentor and guardian Deepak, and he could hear him talking again in his head. This time it was clearly about the three Unstoppables:

Remember how your planet's magnetic field is much weaker. You should expect a major magnetic event every 12,000 years and the next one is overdue.

See how the rotation of your planet has slowed, the magnetic poles will spin off towards the equator. This is a polar flip and will only begin to reconverge over a long period of time.

Then a solar outburst may occur after a pole flip, and this could take the form of a mini-nova.

James saw these thoughts more like a lucid dream, until he realised he was back on the island of Montserrat. He was lying on the grass in Janet's garden, close to the plane, and Ben was holding him in his arms and shouting.

"James, you came back. I don't know what's happened, but you've brought back a dog with you."

"Hang on, Ben, please can you give me a drink from my flight bag. What's this about a dog?" he replied.

"Yes, he's over there cocking his leg against my plane. Did you mean to bring him back?" Ben asked.

"Not really, but I had to leave in a hurry. I think he's the mutt from the first time I was on the island."

Andrew Man

"Oh no, you mean you went back again to that island in 2030."

"Yes, and I found my medallion to travel again," James replied smiling at Ben.

"Really, well that's good news."

"So, tell me what's been happening with you here? Why are you back at the plane during the night?"

"I got the message from Lucy to return here. Some American helicopter came over from Antigua trying to capture our plane. Kiya must have sent several of those tic-tac machines as for a while the night sky was all lit up and that chased the 'copter away. After that I stayed up here to protect the plane."

"Okay, so what do you want to do next?" James asked.

"I'm waiting for my mum to arrive and then we all want to return to England, even if it is half flooded with water. Michelle is going to join me here just as soon as she wakes up at the hotel. This has been a good trip for us, as she told me she's pregnant. Now we just want to go home."

"Thanks, and many congratulations," said James.

"What are you going to do now?" Ben asked, while the dog ran back and started to lick James. "Boy, that dog most certainly likes you. You really did find him on that island?"

"Yes, but I need go back to the cylinder and talk to Kiya. I was told to help rescue the other travellers again, so will most likely return with her," James replied.

"That sounds like a long journey, James. Have you got any food or water?"

"No, not really, anything on that plane of yours you can offer?"

"Only snacks and more bottled water, but it might help you," Ben replied handing some to James. "What should we do with Lucy, is she still down there on the cylinder?" he asked.

"Yes, I suppose so and now that it's starting to get light, I had better get a move on down there, before they leave," James replied.

96

"All right, good luck, and please take that dog with you," Ben said laughing at James calling to his dog.

"Come on Mutt, we're leaving, come on boy," said James.

"Mut, what kind of name is that for a dog?"

"That's all I can think of for now," shouted James, walking down the driveway with his dog. He paused at the top of the Bluff and then walked down the road towards the beach. When he reached the Kiln Beach road at the bottom it was deserted, but in the morning twilight he could see the cylinder further down the road, with the entrance still open. Standing in the doorway was Lucy, waving at him.

"James, James, you made it back," she shouted.

"Yes, and look what I brought you, a dog."

"Really, where did you find him?" she asked.

"Bit of a long story. Are you all loaded and ready to leave?"

"Yes, Kiya's been waiting for you for an hour, where have you been?"

"I've been talking to Ben up on the Bluff, he wants to go back to England with his mother and Michelle, so what do you want to do? Don't you want to go and try to find your mother now?" James asked.

"I don't think I really belong on this island. Kiya says I can come with her," Lucy replied as James and his dog walked up the entry ramp towards the stairs. "Hurry up, James, Kiya needs to talk to you urgently. Can you run up the stairs quickly and I'll bring your dog."

On entering the control room, James could see Kiya had a problem. Some of the control panel had been taken apart with exposed wires all over the floor.

"Ah, James, I've been waiting for you, what took you so long?"

"Long story short, I went back to Janet's house and found my time travelling medallion," James announced proudly, showing it off around his neck.

"Very good, do you think it might help us fly this ship?"

"Not really, so what's the problem? I thought you just needed to reverse the co-ordinates to find the way back to the other planet."

"Yes, James, but the other planet isn't in this dimension and the wormholes have moved around so I can't get a link. If we can't link, we can't lift off. It's all as simple, or as difficult as that."

"Okay, how far have you got with this voyage?"

"We can leave down the Orion arm, but can't get past Alpha Centura at the centre of your galaxy. It looks to be flashing again with high energy voltage, but that's dangerous," Kiya explained.

"But isn't Alpha Centura just one giant black hole that would suck you in?"

"Yes, and crush us into tiny pieces. What do you suggest?"

"Are there any other habitable planets in our galaxy we could stop off at on our way? I've never done galactic travel before, only time travel, and I don't think we can stay here for much longer," James replied.

"You think we should stay in your solar system and just move forward in time," she replied.

"It's an option, to give us time to set something up in the future."

"That leaves just two planet options, Earth or Mars."

"Yes, but Earth in ten years is most unstable as I've been there. Mars is no better at present with no atmosphere or water."

"James, where exactly have you been in the future?"

"After I left here, I met my guardian in 2030, where I saw a large comet was going to hit this planet. My guardian is a time traveller like you and confirmed there have been three major cataclysmic events on our planet. They appear every 12,000 years, so we need to be very careful about jumping into the future."

"Sounds similar to my planet, where a big moon kept appearing every 10,000 years and caused similar damage, with earthquakes and magnetic pole shifts," Kiya remarked.

James saw a red light flashing on the control panel. "What's that," he shouted, pointing at the light.

"It's a warning. High energy from your black hole is coming our way and may create big solar outbursts. Don't worry, it's years away from your system of planets," replied Kiya.

"No, that's not correct, that's what will hit our planet in ten years' time and cause huge damage – and I've seen it."

"What date do you think it might be safe to jump to?" Kiya asked.

"I don't think it's safe to jump to anywhere in our solar system. Even if you extend a time jump to forty years in the future it won't be safe, and the planet Mars will still not be habitable."

"All right, let me try the navigational controls in time-space and see if that's accepted," Kiya replied, resetting the co-ordinates again. "Look, James, come here. It works on these sensors for a long distant time zone and shows an atmosphere fit for humans to breathe," Kiya announced with delight.

"Sorry, Kiya, I'm not going anywhere with you in time-space, that nearly killed me last time. It's too dangerous, but go ahead on your own if you want to try such a jump," replied James, looking at her with alarm.

"All right, I can give you two minutes to decide, then I'm closing the outer door and starting the launch procedure," she said, just as Lucy walked into the control room holding the dog.

"Lucy, I think we have to leave. Please turn around and go back down the stairs. We need to leave this ship as soon as possible," James said, pushing his way past her and taking the dog in his arms.

"Really, James! What's happening? Why's it no longer safe to remain on board?" Lucy replied, confused.

James took her hand and pulled her out onto the stairwell. "Come on, we have to move quickly. She's going to close the outer door that will trap us inside," he said panting, and held her hand tighter as they rushed down the stairs.

Once at the bottom they ran down the ramp before the entrance door started to close and jumped down onto the road.

"Come on, stand back. We need to hide in these trees before the craft lifts off," James explained as the air filled with static electricity and the hairs on his arms stood on end.

"But where's Kiya going?" Lucy asked.

"She wants to go back to her planet in another universe, but it's too dangerous for you and me. You do want to see your mother again, don't you?" James replied putting his dog back on the ground.

"Yes, but get down on the ground, I think the cylinder is about to take off," shouted Lucy, as the craft lifted off the ground, pulling the air behind it and taking the dog with it up into the sky.

"My God, that was not good for my dog," said James standing up and looking at the empty space on the road.

"Don't worry, James, we should find your dog further up on the road, if you follow me," replied Lucy, as they both started walking up the deserted road.

After walking for ten minutes, they found the dog lying by the side of the road, alive and not hurt.

"Look, James, he's still alive, do you want me to take care of him?" Lucy said picking the dog up in her arms.

"Yes, I think that might be for the best," James replied and they carried on walking towards her house in Woodlands.

"James, I've been thinking about Ben. I suppose he will be returning to the future with his mum and his girlfriend," she said.

"Yes, I expect so," replied James.

"Can you tell me what's it like?"

"Lucy, you know I'm not allowed to tell you about the future, because the time lines are never certain."

"But what can I do?"

"When you get older you should go and study in England. When you get there, go to an airbase called 'Group 22' in some hills north of London and ask to see Ben. You should do this in the summer of 2030, as Ben should be there," James told her.

"Okay, Group 22, thanks. Oh look, my mum's at the door of my house. I have to go now, James, and I'll take care of your dog."

James gave her a kiss on her forehead and she ran inside the gate into the arms of her mother. James waved goodbye as he realised he would have to go back to meet with Janet and Ben in the future.

PART FIVE
JUNE 2062

18 – THE SHIP

Captain Claude Duquette stood on the bridge of his ship *The Destroyer*, listening to the sound of the sonar.

"That's at least two military ships, approaching fast," he shouted at Anita, watching the horizon with binoculars as she moved to the engine control.

"Stop both engines," he ordered and leaving his seat walked across to the voice pipe to a cabin below and reported, "We have company."

"I'll be right up," was the reply, and returned to watch the horizon with binoculars and waited.

"Thank you, number one, I have the con," was all Nathalie said, and taking her position on the Commander's seat she opened her control panel and checked the ship's status.

"Engines all stopped, ma'am, awaiting your orders."

"Good, closing outer watertight doors and flooding ballast tanks port and starboard, we're going to disappear from these people," Nathalie replied.

"I can see them, two masts dead ahead, moving in a parallel line," reported Anita as the hull of the ship became awash with seawater.

"Diving to one hundred feet," Nathalie advised. The conning tower disappeared below the surface of the water and then levelled off.

"What do you suggest, Captain?" Nathalie asked.

"Best action is to remain dead in the water and let them pass on each side of us. Let's hope that confuses their sonars," he replied as the sound of their propellers grew louder.

The Destroyer was one of the last ships built in their world. It was nuclear powered and could travel at up to twenty-five knots on the surface and fifteen underwater. It was equipped with computer-controlled laser guns, for a crew of up to twenty. Nathalie had found the ship close to the Armana dome, abandoned for years, and had put the vessel back into service with the help of a group of survivors from the dome, mostly young women. The only seaman onboard was Toby, the ship's cook.

The ship's officers included professional military personnel from planet Earth; the captain, an ex-French naval officer and Anita, who had trained with US Special Forces. Two British scientists were also onboard, Susan and Bee, with their two children. They had been on the first expedition to the exo-planet more than ten years ago. Susan was an astronomer, who specialized in Astrophysics, while Bee was a biologist by training.

Claude had trained this unlikely crew along traditional navy lines following their escape from the dome over a year ago. During that time, they had survived a cataclysmic pole shift with earthquakes and tsunamis in search of a new safe land – post the cyclical deluge and flood.

As the two surface ships passed above them, they heard a new noise on their sonar, like a baby crying.

"Whales!" shouted Claude with glee. "Anita, can you get a fix on them?"

"Yes, they're quite faint on the starboard side, moving NW away from us," she replied.

"Captain, do you want us to follow them," Nathalie asked to which Claude nodded.

"Very well, now these visitors are gone, you have the con. I'm going below to explain to our crew why we have dived. They must have heard the noise of the surface ships. I hope there's still some lunch," she said, leaving her chair and going below.

"Slow ahead both engines and set a new course 045 degrees," the captain instructed Anita and then explained, "We should be able to hide behind these whales and then turn back to follow those two ships. I want to see where they are heading and why they are sailing at such a fast speed."

After ten minutes, Claude smiled at Anita and ordered a new course.

"Right full rudder to a heading of 180 degrees and increase speed to full ahead."

"But Claude, that will take us back to the island," Anita said.

"Yes, that's where I think they must be heading. There's no other land around here, Anita."

"Agreed, but now we know there's a military force to the north of us. They appear determined, organised. They must have access to a supply of fuel oil to be running ships like that."

"Exactly, so we don't want to go any further north. But I want to know what business they have with this Lyonesse island. Think about it, some of our crew were injured there only a day ago."

"I know, but what are you planning to do, land there again?"

"No, not yet. Let's go back and see why this island is so damn important to these people," Claude replied.

"I think you should tell Nathalie about this plan."

They sailed on for another hour as Claude calculated their distance to the island, when Nathalie appeared back on the bridge.

"We've followed those two vessels back to the island and with your permission would like to take a look."

"All right, what's your estimated distance to the island?" she asked taking her place back in the control seat.

"About five miles by my reckoning," Claude replied.

"I'll reduce our depth to twenty feet. That should expose just the conning tower, since we don't have a periscope. Stop all engines," she ordered.

Slowly, very slowly the ship rose in the water and they could look outside. When the water cleared from the small windows on the bridge, they were some miles from a rocky shore. In the distance they saw the two ships tied up on opposite sides of a jetty.

"Slow astern both engines," Nathalie ordered in alarm. "Your DR position was out by a couple of miles, Captain. What do you suggest we do now?"

"Maybe the whales screwed up my calculations. Can we go around the north end of the island and see what's on the east side? There's something about this that makes no sense," he replied.

"All right, I agree. We were met with excessive force the last time we landed and some of the crew are still recovering in the sickbay," Nathalie replied.

"Yes, that's why I think it's important," said Claude.

"But this time, Claude, I want a covert operation. Is that understood. If you can't find a safe place to hide, then we sail away to the west and say goodbye to this place," Nathalie ordered. "Set the course, Anita, to take us around the north coast and then south. You have the map of the island, don't you."

"Yes, ma'am. Altering course now to due east, 090 degrees," Anita confirmed.

Claude moved across to Nathalie. "I think you know what this is about, don't you. That's why you sent Kiya back on the spaceship we saw on the island. Are you going to admit that you're looking for aliens?" he whispered.

"I think you may be right, Claude. Now keep your eyes on the coastline and make sure we don't run aground," she replied and went below.

The ship continued on around the north coast of the island and then turned south, following the coast, when Nathalie returned.

"Claude, come here and look at this old map of the island we used last time," she said. "Now, about five miles down the coast you will see an inlet with a sandy beach and a headland of rocks."

"Yes, I remember that map, it was most useful for our landing on the other side of the island," he replied.

"Under that headland is a natural cave that was converted into an underground base for submarines, done a long time ago. I know our ship is a lot bigger, but I want to try and enter this base. That's better than surfacing outside," she proposed.

"Okay, sounds like a good plan, if we can get inside."

"Tell me when we reach the inlet and we can see if that's possible."

The submarine continued down the coast until Anita reported she could see the inlet with a sandy beach.

"Stop engines," Claude ordered to Anita.

"Turning hard starboard," he added to Nathalie who nodded in agreement.

Slowly the hull turned to face the headland with just the conning tower above the water, as all eyes focused on the cave.

"It's going to be a tight squeeze to get us in there," Claude announced looking through his binoculars.

"But is it possible?" Nathalie asked.

"Maybe, just after high tide would be best. Let's hope the entrance opens up higher once we get inside. But I think we should try," he replied.

"All right, I'm going to flood both ballast tanks and sit on the seabed until it gets dark tonight. Then we will have to surface. What's the depth here, Anita?"

"Looks flat and quite shallow at fifty feet."

"Good, let's sit on the bottom and wait for the tide tonight," she advised and the submarine quietly descended onto the seabed.

"Claude, you and Anita have been on watch for hours. Both of you go below, get something to eat and rest. Can you send Susan up to talk to me, if she feels well enough," she ordered, as the other two smiled in relief and prepared to leave the bridge.

19 - LATER

Claude and Anita went down the accommodation ladder and walked aft towards the galley.

"Well, Claws," Anita said using his nickname, "what do you think of her plan, sounds madness to me."

"Yes, it's not without some risk, even if we can inside the cavern."

When they reached the kitchen, they found Scota there, cleaning up after serving lunch. Scota had been the daughter of the king under the Amarna dome and a close friend to Kiya.

"Ah! We have two tired watchkeepers who are looking for something to eat?" Scotia asked smiling at them.

"Yes, looks like we missed the main dish, do you have anything cold we can eat?" Anita asked.

"No hot course today while we submerged. But for you I heat up some vegetable soup with bread, that okay?"

"Great, and some hot coffee would be good," replied Claude.

They sat down at one of the tables just outside the galley and continued the conversation.

"Getting inside that cave may look difficult, but I think I can help with the lasers inside the forward laser dome," Anita offered.

"How's that going to help?"

"If it's anything like the rear dome, I should get night time vision of the coastline with full magnification of the cliff. If I can shine two lasers on the entrance, it should help you line up the ship."

"Yes, but if the entrance is not big enough for the conning tower to enter, we would get trapped," Claude replied.

"Not on a falling tide, and perhaps I can cut away some of the rock with the lasers," she explained.

"Are you mad! That might bring down the whole cliff face and block the entrance forever."

"We both said this was a high-risk plan," she said as Scota returned with mugs of coffee and two bowls of soup.

"There you are," she said placing the food on the table and sitting down next to Claude, who was drinking his coffee.

"I hear we've gone back to the island again," she said as the other two looked at her in surprise.

"Nathalie told us, after you followed those two loud machines. Made a bad sound down here in the galley, frightened everyone."

"Sorry about that, Scota, but now we're hiding on the seabed so all is quiet," Claude replied smiling at her.

"I remember from the map you gave us last time; we must be near that enemy base we found on the north of the island. There are some very bad people there you should be afraid of."

"What do you mean, Scota, tell us what you have seen before," Anita asked looking at her soup.

"These people come on a big ship from the sky and take all our men away at Amarna. Didn't Kiya tell you," Scota replied.

"So you think these are the same people here on this island?" Claude asked.

"Yes, most certainly, and that noise above can only mean they come back to pick up more people here. Maybe today, maybe tomorrow, we don't know," Scota warned and standing up she walked back to the galley, leaving Claude and Anita looking surprised.

"Is this what Nathalie has been hiding from us all this time?" asked Anita.

"It's all starting to fit together. How we lost Kiya during our mission ashore and watching them load plastic chambers onto the ship would explain all that," Claude replied.

"Do we ask Nathalie what's her plan."

"No, not for now. But I understand why she's so determined to risk everything and hide *The Destroyer* in the base under the cliff," Claude replied.

When Scota returned to offer them more food, Claude decided to explain the plan to her. Scota had helped Claude lead the shore party on the island with success and since Kiya had left the ship, was now the leader of the female crew.

"Scota, we may need your help with the ship tonight. We are going to hide the ship in a cave, under some cliffs on the island. Can you make two mooring parties available?" Claude asked.

"From what time you think my crew will be needed?"

"In the early morning before you start your duties in the galley. Let's say from when the small hand on the clock is on four and the big hand on twelve."

"Understood, I bring three seamen with me to the main accommodation door to help with the ropes like last time," Scota replied and left Claude and Anita sitting alone.

After that Claude went up to his cabin for a sleep and Anita went up to the bridge to tell Nathalie of her plan with the lasers.

"I understand that we should try to enter on a falling tide and your lasers may help, but if high water is at 4:00 am that only leaves us a short window. Do you know what time sunrise is tomorrow?"

"It was around 5:30 this morning," Anita replied.

"That gives us a window of just over an hour to get hidden inside, assuming no other delays with the entrance. I expect to see you and Claude on the bridge at 0400 hrs.," replied Nathalie.

Anita left the bridge, deciding not to mention anything about blasting the rock away with her lasers. Instead, she went to make sure she could find the entrance to the forward dome compartment and that she could get inside.

Early the next morning Claude and Anita met on the bridge just before 0400 hrs. The control room of the ship was dark, with only green lighting to give the occupants time to gain their night vision, as they waited for instructions from Nathalie.

"Good morning," she started. "Let's get to the surface and inside this submarine base, and good luck to you all," was all she said, when she saw Scota hiding in the shadows.

"Hello, Scota, and to what do we owe the pleasure of your company?"

"Claude, er, the captain, asked me to provide a mooring party and I thought I might be of help before we get alongside," she replied.

"Did he now, and Anita's going to the laser dome so yes, you can stay and help, as you say," Nathalie replied.

"Good. Anita, take this short-range walkie talkie we used last time and keep it open all the time. Oh, and take the signal light with you from the bridge. You can shine it down the chamber inside to show me where we can tie up the boat," Claude said.

With that, Nathalie took her seat of command and pushed the buttons to expel the water from the ballast tanks, and the submarine rose up from the seabed.

"Anita, take Scota with you and night glasses also. She can stand watch on the forecastle and see if we are spotted by anyone on the cliffs. Off you go now, hurry," Nathalie ordered.

When the submarine surfaced Nathalie looked at Claude and smiled. "You have just over an hour, Captain, to get this boat inside before the sun comes up. Can you do it?"

"Yes, with help from Anita. It may be difficult, but not impossible," he said and they both trained their glasses on the cave in front of them.

"Claude, you have to open the outer hull doors as Scota can't get outside," Anita reported.

"Okay, the doors are unlocked now. Can you tell us what you see?"

114

"Give us a minute, we have to climb up… It looks all right, there are no lights or people on the cliff. You should commence approaching the entrance and I'll go down to the laser pod," replied Anita.

"Okay, tell me what you see down there."

"What's happening, Claude, what's Anita telling you?" demanded Nathalie.

"It's all right, there's no one on the cliffs and Anita is going down to her laser room. Look, I'll put this on the speaker and you can follow her observations," replied Claude, when he noticed the ship was drifting to the north of the cliff.

"Come in, Anita, are you in place to see the entrance?" asked Claude.

"Yes, just made it inside. You should see the two laser beams on the entrance now," reported Anita.

"Thanks, I see them – moving dead slow ahead now," Claude replied as the ship moved forward towards the cliffs. When it reached the entrance the conning tower was far too high to get inside.

"Claude, we have a problem. I don't think we have reached high tide yet. You have to back off and let me work with the lasers," was all Anita said.

"What are you going to do?"

"What we said before. I need to cut a meter off the top of the rock at the entrance. It's the only way."

"What? You can't do that; it might collapse the whole rock face!" shouted Nathalie.

"Claude, can you back the ship off from the rock face. Don't want any debris falling on Scota," Anita replied.

"Okay, you are clear," replied Claude as he reversed the ship.

"Now watch me. I have the lasers on low power with a setting for cutting through granite, but it may take a while," said Anita.

"What the hell is a meter?" shouted Nathalie at Claude.

"Oh! That's about three feet," Claude replied. They both watched the laser cutting away at the entrance. Claude noticed that the ship was now in dead line with the entrance, so the ship was being held at the top of the flood. They watched huge chunks of rock fall harmlessly into the water at the entrance as Anita cut her way around the top. After another half an hour, it looked as if Anita was finished.

"Claude, you are cutting this fine, in another ten minutes it will be light," announced Nathalie.

"Anita, are you finished?" Claude asked.

"Yes, line up the ship and you should be able to enter. Now the tide is ebbing the ship must be lower in the water," Anita confirmed.

"Okay, thanks, lining up now and going dead slow ahead," he said.

Much to Claude's relief *The Destroyer* sailed slowly into the submarine base and they all looked in amazement at the size. The basin was over a thousand yards long, two hundred yards wide and they couldn't see the height of the roof.

"There must be room for four submarines in this base," shouted Claude at Nathalie as the ship continued inside, with Scota's light at the front. Claude ordered stop engines as he could see the whole of their ship would be hidden inside.

"More lights please, Captain," shouted Nathalie, and the ships flood lights lit up their ship fore and aft. Anita and Scota ran down the fore deck to moor up the ship. Anita jumped ashore onto a narrow walkway as lines were lowered, and the ship was secured at both ends. When Anita jumped back onboard, she came face to face with Scota.

"Thanks, Scota, that was work well done," she beamed, but then saw the women were all holding ten-inch knives.

"The guards up there will come to the ship to kill us, don't you understand? Coming in here will have triggered some alarm, this place is not safe for any of us," Scota said.

"All right, close the inner door here and post guards on all the outer doors until we discuss this with the captain. Now, Scota, follow me to report this to the Bridge," Anita replied.

The two of them quickly climbed the stairs, letting Anita question Scota some more. "So have you been here before?" asked Anita.

"Oh yes! I was a prisoner here for several years, and you don't want to know what their people can do," Scota replied.

On arrival at the Bridge, they not only found Claude and Nathalie, but Susan and Bee as well. All of them turned as they entered the compartment.

"Claude, I think we may have a problem," Anita began, but then let Scota talk of her fears.

"How do you think we may have triggered an alarm entering this submarine base?" Claude asked calmly.

"When I worked here as a prisoner there were doors at the entrance to keep some water inside during low water. Some of the small submarines would damage the doors and we repaired them. My mooring party at the back of the boat say the doors have been torn away. That most certainly make alarm and guards come to see," Scota explained.

"All right, I agree it's a risk, but no one has come so far," Claude replied.

"No, Claude, but we don't want a gunfight on our hands either. Maybe it's better we turn off the deck lights, keep all the outer doors closed and wait to see if anyone comes for a few hours," Nathalie ordered and they all nodded in agreement.

"Thank you, Scota, for the warning. When your crew are rested and the tide is out, can you go outside again to see the status of the gates and report back to me. It would be most helpful," Nathalie said, smiling at her.

Scota and Anita took the stairs to leave the bridge, but Scota stopped to ask a question. "What Nathalie mean by 'status of the gates'?"

"That's just a way of asking how badly the gates are broken," Anita replied, smiling at her. Anita then stopped outside her cabin door marked 'Chief Gunnery Officer' and beckoned to her to come inside.

"Look, I know it hasn't been easy since you lost Kiya, but I prefer you ask me before you take weapons from the cabinet here. Now tell me what you think you need," Anita asked, unlocking the arms cabinet, as now Scota smiled at her.

"We need to make lots of smoke, so my crew can move to kill the guards. Also we need bombs to make big noise. Ah! Some more knives as well," Scota replied handing the weapons to Anita, who had found a canvas bag and carefully placed the items inside.

"You don't want any guns or pistols at all?"

"No, those for your people upstairs, okay."

"Now think, Scota, you must keep the bombs dry and away from any heat. It's all very dangerous, so not in your cabins, okay," Anita tried to warn her, but Scota took the bag and left the cabin to return to the galley below. Meanwhile, Anita threw herself on her bunk and slept from exhaustion.

20 - ANITA

Life on the ship continued without incident for the rest of the day.

Scota and Toby worked in the galley preparing lunch for the crew of six women, while Claude kept a watch on the bridge for any intruders outside. Nathalie went down to her cabin to sleep, while Susan and Bee played with their children near the galley, with all the outer doors locked down.

"Do you know why Nathalie wanted to come back to the island and hide in some underground base?" asked Bee while they were sitting at a table near the galley.

"I think it must have been to do with the rocket launch site we saw on the island. I bet that's not more than a couple of miles from there," Susan replied, watching their daughters busy drawing on some old paper they had found from the past.

"Have you looked outside?" Bee asked.

"Yes, but only from the bridge, and it's enormous. Nathalie wanted the outside lights turned off, so not much to see now."

"Okay, but what did you see before?"

"Nothing special, just a narrow walkway all along from the entrance. Then stepped terraces going up to an entrance higher up, and small stairs running down from the top, every hundred feet or so."

"Not a lot to see then."

"No, but Scota tells me there are some ancient paintings outside that might be of more interest," Susan explained.

"I need to get up to the bridge to look at that map of the island again. Something about this place doesn't feel right," Bee replied.

"Bee, have you looked at the time! We need to leave here soon to let the Armana women eat lunch first," Susan announced.

"All right, we can move back to my cabin and take some food with us and for the children to eat there," Bee replied. They cleared the table and went to look to see what was for lunch, taking their children with them.

Anita woke up starving. Looking at the clock, she saw it was late afternoon. She washed her face and hurried down to the galley to look for food. She was pleased to see that Scota was still there.

"Hi, Scota, sorry I overslept, is there any lunch left over?"

"No, it's all gone, but you can have some dinner. It's a beef stew that Toby made, should be ready shortly. You want some coffee?"

"Yes please," Bee replied, sitting down at a table. Scota joined her with the mug of coffee.

"Listen, I want to ask you something about that room where you go to fire the light."

"Yes, what do you want to know?"

"How much can you see from inside there?"

"Almost everything, why do you want to know?"

"I'm sending some of my crew outside when it's dark and want to ask if you keep a look-out for us? Just in case some of the guards come down here tonight."

"Yes, of course, I can do that. What time do you want to leave?"

"Your captain said in about an hour," Scota replied looking up at a clock on the wall. "So that's about 5pm."

"Good, let me eat an early dinner, and then go up and tell Claude."

"Thanks, Anita. I'm really scared of this place," she replied.

"Don't worry, I can see everything that moves, even in the dark. Remember to take the smoke bombs with you – I can even see people through the smoke," replied Anita, smiling at her.

After she had eaten, Anita went up to the bridge to tell Claude of her conversation with Scota.

"I also gave her smoke bombs, Claude, and some more knives, but she didn't want any guns."

"Sounds like we'll have a fighting party outside tonight, if you don't mind keeping a watch in the laser turret. Can you take a walkie talkie with you to keep in touch with us here?" Claude asked.

"Yes, of course. I think I had better get going down there to check there's no one about before they leave."

"Very good, I'll call Nathalie and ask her to come up to the bridge, while I go down and open the door to let the crew outside," he replied.

"Looks like it may be a long night," sighed Anita, leaving the bridge.

Anita first went down to the galley and gave a 'thumbs up' to Scota who was preparing her crew with dark clothing. She then went down a level and walked forward along the boat deck to the entrance to the laser turret. Climbing inside, she placed her hand on an identification pad, settled into her seat and looked at the dock outside. It only took a few seconds to power up the lasers, and not seeing any movement she called Claude on the short-range portable.

"Everything looks quiet outside; you can open the outer door."

"Confirmed, opening the door now – over," Claude replied.

Anita saw four human shapes appear on the walkway. To her surprise two of the shapes ran down to the stern of the ship and the other two ran up towards the bow and were then out of her sight.

Everything remained quiet for another ten minutes as Anita watched the entrance high up above their ship. Then the door opened and more shapes appeared at the entrance.

"Claude, we have company, have you shut the door?" she asked.

"Yes, back on the bridge, what do we do now – over."

As suddenly as the men had appeared the whole dock was covered in thick yellow smoke with explosions taking place everywhere outside. Anita immediately switched to infra-red vision and watched as two of the intruders on the left were attacked and left on the ground, while two more on the right suffered the same fate.

"What's happening outside, Anita, we can't see anything from up here – over," Claude shouted down his portable.

"Don't worry, Claude, I'm watching with my heat vision and our crew has already taken down four of the guards – going after the rest now."

"But what was all that gunfire, who was shooting at who down there?" Claude asked.

"That was not gunfire, Claude. I forgot to tell you, Scota took stun grenades to confuse the attackers, that's all – over," she replied.

"Can you see if any more people are entering the base – over," Claude asked.

"Negative, there are just four small people coming towards your door now. I think by their shape they're all our crew members."

"I hope so, because I'm going down to open the door now," said Claude, while Anita watched the entrance again.

"No more intruders coming down, Claude, you can open the door – over," Anita told him.

The door hissed open and Claude stepped out to face Scota. "What happened," he exclaimed, shocked at seeing blood on their clothes.

"We killed them all with our knives," she replied calmly.

"Right, you had better come inside and get cleaned up," he said standing aside as the crew members climbed aboard and the outer door was shut again.

"Anita, if it's still quiet outside, you can come back to the bridge – over," Claude said.

"Negative, Claude. Now the smoke has cleared I can see five or more bodies lying on the terraces. I don't think this is over. I'm staying here and you should ask Nathalie what we do next – over."

"Okay, will report back shortly – over and out," Claude replied.

Anita watched for the next few hours and saw two crew members drag the bodies down from the terraces towards the walkway. Then she lost sight of them but shuddered at the thought of the corpses being dumped in the water. After that, a fire hose was sprayed on the dock to remove all traces of the bloody incident. She waited until she thought the crew were back on the ship and then decided to call it a night.

She squeezed back out of the tunnel, and securing the hatch walked back along the cargo deck to look at one of the launches lashed down. Then she stopped, looking at the covered hull.

We've been too long on this planet and need to go home. It shouldn't take me long to prepare this boat, she thought and started to work away on the boat. Then she walked over to the entrance door and pushed the button to open the inner door. As soon as it was fully open, Anita opened the outer shell door and looked out. It was pitch dark with a cool breeze blowing in from the sea outside. She could hear the ship straining against the jetty as an incoming tide flowed into the cavern.

In five hours it will be high tide, ready to go outside, she thought and quickly closed the outer door again.

With that done, she went straight up to the galley to find Toby and tell him of her plan. Then, pouring herself a mug of a hot drink that passed as coffee, she climbed up to the bridge to find Claude. She handed over her mobile for charging and looked at him.

"So, Claude, tell me what you have decided to do next, because your crew just murdered at least five of those men. Whoever follows is not going to be so careless," she said.

"Nathalie wants us to go and recon that landing site as soon as it gets light. Do you want to come along?"

"What! You're inviting me to some sort of safari outside now."

"No, Anita. Nathalie thinks that one of those craft may land there in the morning and she wants us to watch and observe, that's all."

"All right, let me go and sleep. You can wake me when you're ready to leave, okay," she replied.

"Thanks for your help and goodnight," Claude said.

As she walked back down to her cabin, Anita thought that this might be a chance to leave the planet for good.

21 – LAUNCH PAD

Anita felt a hand shaking her as she woke and finally remembered there was something important she needed to do.

"Anita, wake up. Can you give me the key to the armament cabinet, I need to get some weapons," Claude said.

"You might at least knock on my cabin door. What time is it?"

"It's nearly 4 am and Nathalie wants to see us all on the bridge," he replied.

"Okay, okay, I'm coming. The key is on the top of the cabinet," she replied turning on a light.

"Right yes, found it! I need to take pistols and enough ammunition for this mission today."

"Take what you want, except the rifle with the telescopic sights, that's mine," Anita replied.

"Thanks, see you up on the bridge for the briefing," Claude said and left Anita alone again.

She sat down on her bunk and put her face in her hands, as a few tears ran down her cheeks. Then pulling herself together, she washed her face in the basin, brushed her hair, and pulled on her camouflage jacket again. Lifting the rifle out of the cabinet she placed a box of cartridges in the pocket of her jacket and left the cabin.

When she reached the bridge, she found everyone there already. Claude, Bee, Susan, Toby and Scota stood in a circle around Nathalie.

"Good morning, Anita, and welcome everyone," Nathalie started in the green night vision on the bridge.

125

"What are plans, Captain, for this mission ashore?" she asked.

"It's purely a recon mission to observe the people at the landing site and to see if a space craft lands later this morning," he replied.

"How many crew do you want to take with you?"

"I think just Scota and one other crew member who I'm told has experience of these tic-tac craft," said Claude.

"Right, any questions from the rest of you?" Nathalie asked.

"Yes, I think we need a parallel team to observe from the seashore and provide an exit route, in case the land mission is compromised," Anita proposed.

"Do you now. Any objections, Captain."

"Yes, I think that's an unnecessary risk of manpower," Claude replied, looking at Anita.

"In fact, I think a sea mission is a good idea. Thank you, Anita. How are you going to achieve that without any delay?" Nathalie asked.

"I prepared the starboard boat last night, charged up the battery and transferred the fuel from the other launch. It's ready to go as soon as we finish here," Anita replied.

"Really, such precise preparation without telling anyone?"

"Toby is advised and ready to help with launching the boat on the starboard side. With high water in an hour, there should be no problem to sail out to sea and up the coast before it gets light," Anita replied.

"Excellent, I'm going to approve your mission. There's a small landing place on the northern coast you can use that's closer to the landing pad. How many crew will you need?" Nathalie asked.

"Just two crew members for the boat," Anita replied looking at Scota.

"Very good, and you will work together with Claude. Each of you take a portable phone. I suggest you call each other at 0500 hrs. Are there any other questions?" Nathalie asked and with a shake of heads everyone started to move down towards the companionway.

"Just one moment. Susan, can you stay behind for a word please?" asked Nathalie. "Susan, I know you were injured last time ashore, but can you climb up the steps outside to the entrance?"

"Yes, I think that should be possible," Susan replied.

"Good, then take this camera and go up with a crew member to see some ancient paintings on the walls. Then come straight back and tell me what you think of these."

"Very good, do I need to take anything else?"

"Yes, take this revolver with you. Claude gave it to me, but you should have it if you're going outside," she said, handing her the pistol. "Let the others go on ahead and wait until it's light. You can get Bee to look after the children while you're away."

Susan took the camera and the gun and went down below.

Anita went straight to the galley to look for Toby but found Bee standing in front of plates of half-eaten sandwiches.

"Do you know where Toby went?" she asked.

"He's already down below with two of the crew… Do you know what you're doing, Anita?" Bee asked.

"What do you mean, taking a boat out? We've done it before, remember, and we all came back," Anita replied.

"Yes, and two of the crew were injured. Susan was hurt in the leg, so you had better be more careful this time," Bee said.

"Don't worry, I will," she replied. Wrapping some bacon sandwiches in paper and placing them in a backpack she left to go below.

After Bee watched her leave, she waited for Susan to arrive and saw she was holding a camera.

"Nathalie wants me to go up to the entrance and take some photos," Susan explained, holding up the camera.

"I don't know but everyone here has gone mad," Bee replied.

"No, not really, but I think we should prepare. Remember when I came back last time there was no infirmary for me to go to with my bad leg. Our girls won't be awake for another few hours, so let's get to it," Susan said.

"Good idea, but where?"

"Let's put a bed in the room where we held Bill as a prisoner and gather as much first aid in there as we can find," Susan proposed.

"All right, might as well do something. Oh, there are some sandwiches here if you feel hungry," Bee replied.

"Great, bacon! I don't know how Toby finds the time to prepare this at 4 am, but I could smell it coming down from the stairs."

****

When Anita went down to the cargo deck, she found Toby with the outer door open and the boat already swung outside the ship.

"Here you are, Anita, all ready to go? I started the engine and checked the fuel. You have enough for a couple of hours, no more," Toby advised.

"Thanks, Toby, you're the best," she replied giving him a big hug, and seeing the two crew were already onboard, she jumped onto the cockpit at the stern to take command.

"Lower away," she shouted at Toby who pushed a button, and the launch went down the side of the hull into the darkness. As soon as the hooks were released, Anita engaged the drive and the boat moved in a circle and back out towards the dim light at the entrance.

The small craft sailed down the side of the ship and immediately felt a strong wind blowing in from the sea outside. As she approached the entrance, she saw white horses on the waves from a strong southerly wind outside. Anita signalled to the crew members on the fore deck to join her in the cockpit as the boat hit the open seas and she turned north with a following sea. With the wind behind them, she thought they would reach the north of the island in under half an hour, as the boat pitched and rolled in the waves.

As dawn started to break, the coastline north became clearer to her and the high headland gave way to low land in the north. She looked at her two crew members huddled together in the cockpit and realised they were feeling the cold from the wind, dressed in only cotton shirts and pants.

"You know how to steer," she shouted at the women and getting no reply, pulled the one closer to her up to the boat's wheel.

"I'm going to get us some jackets," she shouted, remembering having seen clothing in the other launch. "Can you just steer straight like this. I'll only be a minute," she said, handing the wheel over to the crew member and watching to see if she understood before dashing below.

Finding the locker, she pulled out three leather jackets and started to put one on, balancing herself in the small cabin. At that moment a big wave hit the boat and she was thrown off her feet as sea water poured over the stern of the boat.

"Christ, we've been pooped," she shouted and jumped back into the cockpit. Taking the wheel again she was able to turn the boat back on course, just in time. Then she saw that both crew members were not only cold, but now soaking wet.

"Your jackets are in the cabin below," she shouted above the wind, showing them what she was wearing and pointing below.

They went down and returned to the cockpit, smiling with some weather protection.

As the launch reached the north of the island, Anita turned west and the wind went down to a strong breeze. They followed the coast for another ten minutes, looking for a small cove that Nathalie had mentioned where it should be possible to land.

"Do you remember how to moor the boat from last time?" Anita asked the tall woman she remembered from before.

"Yes, I take the rope from up the front to hold the boat steady," she replied as a quay appeared with steps down from above.

"Do you see anyone around?" Anita asked urgently.

"No one around. Think it safe to go ashore," replied the other woman.

Anita turned the boat in a circle as they slowly approached the quay and reversed so that the bow was pointing out to sea. One crew member ran up to the bow and jumped ashore to secure the boat while the other secured the stern. When they finished, Anita jumped ashore with her rifle and backpack and signalled them both to come to her.

"From now on, no loud talking, only whispers. From now on we lie on the ground. No one stand up, do you understand?" Anita asked, crouching down, as both women did the same and nodded.

"This place is very dangerous for us. You, lie on the ground and look up at the land all the time, and tell us if the boat has been seen. You," she said pointing to the other woman, "come with me up the stairs to see what's above. Is that clear."

The two women looked at each other and agreed without saying a word. One went to lie down on some grass above the front of the boat and the other gave a thumbs up.

"All right follow me," Anita said in a whisper, and they moved up each side of the stairs to give them more cover. Once they reached the top, they both lay down on the ground and Anita looked around her. There was a three-foot wall all along the base and 500 yards up the coast was a low building that looked out onto the sea. The only cover they had were the brown leather jackets they wore, but the hull of the boat below moored on the quay could not be hidden.

"What can you see outside?" whispered Anita.

"No one there," she replied, giving a thumbs up.

Anita remembered she had to call Claude. Opening her backpack, she took out the portable and slid a few yards down the stairs to talk. Looking at her watch she saw it was already past 5:15 am and turned on the receiver.

"Base to Claws, do you read – over," she said in a low voice, but only heard static, so she waited and repeated her message every two minutes.

"Hello, base, we hear you. What's your status – over?" Claude replied.

"We are in position in front of the base, what's your position – over," Anita asked.

"We are at the wire around the base and have a key to enter, but no cover inside – over," Claude replied.

"Understood, will advise as soon as we see movement here. Stay online – over," Anita replied.

"Roger that," Claude confirmed, and Anita switched off, moving back up the bank on the side of the stairs. When she got back to the top she signalled to her partner if anything was new and looked outside.

All she saw was a flat area of green grass and in the distance some sort of circular landing pad painted white. Looking around there was no one to see at all, but as the sun started to break through the clouds it made them even more exposed. Another half an hour passed, and she opened her backpack again and took out some sandwiches, handing one to her colleague.

She shook her head and pointed to the woman on lookout below, so Anita gave her a second sandwich. With a thumbs up, she scooted down to her friend and was back in a minute. After that they both ate their bacon sandwiches in silence, with their backs to the wall. The only things moving were what looked like seagulls, flying in circles above them.

22 – NUMBERS

"All this work for an infirmary, Susan… it's very good. But aren't you meant to be going outside?" Bee reminded her.

They were sitting in the galley having a hot drink that just about passed as coffee, both feeling tired after moving a bed into the makeshift infirmary.

"Yes, I haven't forgotten. Nathalie told me to wait until after sunrise to take the photos," she replied. The last remaining crew member was hovering around them preparing food and water for when, or if, the other crew members returned.

"All right, it's time to go," she announced and stood up to leave, holding the camera in her hand.

"Can we meet at the outer door, as I need a jacket. I'm meant to take this girl with me to help climb up the stairs," Susan remarked, nodding to the girl to leave.

Two minutes later, Bee opened the main door and the two women started climbing the stairs to the entrance of the cavern. When they reached the top, Susan waved and Bee closed the outer door again.

"You come with me this way," the young woman said.

"You've been her before?" Susan asked.

"Yes, many years ago when I was a little girl. Will show you the paintings inside," she replied, and led her down a path to a small cave under a rocky overhang.

"When sun rises, it shines into this cave, but no sun today."

When she looked inside all she could see was darkness and kicked herself for not bringing a torch.

"No worry, you stay," and the woman lit some candles on a shelf at the back of the chamber. At the same time, the clouds parted and sunlight streamed into the cave, revealing the paintings.

"Wow," exclaimed Susan taking photos of the paintings until the sun disappeared again.

"Tell me what your people think this painting of your planet means?" Susan asked.

"That is how our planet turns over every time the big moon returns," she replied.

"And all the numbers?"

"That, I have no idea. But if you study numbers, you will see how many times they return. Are you finished, we must get back," she replied in haste.

"No, wait a minute, I just want to touch this carving," Susan said, but the candles were blown out and they returned inside the submarine chamber again.

When they reached the outer door, it opened and Nathalie was standing there.

"Were you able to take some photos? Come, we can enlarge them upstairs," she said, telling the girl to close the door again.

Nathalie transferred the four photos to her personal screen and looked at them closely.

"You did well to catch the paintings in sunlight. This first one shows the planet with the continents at the position when we left Armana. But the second has most of the northern continents in the southern hemisphere with the equator now close to where the north pole was before. Do you think that's possible?" she asked.

"Yes, we know the ship experienced a real pole shift from that moon, but then it flipped back again. I'm sure we're not on the equator now, it's not warm enough here. Remember, on our planet Earth they found that 18,000 years ago the equator was much further south of Arabia, right on the Indus valley and on Easter Island, so it's possible it moves around here too," Susan replied.

"All right, and what about these two photos with all these numbers?" Nathalie asked.

"I'm not sure, I need to study them more closely. But, and it's a big but, I have seen this mathematical series of numbers back on Earth."

"Really, so where were they found and who made them?"

"The numbers were carved on clay tablets and found by archaeologists around the 18th century. They were written by Sumerian astronomers, some estimate as much as 6,000 years ago."

"All right, go on, what do they mean?"

"If you look at the first photo, it starts with just the numbers 60 and 70 that are multiplied together to give a range of periods of time."

"What's so special about these two numbers?"

"They are an exact multiple of the astronomical cycles of the outer planets Uranus, Neptune and Pluto in our solar system."

"Why would anyone want to know that?"

"Because they were looking for the sacred number called the 'Great Year' – the great constant of our solar system. That's what I remember. If you look on the last photo the largest number you will see is 195,955,000,000,000. That's the number in seconds, not years. The Sumerians were credited with the idea of dividing hours and minutes into equal parts they called seconds," Susan said, pointing at the screen.

"But why seconds? Come on, Susan, what's the real number in years, on our planet Earth?

"The number for one rotation is 25,900 in our Earth years."

"So, if this planet is in our galaxy, are we close to Earth?"

"The Milky Way galaxy is huge, some 100 light years across. But all planets will take the same time for one rotation around the centre," she replied.

"What's the distance from our solar system to the nearest star?"

"Our nearest stars are Alpha Centauri A and B, about 4 light years from Earth," replied Susan.

"Wasn't there hope of life on a planet close to one of those stars?"

"Yes, that was Proxima Centauri that rather came to an end with a solar flash we saw on Earth in 2021."

"Yes, I remember Christmas day 2012, the end of the Mayan calendar. So how do you think that happened?" Nathalie asked.

"They think our neighbours passed through a huge galactic energy cloud when the star heated up until it gave off a solar flash."

"If we saw that in 2012, is it possible our sun has moved into the same energy cloud by now?" asked Nathalie.

"Yes, it's possible. The sun is moving through space at 500,000 miles an hour, dragging all the planets and Earth behind it. That was thought to be empty space, but it's not always so empty," said Susan and continued, "Doing the math's in my head and working forward from 2012, our Sun would need to be in such a high energy cloud for about twenty years before it released a solar flash."

"So, when do you think it might happen?" Nathalie asked.

"The earliest that might happen would be 2030 or 2031, but would not kill everyone on our planet. But most of the electric machines would be dead," Susan replied.

"But if this has happened several times before, how did these Sumerians know all this 3,000 years ago?" asked Nathalie.

"Someone, maybe someone from here, must have given this calculation to people on Earth because none of the outer planets were visible to the human eye 3,000 years ago. We also have to accept that our ancestors may have come from outer space," Susan replied.

"Yes, and that brings me to another question and that's the female monthly cycle, that depends on the moon on our planet. But here the moon only returns every ten years and most of us only experienced periods when the moon returned in Amarna. So do the Amarna women only become fertile every ten years?"

"Yes, that's a good question. A species that only recreates every ten years would be quite different to us humans. I did wonder if the attack on the dome was triggered by those men in the north, wanting to harvest fertile females before the pole shift event occurred."

"Does that mean that every Amarna woman may live to be over a hundred years old, if they can only conceive every ten years?"

"Oh, Nathalie, I don't know. I'm not a doctor of human DNA. But our human DNA has made some big changes in the last hundred thousand years. Look how it replaced the Neanderthal with Homo Sapiens," Susan replied.

"So, in the distant past in Europe, when cavemen were painting in caves in France, people were writing numbers on clay tablets. Then some people knew the number of years for the solar system to make one revolution around its centre."

"Yep, that's about it, although it sounds impossible."

"Right then, let's keep this to ourselves for now," Nathalie said, closing down her screen and getting up. They both walked towards the exit from the bridge, but then Nathalie stopped.

"Thanks, Susan, for giving me your ideas on some questions that have been swirling around in my head for weeks. What do you really think of our captain Claude, were you ever attracted to him?"

"Yes, when we trained, I couldn't get enough of him. At that time ten years ago, if he had made a pass, I would have hopped into bed with him. It's not difficult to explain, with a one-way dangerous mission to the unknown. He was a man who was calm, protective and I admit it made my knees go wobbly. I think women are hard wired to follow that kind of man and before long you know you're going to have sex."

"But as an astronomer who trained for a mission to an exo-planet, do you have any personal ideas of where these people might have come from in our universe?" Nathalie asked.

"Before I left that cave outside, I saw something that had been carved on a rock near the entrance and recognised it as a group of stars in the constellation that's over a hundred light years from our home planet. The big star in that constellation is Arcturus, you can easily find it on the star globe up here. But why someone should etch that on a rock here is beyond me," Susan replied.

"So, we really are no closer to an answer."

"No, and I don't want to gossip, or criticize the behavior of anyone on the ship, but we both know that our virile captain has been intimate with both Kiya and Anita, on and off. Having sex with two women at around the same time and yet neither of these women conceived, that's what I couldn't understand," Susan replied.

"Yes, that's true, but it might be something to do with the stress of living on a submarine. Confidentially, I can tell you that Captain Claude is going to be very surprised, when and if he returns here today," Nathalie said, placing a finger on her lips and smiling as she walked back down to her cabin.

23 – TIC-TAC

Meanwhile, back on the north of the island close to the spaceport, Anita could hear men moving around. She took the telescopic sights off her rifle and looked at the scene outside. Two men were dragging something that looked like pipes across to the landing pad, while other men were joining them from the building just down the coast.

She signalled to her assistant to keep a watch, while she slithered down the stairs to call Claude.

"Base to Claws – over."

"Claws here, we are seeing movement, do you copy – over."

"Yes, looks like they are expecting a visitor – over."

"Roger that, will keep you posted – over," Anita replied and returned to keep watch. Another half hour passed and still nothing, as the men kept looking up at the sky.

Just when Anita had almost given up, her companion looked at her with a smile on her face and pointed. Then she saw a silver shape moving across the flat land towards the landing pad. As it approached it got larger and larger. A huge flying cylinder, bigger than their ship, was approaching with no engine noise at all.

It appeared to be coming in to land on the white pad and hovered a few feet off the ground, then continued down, throwing soil and debris high in the air. The men ran out of the way as it finally came to a stop a hundred yards from Anita, with one end facing the sea, towering above them. The only sound was the wind blowing across the landing site and a crackle of electric shocks that were now earthing

138

themselves. Anita watched as the men returned and began frantically dragging the pipes towards the cylinder. Perhaps they planned to wash the cylinder with seawater to cool it down?

Anita felt they were much too close for comfort and signalled her companion to come up from the boat, and the three of them ran to take shelter under the wall of the building further up the coast. Hiding above the rocks, they watched as the men sprayed water on the craft where it hissed into steam and crackled in the air.

Finally, as she watched through her telescopic sights, she saw the outer door of the cylinder partly open then close again. The guards returned, shouting at each other until they saw a man holding a black tablet in his hand and the door descended again. When it reached the ground, it exposed an inner vertical door that slowly rose to the top of the cylinder. Inside, people appeared who started to walk down a ramp in a daze.

"You see, all people in a trance and now leave tic-tac to go to boats," her companion whispered.

"Why did you call it a tic-tac?" Anita asked.

"We saw them in Amarna before the dome was built. I came here once as passenger when I was a girl. This one had a big problem to land and then problem to open door. Never seen that before," she replied.

"Can you guess how many passengers on this tic-tac?" Anita asked.

"Maybe... what you call a hundred," she said and held up five fingers.

"You mean, five times a hundred, or more." Anita gasped as she watched the men and women walking off the cylinder and down the path towards the quay where the two military ships were moored. The guards were keeping the people in two long lines, armed with wooden sticks and spread out all along the path to the quay. Taking her chance, Anita moved down over the rocks to call Claude.

"Come in, Claws, urgent – over."

"Receiving you, base, what's happening there? We can see people – over."

"Roger that, the cylinder is discharging its human cargo. We think it may be as many as 500, expect to take an hour or more – over."

"We may be able to move closer now the goons are occupied – over," Claude replied.

"Okay, but be aware there is a force at the front door. Repeat, we have eyes on guards there – over."

"Understood – over and out," Claude replied, but Anita couldn't understand why he was in such a hurry to get to the cylinder.

Claude and Scota had already entered the base and were lying on the grass two hundred yards from their target, watching the movements around the cylinder through binoculars.

"If we crawl slowly towards the back of the cylinder, where they can't see us, can we get onboard?" Claude asked Scota.

"Yes, there is a maintenance door that we may be able to open," she replied.

"How long do you think it will take for all the people to leave? Anita thinks there may be five hundred on the ship," Claude said as they kept moving forward on their stomachs.

"Too long, we need to get to that control room to find out the problem. Maybe the pilot is dead," Scota replied.

"Okay, let me take another look, as I think we can run to the back from here," said Claude, but Scota didn't wait, she ran forward ten yards and lay flat on the ground.

Claude watched again to make sure they weren't seen, and when he gave her a thumbs up, she ran the last fifty yards to the back of the cylinder. After that, Claude ran the final distance to join her, only to find the other crew member already there, hugging Scota and smiling.

"Great, who did you say this assistant was?" Claude asked.

"My best friend here was a pilot on these tic-tacs. She knows how to open the door here," Scota replied, pointing to the shell casing that was still hot, but Claude couldn't see any door.

"You have bottle of water please?" Scota asked.

"Yes, thirsty work," Claude replied pulling the bottle from his backpack, but Scota poured the water onto the shell plating. The other woman knelt down and placed a black box on the surface and a small door slowly slid aside.

"Wow, that's cool," Claude exclaimed.

"Yes, but entrance too small for a big man like you. I go with my friend to see the problem and you stay here to keep watch, okay," Scota insisted as her friend climbed inside and Scota followed.

Claude, now left outside, carefully looked down the side of the cylinder to check that people were still leaving. He could see one guard on his side of the entrance and guessed there was at least a second on the other side. He pulled out his revolver and sat down on the dry earth, wondering how long this would take. He considered calling Anita, but thought it too risky and checked to make sure his receiver was switched off. After some time had passed, he checked his watch and saw they had been inside for over half an hour, when he heard a small voice.

"Claude, Claude, can you come inside," said a voice sounding like Scota. Taking his backpack off, he squeezed inside, to see a vertical ladder in the small chamber with the figure of Scota at the top.

"I'm going to lower the pilot down. It's someone you know, but she's unconscious. Can you help us?" Scota asked.

"What do you mean, someone we know," Claude asked, watching a slim woman dressed in grey shorts and a pink top being slowly lowered down the ladder, into his arms.

141

"Can you put her body on the floor and climb outside? It will give me the space to pass her out to you," Scota shouted down at him.

Claude squeezed out and waited as the head and shoulders of a young girl appeared at the entrance. Holding her body under her arms, he carefully lifted her out onto the ground. Next, Scota appeared and looked at Claude closely.

"You don't recognise her, Claude? It's Kiya!" Scota exclaimed.

"Kiya, that's impossible, she's dead," Claude replied.

"She would have been in another hour in that control room," replied Scota.

"What was wrong with the ship?" Claude asked.

"Something to do with fine grains of sand. Do you have a lot of sand on your planet?"

"Is she injured?"

"No, I gave her some medicine to make her sleep while we take her back to the ship, if you can call Anita."

Claude nodded and took out his walkie talkie. "Claws to base, can you read me – over."

"Yes, Claws, what's your status, we can't see you – over."

"We are without eyes and have one person for medical extraction. We need to come to you for the boat – over," Claude replied.

"Affirmative, will prepare now. All the people have left now, you should watch for us at the wall – over."

Anita guessed they must be hiding at the back of the cylinder but was sorry to hear one of his team was injured. When she next looked up, the last of the human cargo had left the cylinder. Two guards were following them down the path where all the others had gone.

"We go back to the boat now, as the others will join us there," she explained to her two crew members and they all scrambled along the rocks back to the steps. Anita sent one crew member to meet Claude at the top of the steps, while she went onboard to check the fuel for a return voyage.

Meanwhile, Claude lifted Kiya up into his arms and Scota looked outside to see the last of the people had left the cylinder. A moment later they heard the small access door close shut and the cylinder started to hum.

"Come, Claude, we have to move quickly, the cylinder is going to take off again," Scota shouted and taking his arm she dragged him away and they started running.

"But what about your assistant?" Claude shouted.

"She stay onboard to test the problem again, then land craft for repair," she replied. "Okay, now you give me Kiya and lie down. Cover you face and eyes as take-off makes a lot of dust."

Anita, looking up from the boat, saw the enormous cylinder pass over her head. The wind from it strained the mooring lines and the craft moved further out over the sea.

When the noise stopped, Claude looked up and saw they were alone on the landing strip, the cylinder was gone and someone was waving at them by the sea wall.

"Scota, are you all right?" he asked.

She sat up and spat some dust from out of her mouth. Then she turned to Kiya and pulled her upright to make sure she was still breathing.

"Yes, everything okay, we can go now," she replied looking around the deserted site.

"So, if this is Kiya, why is she wearing a pink tee-shirt and girl shorts?" Claude asked,

"I expect she spent plenty of time on the beach, meet many new boyfriends, Claude."

"What!"

"Come on, I just tease you. Let's go and find Anita's boat. Can you carry Kiya for me?" Scota replied, standing up and looking around.

Claude lifted Kiya up into his arms and they walked towards the crew member to find the boat. Scota led the way to the wall, and Claude carried the young Kiya down the steps to the boat.

News must have travelled fast as a crew member stood on the quay, with her short knife drawn. Scota just looked on and smiled.

"Please, you must let us take her back to the ship. You can see her when she is awake," the crew member said, taking the unconscious girl in her arms and carrying her below to the cabin. Claude jumped onto the boat and came face to face with Anita.

"Let go forward, let go aft," Anita ordered as the boat reversed from the quay and Anita turned the wheel to make a course back along the north coast.

"So, Claude, you have got your old girlfriend back, are you happy?" Anita asked, watching him grip the top of the windbreak with his hands.

"Are you able to handle this boat, Anita, or want me to take the wheel," Claude replied.

"I'm quite capable, thank you. It was rough when we came up here this morning, so you can expect a strong headwind to get back," Anita replied.

When they rounded the headland and sailed south the little boat felt the full force of a head wind again. Anita sent one of the crew inside, who gave her jacket to Claude and went to sit at the back of the boat.

Scota came out of the cabin wearing one of the leather jackets and came to talk to Anita at the helm.

"What happened to Kiya, is she all right?" Anita asked.

"Yes, she's sleeping on the bed inside. How long will it take to reach our ship?" she asked.

"Maybe another hour, as we're not going very fast with this wind or I will make you all sick. I heard your assistant was once a pilot of those cylinders you call tic-tacs, is she coming back?" Anita asked, shouting in the face of the wind.

"Yes, she went to land somewhere close by and you may see her shortly," Scota replied as they both scanned the horizon ahead.

Nothing happened for a few minutes as Anita looked down at the fuel gauge that was showing nearly empty and the boat continued to pitch up and down in the rough seas.

"Look, look, right ahead, that looks like her tic-tac," Scota shouted in excitement, loud enough that it brought Claude to his feet to see.

"Yes, but what's it doing? It's going to be hovering above us in a few minutes," Anita replied.

"Right, but look at the sea ahead of us, it's flat calm. Full speed ahead, Anita, the cylinder is helping us get back without all that unpleasant pitching," Claude shouted.

For the next twenty minutes the spaceship followed them down the coast until the headland came into view at last.

"Great, I think we're going to make back," said Anita, pointing out the fuel gauge to Claude, as she steered the boat towards the entrance to the submarine base.

"Now look," Scota shouted again as the cylinder descended further into the sea and landed on the water.

"What in heaven's name is the pilot doing?" replied Claude.

"I think it's okay. She will let the tic-tac sink under the water and stay hidden down there, like we did, you see," Scota replied.

"Your English has improved, Scota, and you're right, that's exactly what we did," replied Claude, as the cylinder sank below the waves and disappeared. When the boat finally entered the cavern Anita saw their huge ship sitting on the seabed, only shallow water around it.

"Claude, look, there's little water inside here. Can you go up on the bow and guide me? We need to get up into a channel or we will be stuck here for hours," she said, cutting the power to the engine as the crew members came out to see what was happening.

"Okay, give me a torch from the cabin to help me see, can you?" he replied and then Anita had a better idea. She pulled out a distress flare from a cockpit locker, ripped off the protection and fired the rocket up into the air. Immediately the huge chamber was lit up with red light, so that anyone on the bridge would know they had returned.

"Keep going straight ahead, we are almost back at the hooks," shouted Claude. Then the lower access door opened and bright light flooded down onto the little boat. Looking up, Claude could see Toby lowering the two hooks to lift their craft out of the water.

Holding a mooring hook, he pulled the wire with the steel hook towards the boat, as crew at the stern did the same.

"Forward hook connected," he shouted to Anita. Seeing Scota was struggling with the aft hook, he ran down to help her.

Once that was connected, Anita shouted up to Toby, "All connected, Toby. Lift us up now." Slowly, the wires took the weight and the boat was lifted up the side of the ship.

As the red light from the flare died away, they were back into darkness. When the boat reached the cargo deck, they saw Susan, Bee with their children, and Toby all smiling at their safe return. Susan was holding what looked like a stretcher.

"Can you pass me that stretcher," Scota ordered and disappeared into the cabin. The other crew members huddled around as finally the body of a person was lifted out onto the stretcher, while Claude and Anita watched.

"Claude, what happened?" Susan shouted at him in shock.

"They found Kiya on that spaceship. Do you have a place we can take her?" he replied above all the activity.

"Yes, we have made a sick bay. Is she still alive?" Susan replied.

"She's been sedated for the journey back here, but let Scota and her crew handle this. We have been asked to stand aside," Claude replied.

"I can show you the way to the infirmary," Bee said as the stretcher came onboard, carried by two crew members and Scota.

They watched in amazement as Anita jumped onto the ship in tears and ran inside as fast as she could. She ran up to the galley and then up the stairs to the bridge, where she found Nathalie waiting for her.

The two women hugged each other and Anita wept in her arms.

"There there, my dear. I knew this would be a shock for us all and for you in particular," Nathalie said, trying to soothe her emotions.

"But how did you know, that's not possible," said Anita.

"Yes, it is. I can't talk to them but have been monitoring the movements of these spaceships for some time now and it sounded like something was arriving from our planet Earth, so I took a chance."

"Really, and one of the crew is flying that thing now, because we just saw it submerge in the water outside," Anita said catching her breath.

"That was just luck. We found out that one of the Amarna women was a pilot in the past and when we have all adjusted to this new situation, it may be possible for you all to go back home," Nathalie explained.

"You mean go back to our planet?"

"Yes, my dear. You, Susan, Bee and Claude have all been here for far too long. Your mission to this planet is almost over. Leave me and the Amana women to find a new home here."

"You don't want to come?"

"Yes, maybe, but not now, sometime later. You and Claude have both been a great help, but now you have to let go and go back home," Nathalie replied with tears in her eyes.

24 - SCOTA

Perhaps that would have been how it ended, Nathalie thought making her way down to the galley where she knew Claude and all the Amarna crew would be celebrating the return of Kiya.

Toby had prepared hot soup, fresh bread and a drink that most certainly was not the usual coffee. She walked around all the crew members, smiling and shaking hands until she reached Claude.

"Well done, Captain, that was a very successful mission for us all. Can I have a word outside for a moment," Nathalie asked.

"Yes, of course, right now?"

"I don't want to spoil your party, but I need to see all the team on the exo-mission on the bridge in an hour, at seven pm. That's you, Anita, Susan, and Bee. You had better include Scota, but no one else. I'm afraid it's not good news," Nathalie said, then turned away and left to return upstairs.

Claude returned to the party and made his way to Anita to see what she knew.

"Nathalie wants to see us all upstairs on the bridge at seven. Do you know what's this all about?" Claude asked.

"Yes, I spoke to her earlier, we're all going home, Claude!" she said laughing at him.

"You're drunk. I don't think that's what this is about," he replied.

"Why don't you go fuck yourself, since you've fucked most of the women on this boat," she replied.

Claude quickly retreated and sought out Susan, who was standing next to Bee.

"We have to meet on the bridge with Nathalie at seven. Can you put your girls to bed early and join us?" Claude asked as Bee looked on in surprise.

"Yes, I suppose so. We need to take some dinner to the girls and get them asleep. Is it really that important?" Susan asked.

"Nathalie was most insistent with me. That's all I can tell you," he replied.

As Susan turned away, he touched her on the arm to add some more. "Susan, can you take care of Anita, she looks to have been drinking too much tonight."

"Yes, we will bring her with us when we are ready," Susan replied, not looking surprised.

After that he moved around to find Scota, but she was nowhere to be seen. Five minutes before seven Claude left the party to find Scota standing outside the sick bay, talking to one of her crew members.

"How's our patient tonight?" Claude asked.

"Doing well, thank you, she's awake at last. Are you going up to the bridge? I hear Nathalie wants to talk to us," she replied.

"Great, do you want to join me?" Claude asked.

"Yes, lead the way," she replied and they climbed up the stairs to the bridge.

It was fifteen minutes later before the others arrived, and while they waited Claude offered his Captain's chair to Scota. When Anita, Susan and Bee finally arrived, Nathalie started the discussion.

"This was not the discussion that I wanted to have tonight. I spoke to Anita earlier and told her that I had plans that with the space craft Claude and his team secured, it was time for you all to return to our planet Earth. So, bear with me as I need to ask some questions about what really happened today," Nathalie said.

"You mean we're not fucking going home," Anita shouted and slid onto the floor.

The whole room realised this was not going to be a pleasant discussion and everyone started talking at once.

"Please everyone, calm down and I will explain. As I told Anita earlier, I found a way to track the movement of this space craft that I think returned from planet Earth, with Kiya."

"Why didn't you tell us earlier?" Claude asked.

"Yes, that was wrong. But I couldn't be certain and didn't want to raise your hopes," Nathalie replied.

"How long ago did this cylinder leave our planet?" Susan asked.

"In Earth years, about thirty years ago," Nathalie said and everyone gasped.

"Yes, that's quite possible with our theories of space-time. Time moves at different speeds to different observers across the Milky Way galaxy. To someone on Earth, it looked to have taken thirty years, but to us here it may only have been a few days," explained Susan.

"Why have you called this meeting?" Claude asked.

"The problem is that although I tracked the cylinder to the island today, I can't communicate with it. I saw it take off again, but fifteen minutes before you arrived it disappeared," said Nathalie.

"That was when it landed on the sea outside, we all saw that," Anita confirmed and looked at Scota for her explanation.

"Scota, can you tell us what you think? Is the cylinder sitting on the seabed outside or has it left us?" Nathalie asked.

"I don't know. At first, I thought it must have gone underwater to hide, but there's another possibility. If the pilot wanted to leave without any trace, my friend Tia might have done a time jump under the water. If that's correct, it's almost impossible to track," she replied.

Everyone looked at her more closely, realising these women knew a lot more about time travel than they had understood.

"Who exactly is Tia?" Claude asked.

"She was a princess at Amarna, before Nathalie helped us build the dome. She was my friend who helped us find Kiya inside the tic-tac," Tia replied.

Postlude

"Okay, Scota, can you tell us what happened when you went inside the cylinder? As you know, I waited outside," Claude said.

"Yes, of course. On the back of the cylinder, Tia opened a small door on the outer shell plating that gave access to the maintenance tunnel that runs the whole length of the cylinder to the control room."

"Then it was possible to walk along the tunnel, while the passengers were still leaving the craft below?" Claude asked.

"Yes, but not walk. It's a small tunnel, you have to crawl on hands and knees in dark for a very long time," Scota replied.

"Did you smell any burning or see smoke inside the tunnel?" Susan asked.

"Yes, very hot and much frightened. I never did this before, but I just followed Tia along to the end," said Scota.

"Okay, what did you find there?" Susan asked.

"At first nothing, but then Tia pulled open a hatch and there was a light below. When we looked, everything appeared operational, except there was a person asleep in the control chair. Then Tia knew how to lower steps for us to get inside and we went below."

"So you didn't know who this person was, no idea that it was Kiya," said Claude.

"No, when we checked she was breathing but not good, so I gave her some medicine for her to sleep."

"Do you remember what you gave her?" Bee asked.

"Some herbs from Amarna, white poppy seeds to make her sleep."

"Scota, that's morphine, how much did you give her?"

"Everything I had, what could I do? I knew we would have to carry her along the tunnel and leave Tia to find the problem. So many other problems at same time," she explained.

"So Tia helped you lift the girl up the stairs and then you dragged her back along the tunnel to me?" Claude replied.

"Yes, it was only when we lifted her up that we both saw that it was Kiya. She was wearing strange clothes I never saw before. As she

151

was still breathing, we decided to push her up into the tunnel. I said goodbye to Tia and she closed the hatch again. That was the last time I saw her," Scota explained.

"Can you think back, was this control room clean and tidy? No sign of a fire or damage at all?" Claude asked.

"No, not tidy at all. There were wires all over the control panel. And an open backpack, with shiny paper and empty bottles on the floor. But no sign of damage from a fire," replied Scota, and everyone looked around the bridge wondering where this discussion was going.

"I'm sorry to ask so many questions, but can you tell us who Tia was in your family?" Susan now asked.

"Yes, she was my grandmother. She must be quite old and knew all the stars in the sky, even when we had the dome over our heads."

"Did she ever tell you stories of where your people came from, in the distant past?" Susan asked.

"Yes, of course, many stories. Old people like to pass down the history for us to understand. She said we came from the stars called Izar in the sky," she replied.

Everyone watched as Susan walked across the bridge to a locker and pulled out a wooden box containing a star globe.

"Can you find this star system on here for us, Scota?" Susan asked handing her the globe.

After only a few moments she handed the globe back to Susan. "Yes, it's close to the big star we know as Izar, but marked here as Arcturus. I never heard that name before," she replied to Susan.

"Scota, do you think your grandmother may have gone back to Izar or is still sitting under the sea outside? Because for those of us here tonight, that's really important," Susan said.

"Really, I don't know. She may have done either, but I know she will come back to us if you give her some time. I think I would like to return to my friends now," Scota asked so Nathalie brought the discussion to an end.

152

"Thank you, Scota. What you did to bring Kiya back was very brave. We all appreciate what you have done, thank you," Nathalie said and everyone clapped in appreciation.

Finally Scota got down from the chair, excused herself and went down below. After that, no one said a word, until there was a loud shout from Anita and everyone looked at her.

"FUCK, fuck, fuck people! How did we miss this?

"Calm down, Anita, we all missed this," Claude replied.

"We spent months training for an exo-planet mission, hours listening to the best science at NASA. Then we arrive on this dumb planet with a group of women in a harem, only to find out that grandma is flying hypersonic craft that can time travel. Did I miss anything out?" Anita asked, looking at the crowd of surprised faces.

"Ever since the attack on the dome we've been living in survival mode, running from one crisis to the next," Susan added.

"Tell us, Susan, you and Bee were living with these women as your 'hand maidens' and yet you never noticed anything?" Anita asked.

"Oh my god, Anita! If it makes you feel any better, I did have sex with Kiya, when Susan was out on her ceremonial duties," Bee replied, much to Claude's surprise, as the others looked out of the windows. "I mean, it took you five years to come and rescue us, Anita, what did you expect?" Bee added.

"Susan, what did you feel about these women at your palace?"

"Nothing except sadness for them, having lost all their men. It was not until we got into the Great Palace that we saw all those androids sitting in rows and confirmed we had been living in a fake Egyptian world. Still, I never connected any of the women to higher intelligence. It only reinforced my view that they were an oppressed group of people living on the planet," Susan replied.

"Does anyone know how old our crew members really are?" Anita asked.

"Yes, Nathalie and I have discussed this. We think most are in their seventies or eighties, that would make grandma some two hundred years old. They can't have the same DNA as us, and a lot longer life span than we can imagine," Susan explained.

"What do you mean, imagine? When I went to Sunday school as a girl, we were taught in the Old Testament how the 'Elohim' came down from heaven and lived amongst us for centuries. Ancient tablets show that the early Gods lived on Earth for hundreds of years but no one believed this. Well, here we have the proof. We're living amongst women who may look like us, move like us, have learnt to talk like us, but definitely have superior knowledge to us," Anita said.

"Yes, Anita, all that may be correct. I'm not going to argue," Nathalie replied, then paused and continued, "Claude, please take your place in your Captain's chair. I'm going to send some photos to your screen that were taken outside, and Susan will explain more of this history to you. Now, I need to go down below to check on the patient Kiya and hope to get more confirmation from other crew members."

As soon as she left the bridge the others crowded around Claude to look at the cave paintings. Anita managed to stand up and went to the screen with Susan.

"This first painting is a view of the planet with a black line across the centre that represents the equator. You can see that most of the Americas continent is in the southern hemisphere, with a new large island on the equator," Susan explained.

"Is this what the planet looks like now, or in the distant past?" Bee asked.

"No, it can't be now as we found from the star sights our position was some 41 degrees north," replied Claude.

"Nathalie and I think this painting was done some time ago and long before the last pole shift," replied Susan.

"But if India has moved up to the north pole, then we are in an ocean close to the south of it!" Bee exclaimed.

"Remember that globe thing on the Palace door in Amarna? You pulled the continent of the Americas down and I pushed the Indian continent up and the door opened, didn't it," Bee said.

"Yes, Bee, that's correct, but I think we are a long way from Amarna now," Susan replied, and Bee groaned.

"What else did you find," asked Claude.

"The rest of the photos are images of a mathematical series of numbers that may not be of much interest," Susan said.

"No no, please, we want to see them," they all chorused.

"All right, here's the first photo, based on a mathematical progression on the numbers 60 and 70, we think in hours," said Susan. "And on the next image the numbers are the same but in seconds."

"Wait, go back. I've seen that 195,000,000 billion number before. It was at a lecture given by NASA. He said if we ever saw that number on another planet, we would have found the holy grail!" Bee announced.

"Really, you remember that?" Susan asked.

"Yes, it had something to do with the orbits of the outer planets. I don't know how to calculate it or what it means, but we don't have any outer planets here do we?" Bee asked.

"No, you're right, the number is important. It's the time it takes for our solar system to make one circuit around our galaxy. In Earth years that's about 25,000 years, often called the Great Year of the solar system. The question is, what's this number doing on this planet, because it looks like we must be somewhere in the Milky Way galaxy. Our solar system is located some 27,000 light years from the centre so this planet must be about the same," Susan replied, but most people looked lost.

Nathalie returned with a tray of steaming hot drinks, and everyone crowded around her.

"Good news, everyone. I was allowed to visit Kiya in that sickbay you made. That was an excellent idea. She's awake, but still very weak. I tested her for radiation sickness and gave Scota a supply of iodine tablets to take," Nathalie said, finishing her hot drink and looking flushed.

"Thanks, Nathalie, that is good news, anything more?" Claude asked, looking at her more closely.

"Yes, the crew think it's safe for us to go outside, after the crew removed all the guards. The men you saw by the landing site were sailors from the ships, who have left, and they don't expect any more to return for a while," Nathalie said, holding onto the chair.

"That's good news, so can we barbecue outside in the sunshine. I mean close to the entrance would be good," Claude replied, as Nathalie slowly crumpled onto the floor.

Toby and Scota appeared at the entrance to the bridge and watched her fall.

"Claude, what just happened to Nathalie?" Susan asked in alarm.

"Toby put a dose of poppy seeds in her drink. She should be unconscious for the next six hours and in the meantime…" Claude stopped.

"What exactly are you going to do, Claude?" Susan asked.

"Scota here was instructed to check out Nathalie's cabin and found a hand written log of her communications. She appears to have sent a message for help that's expected to arrive early tomorrow," Claude explained. "It's all in her book, Susan, if you can check to see what else she's arranged. Take a seat on her chair and see if you can find anything on her screen," he said.

"But what are you going to do with Nathalie?" Susan asked again.

"Toby here is going to take her down to the sick bay and lock her inside for now. We have just ten hours to re-supply the ship with fresh provisions and leave before the morning high tide," Claude explained.

"So who's going outside to do that? There are almost no fresh vegetables left in the store room and little flour left for bread," Bee said.

"Bee, you can help get some of that onboard, but leave any contact with the locals up to our crew members. They will bring the provisions down to the ship for loading. You can go down with Toby to open the cargo door and prepare the deck to bring the livestock onboard," he explained, and everyone looked at him in amazement.

"Anita, we're going to have to barter weapons with the locals. Scota has some guns they took off the guards, but can you check what spare weapons we might have to trade?" asked Claude.

With that the meeting broke up in confusion. Nathalie was carried below and people rushed back down below. Mothers had small girls to put to bed, Claude went down to the galley to meet with Scota to discuss his plan, while Anita went down to her cabin and threw herself on her bunk not knowing what to think.

25 – LOG BOOK

When Anita awoke next, she saw she had napped for almost an hour. The mattress under her was made of some thin material, probably military issue, with lumps. The rest of her cabin consisted of a little desk and a chair, and some bookshelves. In the corner against the forward bulkhead was the cabinet that housed the ship's weapons. She sat up on her bunk and thought how different her life had been, back at home when she was a small girl and looked at herself in the mirror. When she looked closer, she could see dark shadows beneath her eyes. She moved closer, looking at herself again, and tried to pull away from her gaze but something in her body asked her to stay and look at herself again. All she could see was Claude walking towards her, cradling Kiya in his arms, and big tears fell onto her cheeks. How she longed to get off this ship and away from Captain Claude once and forever.

There was a knock on her door, and when she opened it Susan stood outside, holding Nathalie's log book.

"Come on in and sit down. I thought you would be putting your girl to bed, everything all right?" Anita asked, wiping her tears away and moving a pile of dirty clothes on the floor to the side of her cabin.

"Are you all right Anita? You look upset."

"No, no, I'm fine, what can I help you with?" Anita asked.

"Much of what Claude said may be true, at least the part about requesting assistance, but there's no reply, so we still don't know if anyone even received it," she said.

"That's basic military training. Expect the worst and hope for the best, let me see," Anita asked, taking the book in her hands. "It's all in some sort of code."

"Yes, but pretty simple. Scota must have read it in five minutes, but it took me half an hour of guessing. Here, I wrote down an English version so you can see what she was tracking."

"Okay, I understand, but it looks like there's a lot more."

"Yes, here's the number of Kiya's craft, or tic-tac, or whatever it's called. She was looking at this number for days and from what I found she didn't want Kiya to come back here."

"Why do you say that?"

"Because after some weeks, when someone powered up the ship again these receiver messages were repeatedly sent like some kind of virus."

"Is that possible? If it took thirty Earth years to reach us, how would any messages get there so fast?"

"That's what I wanted to ask you. If Scota read this, and I think she did, then she's right to be very upset with Nathalie."

"What do you think Claude will do with her when we leave?"

"No idea. Have you sorted out the arms trade yet?"

"No, and I don't want to. Scota already has the weapons from the guards they killed, so I'm going to wait and see how that barter trade works out first," Anita replied.

"Right, and how the crew are going to find months of provisions in the next ten hours, at night, is beyond me. If you've not eaten, let's go down to the galley and see what the latest gossip is down there," Susan said, and they both got up and left the cabin.

When they reached the galley there was no one there and Susan started to panic about Bee and the girls. First, she ran down to her cabin, where she found both Mayati and Nut asleep in the same bed, by which time Anita arrived outside.

"Remember, Bee was going to help with provisioning the ship. Let's go down to the cargo deck to see if she's down there," Anita said, and led the way to the stairs to the deck below.

"Here they are, but what in heaven's name is Toby doing?" Susan said when they saw a construction of wooden planks that had been used some months ago.

"Hi Susan, can you come and help? We're building a place to keep the sheep and pigs in pens," Bee said.

Toby didn't look up, but hammered away to make a small enclosure for animals.

"Where exactly are these animals, Bee?"

"They're coming real soon, the crew are bringing them here," Toby replied.

"But Toby, you haven't put down the ramp to get them onboard."

"No, we didn't know how to do that," said Toby.

"Okay, no problem. Susan, can you help me lower the ramp onto the quay. This is madness, come on, I'll show you what to do," Anita replied.

Two minutes later Susan and Anita walked down the ramp and looked up at the steps leading to the entrance.

"This is not going to be easy. If someone drives some sheep down here, they'll run all over the place. I'm going up to the entrance to see what I can hear and warn you when they come," Susan said.

"Do you have a gun?" Anita asked.

"Yes, Nathalie gave it to me."

"If we can't get these animals up the ramp, I suggest you shoot them, because that will be your dinner," Anita replied.

Nothing happened for another half an hour. Susan looked at her old wristwatch and saw it was almost midnight and nothing had been loaded. All she heard was more banging and hammering from Toby inside, as she paced up and down one of the lower terraces. Then she heard Anita shout as the noise of animals become clearer.

"Susan, it's not sheep but goats, a small flock of them are coming down your way," shouted Anita.

As she watched, a man dressed in a brown tunic appeared at the entrance with a long thin stick. He was trying to keep the animals under control, guiding them down towards the light of the ship, but the goats were jumping down the levels and going towards the water at the stern of the ship.

"Toby, Toby, you'd better come quickly. The goats are outside and running away," Susan shouted as Bee came to the door, watching the animals disappear from her view with the man running after them. Some minutes later he returned looking angry and upset and looking at Bee, said something she didn't understand and came inside.

"Do you know what he said, Toby?" Bee asked.

"Yes, all his goats jumped into the sea and swam away. He's very upset, but they bring more, sounded like pigs. Come on we need to finish the work on this pen," Toby replied and they went back inside.

Meanwhile, the man on the quay stopped and turned to talk to Anita. "You commander of guns," he said making a salute to her.

"Yes, what do you need?"

"Scota asked for thing, make big bang," he replied laughing.

"Okay, I give to you next time," she said, making a thumbs up sign and saluting him back. She walked up the ramp to board the ship and find the weapon.

"Hi guys, how's it going here? Anita asked, smiling until she saw the pen was still empty. She asked Toby what had happened.

"Oh, the goats, they all ran away. Next time he'll bring some pigs. Even more difficult to handle," Toby replied.

Anita didn't smile at the news as it meant they would have even less meat to eat. Instead, she walked up to the galley and then decided to check in on Nathalie to make sure she was still locked up in the sick bay.

Checking the door was still locked, she went up to her cabin and took out the cross-bow that she had used before, together with all the sonic missiles left in the store. Returning below, she found the man and Bee chasing a pig around the cargo deck until he stopped it with his knife, and Bee collapsed on the deck.

"Bee, are you all right?" Anita asked taking her arm.

"Yes, that was horrible," she replied looking at the dead pig on the floor.

"I'll be needing some meat for cooking tomorrow," Toby added and walked away.

The same man was looking at Anita with the cross-bow and smiled at her.

"You need to take these arrows as well," she said, giving him the weapon and the missiles wrapped in a cloth. Toby returned and speaking to him in his language, they hugged and he left again.

"Toby, is that all we got? One pig – that's not going to feed us for long," Anita said.

"It's a start. I understand Scota is bringing the vegetables and sacks of flour on some old cart, if you can go and help up at the entrance," Toby said. "You might want to take Bee with you, while I deal with dead one," he suggested smiling at her.

When Bee looked at Anita she nodded and they went down the ramp to join Susan and then walked up to the entrance. They waited another hour before a wooden wagon arrived, pulled by a very old and small electric tractor. Claude was at the wheel and it was being pushed by some of the crew walking behind.

"Thank god you made it, Claude, it's almost 4 am, what took you so long?" Anita asked, but Claude ignored her as he came to a stop on the path by the entrance.

"Susan, Bee, can you start taking the fruit and vegetables down to the ship? The rest of us will unload the sacks of flour and the heavy stuff underneath," Claude said.

Susan and Bee ran forward while Anita stood at the stone entrance and watched until Claude looked at her. "Have you seen Scota? She's disappeared," he said.

"Yes, I gave her the sonic cross-bow with all the missiles. I expect she's training up the locals for an attack," she replied.

"She had better be back by 6 am or we'll leave without her."

"All right, Claude, anything I can do?" Anita asked.

"Yes, can you help us unload these sacks and carry them inside?" Claude asked her. His words were almost drowned out by a huge explosion coming from the landing site to the north of them.

"Ah! I expect that's Scota destroying the building now. She should be back very soon," Anita said, finally approaching the wagon and helping to unload the heavy sacks.

"Okay, I'll leave you in charge here while I go and look for Scota. You know what to do, don't you," Claude replied. He jumped down off the tractor and ran off up the path towards the smoke in the early morning light.

Susan and Bee returned. "Toby's put some planks of wood on the stairs so we can slide the sacks down to the ship," Susan advised.

"Can you take some more of these vegetables, Bee, please? They're not heavy," Anita asked.

As soon as Bee left again Susan turned to Anita and asked where Claude was.

"Claude ran off to find Scota, who looks to be starting a war over there," Anita replied, pointing at the black smoke in the distance.

"What! That's the last thing we need, aren't we supposed to be leaving at around six? That's in less than an hour," Susan said looking at her watch.

"Let's start sliding these sacks down the planks and get the last of this stuff onboard before Claude returns," Anita replied.

With the help of the crew they emptied the wagon, slid the sacks down, and lifted them onto the ship. By the time they finished the loading ramp had risen up off the quay with the incoming tide. Toby went and collected the last of his planks and climbed back onboard. Anita retracted the ramp and started to close the outer door.

"Hang on a bit, what about Claude and Scota?" Toby said.

"You wait for them down here while I go up and check we've got all of the crew onboard," Anita told him and led the way up to the galley with Susan following her.

"Susan, that was complete madness, if you ask me," Anita remarked. They both turned and looked down in horror as Toby started work on the carcass of the pig.

"Maybe, but you have to admit that our fearless Captain can do some of what he promises," Susan replied, shaking her head.

"I suppose I'm going to have to find Kiya and ask her to instruct the crew to go to their mooring stations," Anita replied.

"Already? Why not wait for Claude and Scota?"

"Claude will storm aboard and expect the ship to be ready to leave immediately. Don't you just love this man. In fact, I think you should go up to the bridge and see if they're up there already," Anita said and went to look for Kiya.

When she arrived in the galley, she found Bee sorting out the fruit and vegetables for storage and asked for Kiya.

"Kiya, she's in the sick bay," replied Bee.

Anita ran around the corner, but the room was empty.

Fuck, fuck, she thought, *what's been happening?* When she returned to the galley Claude and Scota were coming up from below.

"Claude, Claude, there's no one locked in the sick bay anymore and we need to leave, don't we?"

"Do you mean Nathalie?" he asked. "Scota here asked Nathalie to leave. She packed her things and I agreed. We left her sitting on the quay outside." He asked if the crew were ready to go to mooring stations.

"No, I mean I couldn't find Kiya to give the order and was looking for you," Anita explained.

"The crew must be tired after being up all night carrying all those provisions, can you do it with Scota? You go down aft to let go of the ropes and Scota will go up forward. I need to go up to the bridge to reverse the ship out, is that okay?" Claude said.

"Yes, of course, Claude."

"Right, and as soon as that's done, can you go and sit in the after-gun turret and wait on my orders."

"Yes, but who's going to let the ropes go on the quay?"

"Nathalie, of course, she agreed to make one final gesture for her ship – letting it go," Claude said and left for the bridge.

Anita turned around and on seeing Bee was still there said, fuming, "Did you hear all that?"

"Yes, something about letting go. But I never really liked Nathalie. Not since she made Susan and me pregnant when we first arrived. I don't feel sorry for her, just surprised it took Claude so long to find her out," Bee said.

"Okay, thanks Bee, that's all I wanted to know. Must dash to go up on deck and get the hell out of here," Anita replied and ran upstairs to open the outer door on the after deck.

By the time she reached the stern the ropes had been already let go and the auto mooring system was recovering them for storage. The ship had no guard rails on the upper deck – the shell plating was rounded like a traditional submarine. Moving forward again, she held onto the cold steel of the conning tower and looked cautiously over the side.

In the early morning twilight, she could see no one on the quay, either forward or aft. Looking forward, she saw the ropes must have been let go as the ship was already moving astern out of the dock.

Running as fast as she could back to the after deck, Anita opened a hatch and entered the tunnel to the after-laser turret, activated her code and settled into her seat. Looking above, all she could see was solid rock ahead of the ship and then remembered to put on the earphones. Immediately, she heard Claude's voice.

"Anita, are you there, come in please."

"Yes, I'm here, but it doesn't look as if you can make it," she replied, hoping to scare him a bit.

"What do you mean, it's an hour before high water, there must be enough room to get out of here. Look again."

"Will do," she replied and enlarged the image on her all-round vision to see the clearance again. This time she saw there was not enough clearance from the rock above to make an exit.

"Houston, we have a problem," she replied feeling the engines start in reverse, and watched the conning tower become stuck on the roof of the chamber.

"Claude, I think the stern of the ship is caught on some rocks on the starboard side. What do you want me to do, blast away at the rock?" Anita asked.

"No, don't do that. I'm going forward again and then full astern to force our way out of the chamber," Claude announced. The conning tower grated against the rocks above them until finally the ship was out into the sea again.

"Can you remain in your position for now to see if we have been observed and advise," Claude instructed.

Anita set her screen to cover the headland that was quickly receding behind her, looking for people who might be watching them. Enlarging the magnification, she could see the man with his goats standing on the headland.

"Claude, we are being observed by that man who came on board earlier with his animals. I suggest you proceed with caution," she confirmed.

"Roger that, we are proceeding south down the channel. Please watch and advise," Claude said and she wondered why he was so nervous.

Up on the bridge of the ship, Claude was scanning the sea ahead. He had turned south as soon as they cleared the submarine base and was looking at the old map of the island Nathalie had given them.

On the bridge were Susan and Scota, and Kiya sitting in Nathalie's old chair, looking for any more details about the island. Up ahead was another headland bigger than before, and he altered course to port to give it a two-mile-wide berth.

"Depth report, Scota," Claude asked.

"Three hundred meters and falling," she replied.

"No, two hundred and one hundred," Scota exclaimed.

"Claude, we're going to run aground," said Susan.

"Hard a port," he shouted, then, "Stop all engines."

Fearing the worse he set a course due north, but the ocean depth kept falling, until he realised their system must be hacked.

"Kiya, what's happening on Nathalie's screen?"

"I don't know. We're receiving lots of coded messages on the screen, what should I do?" Kiya replied.

"Okay, I understand. Can you log out and stop the messages?" Claude asked.

"Yes, I'm trying, what else can we do?" Kiya replied.

"Okay, I'm on it," he replied and turned the ship due north.

"Come in, Anita. We have serious interference on the headland to your left. Please check and advise."

"Target identified, do you wish to eliminate, Claude," she replied.

"Yes, affirmative maximum power for elimination."

"Okay, firing lasers now. Target elimination confirmed," Anita added.

Claude took his binoculars and scanned the headland again. All he saw was bare rock, whatever had been there had been blasted away.

"Depth of ocean now, please Scotia," he asked.

"Three hundred meters and falling. Was that something done by Nathalie?" she replied.

"Maybe, or some of the island people, but why?" Claude asked but got no reply.

"Anita, you can come back inboard now," he said.

"Roger that, standing down – over and out," Anita replied, feeling the ship alter course again and increase power.

Back on the bridge, Susan was getting concerned at all the target practice being aimed at the island and went to speak to Claude about the list on the ship.

"What's causing the list, Claude, was the ship damaged when we left the submarine chamber?" she asked.

"Yes, maybe one of the ballast tanks briefly came into contact with an outcrop of rocks on the starboard side. Nothing serious, we can correct it by flooding a chamber on the other side of the ship," he replied, smiling at her.

"But won't that increase our displacement and reduce our speed through the water?" Susan insisted.

"Yes, that will make the hull lower in the water but more stable if we should hit any bad weather," he replied, wanting to ignore her.

"Claude, your actions on the island left a lot to be desired. First you let the crew murder the security guards, then you go on a rampage and destroy their landing base, and finally you failed to find enough supplies to last us a week," Susan said in exasperation.

"I'm sorry, Susan, but I don't report to you and I'm the person responsible for the safety of these people onboard, not you," he replied and walking away from her he made an announcement to all the crew members on the bridge.

Postlude

"I'm setting a new course 090 degrees due east. As some of you know, we didn't take on as many provisions as we had hoped and may need to ration our meals from now on. It will be a race against time to find more provisions, hopefully on the land ahead of us," Claude told everyone as he increased the ship's speed to full ahead.

Susan looked shocked at his arrogance after her discussion with Scota and thought he had no idea what they were up against, or what other people might be ahead of them.

26 - NATHALIE

After Anita climbed out of the aft gun turret, she made her way back down to the galley where Bee was storing the fresh vegetables.

"Hi, Anita, thank goodness you're back. Are we finally leaving that dreadful island?" she asked.

"Yes, out on the ocean waves again. Do you know where Toby is?" Anita asked.

"Still down below, working on that pig," Bee replied with a grimace.

"Come with me, Bee, we have to find Nathalie," Anita demanded. They walked down to the cargo deck to find Toby. As they descended, she saw he was working at a table, cutting up what looked like the remains of the animal.

"Toby, did you see the Captain and Scota come onboard here this morning?" Anita asked.

"Yes, it was shorty before we left. Why do you ask?"

"Did you see Nathalie as well; did she go ashore from down here?"

"Nathalie? No, I didn't see her, she'll be up on the bridge if you want to find her. I'm sure she's still on the ship," he replied.

"I was told that she was left on the quay before we sailed. I thought she was locked in the sick bay, but when I looked just now it's empty," she replied.

"Don't know anything about that," Toby replied.

"Bee, I don't believe Nathalie would leave the ship without saying goodbye. Can you run up to her cabin and see if her gear is still up there?" Anita asked.

Bee ran up the accommodation ladder and Anita stayed to question Toby.

"Toby, where's the best place to hide a body on the ship?"

"You could hide a body somewhere cold so it doesn't start to smell. The cold storage room would be good, but there's only one key," Toby replied, pointing to the keys around his waist.

"Thanks, Toby, that's what I thought, but is it locked now?"

"No, it's open as I've been preparing this carcass," he replied.

"That's all I needed to know," she replied and ran up the stairs to find the cold storage room, bumping into Bee again.

"Well, what did you find?" Anita asked.

"Nothing, she's not in her cabin, but all her clothes are still there. Where do you think she could be?"

"Can you show me the cold storage room? I think I know where Nathalie is," she said.

"Yes, of course, but I'm not going in there, it's too cold," Bee replied. Taking Anita's hand, she pulled her towards the store rooms at the side of the galley. Anita wrenched the cold door open and looking inside, saw there was one remaining meat carcass hanging on a rack.

Pushing her way inside through a lot of cold ice smoke, she moved to the back of the chamber where she saw a fully clothed body hanging on a meat hook.

"Bee, Bee, I think I've found her," Anita exclaimed, dragging the frozen body to the door where Bee looked in, frightened.

"What do you think. It's Nathalie, isn't it," Anita said wiping the ice off her face.

"Anita, really, I don't know. This is all too dreadful," she moaned, putting her hands on her face in shock. At that moment Toby arrived from below and saw the frozen body.

"Toby, you're right, Nathalie is still onboard. She's dead and frozen, by the look of things," Anita replied.

"What? I know nothing about this, really," Toby exclaimed.

"It looks as if you've been framed. If she's found in your storage room you will become the main suspect, as you're the only one with a key," Anita explained.

Toby looked more worried. "So what do we do?" he asked.

"Simple. I know of a great storage place that's not on the ship, if you can help me carry her body up the stairs," Anita said.

"Yes, of course, but we have to be quick. The crew have been sleeping and will return soon," Toby replied, lifting the corpse up in his arms while Anita took her feet. They struggled to carry her body up the stairs to the entrance of the outer door.

"Bee, can you cause a diversion in the galley to give us time to get outside?" Anita asked as they disappeared from her view.

When Toby reached the top of the stairs, he opened the outer door and they were hit by a blast of cold wind, and saw the ship had a ten-degree list to starboard.

"Anita, I don't think I can go out there," Toby said looking at the wind blowing across the deck.

"Leave this to me now, Toby, you've been great," Anita replied, pulling the frozen body outside onto the steel plating.

Anita slowly rolled the body over towards the starboard side of the ship. Getting down on her hands and knees, she waited until the deck rolled, and with gravity to help her she used her feet to kick the body over the side. She then crawled back along the steel plating, not wanting to lose her balance, before climbing inside again.

As soon as she reached the entrance, she stood up and closed the door together before she turned to speak to Toby again. "Thank God that's over. Very windy out there, I thought I was going overboard," she said, straightening her hair and her clothing.

"But why are we leaning to one side now?" Toby asked.

"I don't know, there must be a problem with the ship's stability after we left the island," she replied.

When they returned to the galley below, they found apples rolling all over the floor from the list of the ship.

On seeing Anita, Bee rushed across and hugged her and whispered in her ear, "Is it done?"

Anita nodded, while Toby went to lock up his cold store and then disappeared to his work below.

"This crate of apples fell over on the floor from the list of the ship," Bee said, but members of the crew were starting to eat them. "Right, after all that excitement I'll heat some water for hot drinks, if you want to stay a while," she continued.

"Yes, that would be great. I need to get my breath and can't face meeting Captain Claude right now," Anita replied, taking a seat alone at a table outside the galley and thinking hard about what they had just done and what Claude and Scota may have done.

Now they knew that Nathalie was never left behind, that Claude and Scota must have let the mooring ropes go on the quay before they boarded. That must have been quite an effort with the rising tide holding the ship against the dock, so maybe the ropes had been cut. So many questions and so few answers. Bee arrived and sat down opposite with hot drinks. A few moments later Claude stormed into the galley looking angry and confused. On seeing Anita and Bee he came straight across to talk to them.

"Have you seen Nathalie?" he asked.

"No, why should we?" Anita replied.

"Claude, you told us this morning that you left her on the quay when we departed. Something about letting her go," Bee replied.

"That means she's no longer on the ship, Claude, and you said it in front of Scota, and we all remember," Anita added.

"All right, where's Toby?"

"He was working on that pig down below," Bee replied.

"There he is, bringing the carcass up to his cold store, I guess," Anita said, pointing at him in the galley.

Claude jumped up and ran across to talk to Toby and after a short discussion he left the carcass on a table and followed Claude towards the cold locker.

"Let me go and see if I can eavesdrop on this conversation, it should be most interesting," Bee said, standing up and going in the same direction with a crate of fruit to store in the room next door.

"Give me the bloody key to the cold store, man. I want to see what you have inside," Bee heard Claude demand, as she watched from inside the store.

She heard the cold door open and guessed Claude had gone inside. That was followed by more loud shouting at Toby and she decided to make herself known.

"Everything all right, Claude?" she asked.

Claude pushed her aside and stormed out of the cold store and ran back into the galley. "Anita, tell me what you have done, right now," Claude screamed, then looking closer he saw that she was pointing her revolver at his chest.

"No, Claude, you sit down and tell us what you have done or I'll kill you right now," Anita replied, firing a round over his head that sent the crew running, until he heard another voice behind him.

"Sit down, Claude," Susan said, holding her gun to his head.

When he felt the cold steel of a pistol, Claude finally sat down.

"Now, tell me what you were looking for in Toby's cold store," she demanded. "Do you have the key in your hand," Susan asked, prising his fingers apart to reveal a key. "Thank you, now I'm going to take a look. Can you keep him covered, Anita? If he's any trouble just shoot him in the leg," she said.

When Susan went to the cold store, she found Toby waiting outside, shaking in fear, and handed him the key.

"Can you open it up, Toby, I want to see inside," she said.

"Nothing to see now, the body's gone," he replied with tears running down his cheeks, and Susan entered to see for herself. At the back of the locker she found a frozen gilet on the floor. She knew it had belonged to Nathalie, but found nothing else. Thinking carefully for a moment, she came out from the cold and gave the gilet to Toby.

"Can you give this to Kiya, but don't say where it came from."

Then she turned and went back to face Claude again.

"Well, Claude, I found nothing of interest inside there. We will discuss this again on the bridge when everyone has got some sleep and people are calmer. In the meantime, I don't want to see you threatening Anita or Toby again, is that clear?" Susan demanded.

"You mean he can go," said Anita.

"Of course, we need him to run the ship. He also needs to find out why the ship has this list since we left the island," Susan replied and with that Claude stood up and left.

Once he was out of earshot, they spoke together alone.

"Really, Anita, we can't argue amongst ourselves in front of the crew, let alone firing off your gun down here."

"Sorry, I shouldn't have done that," Anita replied.

"No, but you did well to get rid of the body so quickly. Without a body, Claude will find it hard to accuse anyone about her disappearance. So only you and Toby know?"

"Yes, and Bee. She helped me drag the body out of the locker, and then Toby arrived," she replied, as more crew began to return to the galley.

"Who do you think really put Nathalie in the cold room," Susan asked.

"I assume Claude got rid of Nathalie out of jealousy over his command, but we can't be sure of anything now," Anita replied.

"You can expect the news of this confrontation will have travelled the length of the ship by now, so any minute Scota should arrive," Susan guessed, and sure enough Scota entered the galley to speak to her crew.

"Go on up to your cabin, Anita, and get some rest. I need to stay down here to discuss some unfinished business with Scota. Remember, none of us know anything about where Nathalie is," Susan insisted.

"She's about five miles astern of us by now. Thanks, you really have been most helpful," Anita replied and getting up she left to return to her cabin.

Susan sat at the table waiting for Scota to finish and remembered what happened last night. Her thoughts slid and overlapped in her mind, barring one jagged thought, an important one, that made her want to forget. But it was too late for that.

PART SIX
JUNE 2031

27 - WINDSOR

James had decided to return to Janet's house on the outskirts of Windsor in the UK in June 2031. Old Windsor by then was no longer a small village, but had become a large town in Berkshire, England, bounded by the river Thames to the east and the Windsor Great Park to the west. Most of the low-lying land had been underwater for over a year, flooded by tsunamis after the comet impact and the region was still under military lockdown.

His route back to England had been erratic; he first went up to the airfield base to check that the plane had been returned as he expected along with Janet from the island of Montserrat. When he saw the plane was sitting in the same hangar as before, he guessed that Ben had returned to the UK with his mother Janet. The last co-ordinates he had on his medallion were outside Janet's house in Windsor. He moved the date to June 2031 and pressed the button on his medallion.

He arrived in the morning, on the gravel outside the garage, and was pleased to see there was no water, but also no cars outside. James walked around the house, up to the front door and rang the bell. When he looked across at the grounds, he saw nothing but detritus with rotting wooden pallets and the smell of river mud still in the air. Gulls hopped around, pecking at the newly exposed mud amid the debris.

Ringing the bell again, he waited and rang twice more, but still no one came to open the door.

Hmm, looks like no one at home, he thought, and pressed his medallion against the lock, opening the door. Walking inside he checked the house alarm, but it was dead. Touching the light switch did nothing and he realised the house still had no electricity.

Oh well, let's take a trip down memory lane. He went to look for a bottle of Janet's best wine. Walking through the lounge he saw all the furniture was covered in white sheets and continued into the kitchen. He found a supply of wine in a cool cabinet that was no longer cold and chose a bottle of Pinot Grigio. Finding a bottle screw and a glass he opened the wine and tasted Italy.

Yes, that tastes good, but I need to find my wife and daughter, he repeated to himself until he remembered his promise to help the team return to Earth as well. Taking the glass in his hand and the bottle in the other, James walked on, into the conservatory where all the discussions had taken place ten years ago. Pulling the drape over the table to one side, he sat down at the head of the table and thought of past events.

He closed his eyes and remembered that the table had been laid for five people. Janet took her place at the top of the table and Justin sat on her left with James and Jana on her right. A woman entered with a trolley, on the top of which was a silver terrine of hot soup. Ben followed her in with a basket of bread and Janet told him to sit next to Justin, while James poured everyone a glass of white wine. Ben started the story of the night at his school on Montserrat.

When we arrived, we heard a sound like drones in the sky, so we ran inside the building where there's a shelter from hurricanes, and I took up the story, he thought.

I remember the noise above us, and asked Justin, *But what if these people were all from another planet, coming to Earth like aliens?*

When Ben opened the door to the shelter, he found some of his class already sitting inside, so we both went in and joined them, except the boy who went flying outside, James remembered.

Then Janet stood up and wishing everyone an enjoyable stay in London, time to visit all the theatres and tourist sites, she said.

But of course, they didn't know that London, and the whole of the UK, would be locked down by a virus in less than a month.

If those people on the cylinder were aliens, what type should we expect to find? Perhaps, greys, or reptilians, he thought, *but then nobody went to look at the CCTV or was that also erased by the government?*

We know the people were being attracted to the cylinder by sound waves, James reminded himself. *But who were these people who arrived on the island – most certainly people from another planet.*

After that Elizabeth had walked in and asked that they work together on the Montserrat problem. She had said, *'Everything was difficult to understand,'* and believing her, he had taken Elizabeth to the island. Then a day later, she tried to have him shot. But then he remembered something new. *There must have been something quite dramatic for Elizabeth to change sides against me so quickly.* Now James could see this was little more than a major cover up between two governments.

Hearing a voice behind him he turned to see Justin standing in the doorway looking quite surprised.

"James, James, is that you? So, you have come back at last," he said.

"Yes, Justin, I came back to find Jana and my daughter," he replied.

"They're all well and have been living with Janet close to the airbase. Come on, James, let's go back to the kitchen and see if I can find a beer, this room gives me the creeps," suggested Justin.

James picked up his half empty bottle of wine and his glass while Justin covered the table and chair, and they left for the table and high stools in the kitchen.

"So, Justin, how did you get down here today?"

"I borrowed our postman's motor bike. Janet asked me to come down here from time to time to check there're no break-ins, now the water has gone down."

"Are you stationed up at the base then? I remember there were Marines there during my stay with Ben."

"Yes, and got promoted. I think they realised they couldn't have someone with my knowledge of alien events in the lower ranks, so I got offered an officer's commission. I took the exams and have made it up to Second Lieutenant. I'm now in charge of security up at the base. But tell me, James, what have you been doing for the last ten years?" he asked, opening his bottle of beer.

"That's a very good question. You must have heard from Ben that he came and rescued me from an island off the coast of Portugal, but before that nothing," he replied.

"And you found your medallion again, I see," Justin replied.

"Apparently I was put into a deep sleep to protect me from an old adversary."

"And you've been back to Monserrat since then, I heard as well."

"Yes, I persuaded Ben not to give the plane back to the US military and we stopped off there on our way back. Don't worry, it became just as dangerous as before. I found some of the answers to what happened when you went there, but still not everything."

"I heard that the army was sent to the island to pull the cylinder high up the beach and then overnight, it just disappeared."

"I'm afraid, Justin, it's all about aliens," he replied, swirling the wine in his glass and looking out of the window. The kitchen had wooden units arranged on either side of an old-fashioned gas hob and a window with a view onto the grounds. When he looked outside, he saw the remains of a car had been deposited by the river Thames.

"I was shown photos of people on the beach who had been rescued. Did someone fly the thing off the beach, because the government people were asking a lot of questions," he asked again.

"Yes, I met the alien who did that, and also people with Ben who made us sign a lot of papers so you know I can't say much more," he replied, pouring himself another glass of white wine. "But I can confirm that these aliens are everywhere, living amongst us. The problem is that some can change to look like humans and none of us can tell," James explained. Justin looked alarmed. "Tell me, Justin, where did you do your training, in Devon?"

"Yes, I was at the training centre at Lympstone for another fifteen months. Not as bad as the initial training, but I needed to learn how to lead a team of commandos. After that I was sent to Scotland, where I joined 43 Commando."

"How did you get posted to the airbase here?" James asked.

"After everything went pear shaped with that comet and then the CME, I must have got lucky. When the plane was returned to the RAF base, I was told to report to No. 22 Group and got to meet Janet and your family again. Lots has happened since you were away, James."

"No more questions about Montserrat, then."

"No, not until recently. When I was back in Devon as a commissioned officer, I met the captain who I reported to as a Commando and we talked about that mission again."

"Go on, what did he say?"

"Not a lot, but he showed me a photo. Well, it must have been a satellite image, because it was not very clear, but it showed a naked woman climbing out of a crater, being helped by a couple of the locals."

"Really, did he mention where?"

"Yes, he said the crater was from Janet's house, up on the Old Bluff, wasn't it?"

"Yes, I met her when we went back to the island," James replied.

"Is she an alien?"

"Yes, although I prefer extra-terrestrial. She was found, along with the eight hundred others you saw on the beach," James replied.

"What, that's impossible! Where did they all come from?"

"Really, Justin, they came from another planet in our galaxy, that's all I know. What I can tell you is that I have been asked to assist a team of explorers who went to that planet and now are coming home."

"How do you know all this is true?" Justin asked.

"Because it was an official program of the ESA," James explained.

"So, what's going on here, James? You know, many years ago there was a war in Europe that created four million refugees and quite a migrant problem. Do other planets have some kind of exchange of migrants and that happened on that island…"

"That's exactly what I thought as well. The big question is why both of the Governments involved have been conducting a huge cover up ever since then," James replied, finishing the wine and placing the glass in the kitchen sink.

"No, James, we need to take the empties with us. We mustn't leave any trace of you having been here," Justin said, wiping the glass with a cloth and placing it back in the unit above the sink. Then he placed the empty bottles in his backpack and handed it to James.

"Still no water down here. They promised to get it fixed a month ago. Can you wait for me outside while I check the upstairs, and then we can be on our way."

"Oh, you want me to ride with you on that old motor bike, do you?"

"Yes, James, there's no way we can get you inside the airbase now. Janet has a house outside so I'll take you there."

"I had an official pass last time," James shouted, but Justin had already gone upstairs.

James walked down to the motor bike parked at the bottom of the stairs with a shining Norton sign on the body. He heard Justin return, lock the front door and join him.

"Look, James, you need to know your situation. I recall the UK did a deal that we could keep the plane, on condition we hand you over to US authorities. So, you need to keep a low profile, understood?"

"How far is it up to Janet's house?" James asked.

"Only about twenty miles, shouldn't take us more than half an hour. There's no traffic on the roads these days," Justin replied, starting the engine and with James on the back they set off down the drive.

28 – JAMES

'It was past noon when they reached their destination. The RAF Station at High Wycombe had acted as the liaison between the British RAF and the United States Air Force which was probably why they had allowed the hover plane to be delivered to this airbase in England.

Justin followed the road past the entrance to the airbase and turned left again to what looked like a cul-de-sac with a row of smart houses, ending with a high spiked gate at the end. He parked the motor bike on the drive of the house and helped a by now drunken James up to the front door. Then he rang the bell, to be met by Jana.

"You're not going to believe this, but I found the father of your daughter down at Janet's house in Windsor."

"You mean James!" Jana exclaimed. "He's still alive."

"Yes, and he's been drinking! Is anyone else at home?"

"No, Janet and Ben are working at the base and my daughter's at school in the village," she replied.

"Good, can you help me get him upstairs to bed and I'll have to leave you it, I'm afraid," he said, carrying James upstairs.

"It's best if you put him in my big double bed and we let him sleep it off there. Do you know why he's wearing a tropical shirt and shorts? Did James say where he came from?"

"Yes, we talked a lot about that island from the past, and there's his medallion around his neck, so he may have travelled back from there," Justin replied, heaving James onto the double bed.

"Are you going to tell Janet and Ben?" Jana asked.

"Not right away, or at least until he wakes up. I told him that he'll be arrested if he tries to go into the airbase, so the fewer people who know about his presence here the better."

"Yes, I remember. It would be a disaster for Janet if he was found at her house, but what else can we do?" Jana replied.

"Stay calm and act normal to everyone you meet outside. I will talk to Janet before she leaves work, but we need to find a solution. In the meantime I have to return the wheels I borrowed and appear in charge of security here."

"Thanks, Justin, you really have been most kind. Can you show yourself out, as I'm going to stay next to James until he wakes up," Jana said tearfully.

Justin returned the motor bike to the postman, who asked if there was anything new down in Windsor with the water. Justin smiled, shook his head, and gave the man a small tip for the loan of his bike and the fuel. After that he returned to his office in the base, sat at his desk and poured himself a large glass of whisky.

Knowing that he would have to give the news to Janet before she left for home didn't make it easy. Just before five pm Justin put on his officer's uniform and walked over to the base headquarters to find Janet. Showing his security pass at the entrance, he strode inside to hear the latest discussions on a big screen about US bases.

Seeing Janet seated at a desk, he approached and spoke to her. "Janet, we have a code red at your house, can you come outside with me?" was all he said.

"Right, these people are talking nonsense, I'll follow you out," she replied, and got up to leave. Once outside she asked what was going on and if he had been down to her house in Windsor.

"Yes, I went and found someone from the past down there, who is now in your house."

"What! You mean that person with a medallion?"

187

"Exactly, and asking a lot of questions. It might be best if we walk to the back gate to return to your house, ma'am," he said.

"Stop it, Justin, don't give me that ma'am nonsense. Do your job and have the man arrested, or I lose my plane."

"Janet, we can't, he's got his travel thing with him. We should hurry," Justin replied and saluted the guard at the gate as they approached the house.

Janet unlocked the door and went inside. "Where is he?" she asked, seeing Jana playing with her daughter in the lounge.

"Janet, what's wrong? Did you have a bad day over there? Can I make you a cup of tea?"

"No thank you. Justin tells me you had a visitor at the house today, is that true?" Janet asked. Justin realised that James was gone.

"Yes, Justin came back from Windsor with some flowers over there, aren't they lovely," she replied.

"Yes, lovely. I'm sorry, I was mistaken. Some tea would be good after a difficult day," Janet said and went to sit in the lounge.

Justin looked around the room and saw an old wind-up gramophone and went to look at it while they waited for the tea. He found an old record and the next moment the sound of Vera Lynn singing "The White Cliffs of Dover" reverberated around the house.

"Justin, what are you playing there? Our situation is nothing like the times of WW2, please turn it off," Janet said.

"No, but wasn't it something about 'We'll meet again', and we have just met James again," Justin replied, turning the volume off as Jana brought the tea into the room on a tray.

"Where is he," demanded Janet.

"All in good time," replied Jana, pouring the tea.

Justin sat down on the sofa next to Jana. "James left us a note that I don't quite understand, but perhaps you can make more sense of it," she said, handing the note to Justin.

"Hmm, difficult. *'Going to meet London at the Home Office'*, is all it says," he said, reading out the message and passing it to Janet.

"What happened when James woke up?" asked Justin, trying to be more understanding.

"Well, you know, we talked about where he had come from, but I could see he was very frightened. You know he got his medallion back from his guardian," she replied, and everyone nodded.

"Then he wanted some clothes and while he took a bath I found him a business suit, a shirt and a jacket for him to try on. It was only after that he said he needed to meet someone at the Home Office, but didn't explain why," Jana explained.

"And that was it?" asked Janet.

"No, of course not. Lots of emotional hugs at being away for so long, but you know I can read his mind, so I know it was true."

"What was true, Jana, can you explain it to us," Justin asked.

"Yes, he was on that tropical island during the night and hundreds of people were walking down the road. They all silently entered a huge chamber. Can you explain that to me?" Jana asked.

Justin looked at Janet and she nodded her approval. "I spoke to James down at Janet's house in Windsor, remember? He told me quite openly that what we found on Montserrat was a cylinder to transport extra-terrestrial people from another planet. You may find that difficult to believe, but James said when all the people were onboard the craft lifted off and disappeared," he explained.

"Thanks, Justin, that's what I saw as well, but why does he need to go to the Home Office in London?"

"Yes well, that's where it gets complicated. Janet, do you want to say anything about this?" Justin asked.

"Not really, Justin. I think you can put that record on again about 'Bluebirds flying over the white cliffs of Dover,' while we drink our tea," Janet replied, smiling at everyone.

After that the conversation turned to the current reality, about how Jana's daughter had settled in at the school on the base and Justin's appointment at the base. When Justin announced he had to leave, Janet went to show him to the door and they talked outside.

"Thanks, Justin, for coming and getting me out of there today."

"No problem, I thought you should know," he replied.

"Listen, do you think we should tell Ben about James?" Janet asked, holding up the message in her hand.

"No, you keep that message for now, but it gives me an idea about where to find this Home Office."

"Really, you think you can find the location?" Janet asked.

"It's possible. You know the few flights that land here must be recorded in a log in the Control tower. I can order one of my men to see what was recorded for the flights last month. They won't like it, but it can be done under a review of landing security. We know the date of Ben's flight out of here, so I would expect those people from the Home Office came a day or a few days before. There may even be details of their flight plan when they left. So, let's leave Ben out of it for now. With his girlfriend pregnant he's got enough to think about."

"I know they're still living in that house at the end of the runway, so you think it best if they stay on the base?"

"I think Michelle is happy staying there for now. She has a circle of girlfriends she meets at the NAFFI most days, free transport and medical care if needed," he replied.

"Did you find anything new down at the house in Windsor?"

"Yes, the water around the house has gone, but still no electricity or running water down there, so I think you're stuck here for now. Also, you're close to Ben up here and you can see Michelle, if you can find the time."

"Justin, why did James want a business suit to travel outside?

"Really, I have no idea."

Postlude

"James brings a completely new dimension to the discussions we have been having with our American friends. I can't say much more, but I may need your help in the future," Janet replied, and after giving him a kiss on his cheek she watched as he walked away before she went back inside the house.

29 – HOME OFFICE

James woke slowly, drifting through layers of consciousness until he was staring at the sky. Then in one shift, the shapes around him became clear and he remembered he was searching for one person and a building, as he took in the stark landscape around him.

Jana had told him to find an airport surrounded by water and he thought that shouldn't be difficult after the flood. He had arrived close to the runway that was built on the old London docks. The airport terminal itself resembled a shipwreck stranded on a dried-up sea. James slowly got up and looked around, but could see no one. One end of the runway appeared to have been cleared of debris, making it possible for a small plane to land. Scattered around the terminal building were smaller buildings, now without roofs, only empty walls.

Looking to the south he could see the river Thames, glinting in the sunshine and flowing over much of what had been Silvertown. The tsunami must have swept in from the east, destroying all the hotels and buildings including the Thames Barrier, he thought.

Looking to the north there was one building standing, relatively intact by the sunlight reflected off the windows. Brushing down his business suit, he started to walk north across a bridge to what looked like a hotel, although with all the wooden pallets and boats piled against its east wall it was difficult to know.

Standing outside the entrance was a DUKW, also called a duck, a six-wheeled amphibious vehicle painted in green army colours. James thought it might be the new home and headquarters of the Home Office.

As he approached the back of the vehicle, an army soldier jumped out holding a rifle and James instinctively put his hands up in the air.

"Well, well, what do we have here," he asked laughing at James.

"I was told to report to Ms. London. Ruth London of the Home Office, is this the right place?" James replied.

"It's the only building standing around here, mate, isn't it? Now if you give me your name and security code, I'll check you in," he continued.

James looked up at the roof and saw an array of satellite dishes. "Very well, my name's James Pollack, I'm from Group 22, the airbase in High Wycombe, and I was told to report down here," said James.

"So you must have some I.D?"

"Yes, of course, here you are," he said, handing over his RAF pass.

"Never seen one of these before, are you some sort of a pilot?" he asked looking at the photo. "Right then, I'll take down these details and you can go inside. You may have a long wait as I drove her to the airport an hour ago. She didn't mention anything about expecting a visitor," he said.

"No, sorry, I was delayed. I saw her plane leave just as I arrived, so I had better wait for her inside," James replied, and walked towards the hotel entrance where a new sign on the wall confirmed it was the location of the Home Office.

He could barely believe his luck, not only to find her location, but to find out she would be away for most of the day. If he was careful, he might be able to get into her office and see what he could find there.

He approached the receptionist at the front desk.

"Good morning. Beautiful day outside, isn't it," James said smiling at the attractive twenty something year old woman.

"Yes, but I don't see much stuck inside here. What can I do for you Mister…err," she replied.

"Oh, sorry! It's Mr. Pollack and I'm a bit late. I'm from security up at Group 22 airbase in High Wycombe. I've come here to work with Ms. London on security issues at London City airport," James replied, flashing his security pass in front of her for a moment.

"I'm sorry, I don't know anything about that," she replied.

"No, of course not, you wouldn't know. It's a national security thing, classified. Can you show me the way upstairs and I can get started?" James asked.

"That's not what we normally do here. I think you should wait until she comes back," she said.

"No, no. That's not possible, we have credible intelligence of a bomb alert at this airport. Now please, can you take me upstairs to start on this project," James demanded.

"Very well, but I'm going to call the airbase and speak to the head of security there, if that's all right Mr. Pollack," she replied.

"Absolutely, no problem. Can you get through when all the telephone lines are down?" James asked.

"Yes, we can, but that's a national security thing," was her cheeky reply.

"Right, so lead the way up to your security centre and I'll try to be finished in time to show your boss," replied James.

"But Ms. London has gone to your airbase to take that supersonic plane back to the Americans. She won't be back for a day!"

"What! No, we have to stop that. Can you call Group 22 with your magic thing? I need to speak to the head of security right away," James demanded.

The receptionist looked at him closely, then moved to an inner office to place the call before she shouted out to him. "You want to speak to a Justin Benbow?" She pointed to a phone on the outer desk.

James picked up the receiver and listened.

"Hello, James, where are you, are you all right?" Justin asked.

"Yes, fine, I'm down at the Home Office working on that security problem we found," James said, knowing he was on some sort of short-wave radio communication.

"Yes, of course, I remember that," Justin replied, catching onto the story James must have told.

"Look, the people here tell me that Ms. London left this morning for the airbase, she's going to take the hovercraft back to the States. Do you know anything about that?" asked James.

"No, but I'll call the owner of the plane right away. Is there a problem?" Justin asked.

"Yes, we think some sort of interference has been inserted on the plane that's controlled from the Government offices here. When that plane takes off it will destroy all the people onboard," James replied.

"Right, understood. We will take the necessary measures to secure Mrs. London here at the base and await your report. Thanks, James, that's good work," Justin replied and when James hung up the receptionist returned to her desk.

"That's quite an impressive call, Mr. Pollack, can you come this way?" was all she said and she led James up two flights of stairs.

"Not a lot of people work here then?" James asked.

"No, mostly computer engineers. This building now stores a backup for most of the data for the UK," she replied as they arrived at a door marked 'Control Centre – No Admittance' and using her security pass opened the door.

"Can you introduce yourself to the engineer on duty and I'll leave you to it. When you finish, just call me downstairs," she said, smiling at James.

"Thanks for your assistance," he replied, but when he turned around, he saw he was alone, locked inside a huge room with security monitors and a semi-circular control panel. Protruding from one of the panels on the floor was a pair of men's feet that he assumed belonged to the engineer on duty. James looked up at the screens where he saw one with a view over the Thames, and realised it might be her office. He really didn't want to introduce himself to any more people who might blow his cover. Instead, he quietly withdrew to the door again and activating his medallion walked through to the other side. Now he knew that Ms. London's office must be on the south side of the building, it was only a question of which floor.

James walked back to the flight of stairs opposite a lift shaft and saw a door without a number that looked likely. There was the question of the security camera, so he looked at the room next door. Using his medallion again he entered the room that contained a large furnished bedroom and saw a connecting door. When he entered, he found it was an office with a desk, more screens and filing cabinets. Looking for the security camera he quickly turned the lens to face the white ceiling. Pleased with his find, he started to look for any record of contacts with another world, that was the real purpose of his visit.

****

As the ageing Cessna plane came into land at the Group 22 airfield in High Wycombe, two army jeeps with marines followed the plane down the runway until it stopped and taxied back to the terminal building. Ruth London looked out of the window but couldn't understand the need for such security. When she walked down the steps, a marine asked her to join them in the jeep for the short ride to the arrival building, where she was taken to meet with the head of security, Justin Benbow. His office was small and sparse, with just a desk, a few filing cabinets and two chairs. Ms. London took a seat facing him.

"Lieutenant, what's the meaning of this security for my plane's arrival today," she demanded.

"With the increase of air traffic here, we've introduced tighter security for all planes that arrive. It's just routine security," he said, not wanting to show what he knew.

"I don't appreciate it and will be reporting you to your superior," she replied, about what Justin expected.

"What's your business here at the airbase, as we weren't pre-advised of your flight today," said Justin.

"I think that's none of your business," she replied.

The telephone rang on Justin's desk and he answered. "I think this is a call for you," he said, passing the phone to her and listening to one side of the conversation.

"What do you mean he was in my office! Why was he even let into the building?" she shouted down the phone. "Yes, I know all about James Pollack and I know exactly what he's looking for. Call the army outside and tell them to shoot him," she said as Justin chuckled.

"What's the meaning of this? Is this man working with you, because if I find out he was your career is finished."

"No, not at all. I only joined my assignment here last month and have no knowledge of the person you referred to on your call," he replied, trying to calm the situation.

"I think I have to return to my building to find out about this security breach. Can your men take me back to my plane now," she replied.

"Of course, let me escort you back to the transport outside," Justin said, and Ms. London left on her plane back to London City airport.

When he returned to his office, he found Janet sitting in front of his desk, looking anxious.

"All right, Justin, what the hell was that all about? She arrives this morning and leaves fifteen minutes later?"

"Yes, she had a call from her assistant to say that James was seen in her office and she had to return immediately," he replied, smiling.

"What? How's that possible? He doesn't even know where the Home Office is located, does he?" Janet exclaimed.

"James must have done some research, maybe with the help of Jana, and found the location purely by chance. You know, once inside with his medallion he can move to anywhere he wants. That's the good news, because I spoke to him on some sort of short-wave radio. Did you know about that?" Justin asked.

"Yes, they have some limited communication up and running again but only for government use. What else did James say?"

"You're not going to like this. James told me that she came to take the plane back to the US today," he said.

"So, what stopped her today, Justin?"

"James told her assistant that there was some kind of interference from her office that would kill anyone on the plane," Justin explained.

"You mean something that triggered a bomb – do you believe that?"

"No, of course not. Probably that's how he got access to the building, but it really scared Ms. London," he said laughing.

"What do we do now, await the return of James?"

"Yes, but you have been warned. We may have stopped her attempt today, but if she comes back to return the plane I can't stop her, so what do you want to do?"

"Really, Justin, I don't know. Let me speak to my son and see what he thinks. I'm not giving up the millions I paid for that plane, do you understand?" Janet replied.

"Yes, but did you really purchase the plane, or offer something in return to the Americans?"

"It's complicated, but you're right. I was only given a two-year lease on the craft so that scientists from Harwell could work on the propulsion unit. They wanted to see how it was possible to make a time and space distortion. I'm sorry, but the whole project is now classified."

"Was the negotiation done by our people here or over in Washington?"

"No, it started with NASA who had impounded my previous plane because it had some time travel capabilities. Then I argued for a replacement and lobbied people in Washington for several years. After the Montserrat affair they virtually held me hostage in the US. Fortunately, I found a contact at the Ministry of Defense who supported my research as they were having a problem with cattle mutilations in Wales."

"What has cattle mutilation got to do with time travel?"

"You didn't know the shocking history that 10,000 cattle have suffered mutilation across the American heartland for the last twenty years? And that it was seen to be done by small men in flying saucers that the government couldn't stop?" she said.

"And the connection, Janet, please."

"All right, listen. The British Government works with a number of American agencies on UFO research as a matter of the security threat, mainly through GCHQ. You must have had a security briefing before you were posted here about this hovercraft that was based here. That's why you have Marines all over this base, right?"

"Maybe, but little was touched on about what we were protecting. What's so special about the plane we have outside?"

"Remember the Roswell incident in 1947? Since then, the US has collected five, maybe more, small flying saucers that were used to descend from a mother ship and take body parts from the cattle, and the same in Wales and France. These were piloted by small aliens, but the craft were too small for most humans to fly. Then back in the eighties someone in the office of special investigations in New Mexico found a way to communicate with the aliens and some sort of a deal was done."

"Aw, come on, Janet, you have to be pulling my leg."

"No, it turned out to be true. I heard rumors in the corridors of power that this deal involved a much bigger plane that was stored away in Nevada and never used. So I went to take a look, and after two years of discussion I got approval from the Ministry of Defense to bring it here. Look, it's sitting in a hangar over there," she said waving her arm at the window outside.

"Really, all this happened after I came back from Montserrat? We met at your house in Windsor back in 2021, wasn't it?" Justin replied.

"Yes, and since then we had the tsunamis that flooded most of England, followed by a massive ejection from the sun that finished most air transport as we knew it in the past."

"Thanks, Janet, for that little tour of how we got to where we are today. The question in my mind is the security threat and who's in control of this country today." His phone rang then and Janet quietly excused herself from his office.

When she reached the main building, a marine checked her pass and said she was needed inside. On reaching the control room, two senior Air Force Marshals escorted her to a private office on the side of the building.

"Mrs. Rumford, I'm sorry about the misunderstanding with your plane today, but you must understand that it will be returned to the US tomorrow. Those are the orders we have received from the Ministry of Defense today," he said, passing a message across the table.

"Really? I didn't know the UK had a functioning Ministry of Defense in London or in Blackheath, wherever that may be," she replied, looking at the document more closely.

"Right, if you can just sign these papers to release the plane back to NASA and the United States authorities it would be appreciated. You understand that we are most grateful for the opportunity to study the plane…" he said when she stopped him.

"Yes, yes. I'll sign the papers on one condition, that my son pilots the plane," she said.

"I don't think that's going to be possible after what happened last time," he replied.

"In that case, there's no way I'm going to sign your stupid papers, from some Ministry that we both know doesn't exist. Go ahead and take the plane, do what you like with it, but just remember that's stealing," Janet replied and standing up, she left the room and went to find her son Ben.

30 - WOOLWICH

Having found access to her office, James didn't know where to start. He looked in the desk drawers and the filing cabinets for some record of contacts with aliens, or anything about UFOs.

After fifteen minutes of searching he had found nothing, just Government documents from the past, and then the alarms in the building sounded in the corridor outside and he knew he had to leave. Looking around for a solid wall, he reversed the location from earlier this morning and pointed his medallion at the wall to return to the London City airport with its damaged terminal building.

This time he arrived on the runway that was built on the old London docks, and which looked just as deserted as before. Then he saw the same six wheeled army 'Duck' waiting close to the runway and decided to go and introduce himself again to the driver.

"Hello, we meet again, is Ms. London returning soon?" he asked.

"What's that got to do with you?" the soldier replied, stamping out his cigarette on the tarmac. He turned to look as they heard the Cessna plane coming in to land on the runway. "You had better make yourself scarce, as I've orders to shoot you," he said.

The plane taxied to a stop in front of them and Ruth London walked down the stairs towards them.

"You're going to have to shoot me in front of your boss," said James.

"Put the weapon down, soldier, he's coming with us," shouted Ms. London and indicated for James to climb inside with her before demanding an update from the driver. "What's the current situation with the tide, can we make it across the river?" she asked.

"Yes, ma'am, it's only just past high water, there won't be a problem."

"Very well, let's get started right away," she ordered, taking her place on the bench seat at the rear of the amphibious craft with James.

"Well, James, we meet again at last. I see you have recovered your medallion. You found that back on Montserrat?" she asked.

"No, it was a bit more complicated," he replied.

"But you did go back in time on that plane to the island?"

"Yes, I went with Ben and his girlfriend Michelle to the same place in 2020 again."

"And you also met an alien, who looked rather attractive from the photos. Are you sure she was a female, what was she wearing?"

"Come on, Ruth, she was a young girl, wearing a Caribbean pink tee-shirt and girl's shorts and no, I didn't have sex with her."

"What did you do, because when it got dark all we saw from the satellite were bright flashing lights."

"When I got there, she had already moved the cylinder up onto the road and activated some kind of sound to attract back the aliens who had previously landed on the beach. There were about eight hundred of them who simply walked down the road as if in a trance. Then she closed the door and they all left on the spaceship," he explained.

"And what did you do, go with them?"

"No, this woman was obviously not a trained pilot. She couldn't find a safe route back to her planet or where they had come from. I told her it was too dangerous and left the craft before it took off."

"And then what, you came back here?"

"Yes, I came back to Janet's house in Windsor, in June 2031 as I thought the flood would have receded by then. Any more questions?" James asked as the Duck hit the water in the river and stopped.

"Come on, man, engage the propellers. We want to get across the Thames, not get taken downstream by the tide," she shouted at the driver.

The ancient Rolls Royce engine kicked in and with a cloud of blue smoke the craft moved towards the opposite bank of the Thames, where the Woolwich ferry used to land. Standing up, James could see the remains of the Thames barrier, now shattered by the force of the water, and realised how wide the river was at high tide. Before he could look further, he was told to sit down again.

"Tell me, where exactly are we going?" he asked Ruth.

"We should shortly pick up the road going south to the old Artillery Barracks, about the only safe place on this side of the river," she replied.

"Really, security is as bad as that around here?"

"Yes, the army made an exclusion zone around the city to the north, but here on the south bank we don't have enough military to keep out people looking for food. Other parts of the country are even worse."

"What about the British navy, did any of that survive?"

"Not much. One of our aircraft carriers is about five miles inland, near Southampton, carried there by the tsunami waves. We have no idea where the other is. We now realise that the first wave is not the real problem, but the slosh back wave that comes after is the most dangerous," she said and continued, "After the first wave, the sea goes back down until it hits the coast opposite, like Germany or France, and then sloshes back again. All of the airbases across East Anglia were lost in that way."

"But don't we still have other RAF bases? What about GCHQ?" James asked.

"Whoa there, James. You'll shortly see what the real problem is," she said.

The amphibious craft came to a stop at the entrance to the barracks and the driver jumped out to request entry. James stood up in the 'Duck' and looked around him. The day had warmed up since leaving the airport but hardly an undamaged building was left standing on the road they had driven up. Everything around was covered in debris, decayed trees, cars and trucks piled in a heap and a huge mountain of red bricks. The walls of the barracks looked to have been damaged in places, replaced with concrete blocks and topped off with barbed wire. The sun shone down on the open vehicle and James sat down again, bewildered in the silence.

"What happened out there?" asked James.

"You mean the Georgian façade and Central gateway – all swept away. The Army headquarters were moved out of London many years ago, so all that remains is this gatehouse we use now."

"You mean we still have an Army of sorts."

"Yes, of course. Most regiments were moved out of London to Salisbury Plain, long before the flood. But we need you to work with us now you have your time travelling abilities back," she said as the vehicle entered an enclosed courtyard.

They both descended from the craft where an officer was waiting to greet them.

"Good afternoon, ma'am," he said saluting her, but she waved him aside and walked up the steps into the building.

"And you are?" he asked looking down at James.

"James Pollack. I came down here from the Number 22 Airbase up in High Wycombe," he replied, shaking the officer's hand.

"Ah yes, of course, the man who's been testing the alien craft, must be quite an experience to fly that," he replied. "Right then, come on inside, we have prepared some tea and sandwiches for you both," he continued and James followed him inside.

The room resembled an English style manor house, with an oak table and military paintings along the walls that confused him. James was ushered to a place at the table where Ms. London was in conversation with a high-ranking officer in the Army. He quickly grabbed a plate of sandwiches, remembering he hadn't eaten all day. After that the officer poured him a mug of tea and they sat together talking, until Ruth announced she wanted to show James the basement.

"Come along, James, I want to show you what we managed to rescue before the GCHQ was taken over," she said, and led the way to an ancient elevator in the hallway. The party entered the lift and she pressed a button marked level 4 to silently descend to the basement. James now saw he was in a high security tunnel painted white, with an armed sentry sitting at the far door.

The soldier quickly stood up and saluted when he saw the officers leave the lift. After returning the salute, the colonel put his hand on a security plate and the door slid open. Inside was another door marked "NORAD Personnel Only" and with a violet light James guessed was preparing their eyes for a dark world inside. When the door opened, he found they were in a large dark control room with operators sitting in a row, looking at a huge screen on the wall. They were all standing on an observation platform at the back of the room.

"Don't say anything, James, just watch and listen to what's happening on the screen. Movements on the screen are live in real time, being transmitted by military satellite from the NORAD installation in the Gulf of Mexico," Ruth told him. James could just make out the Texan drawl of a US commentator.

"Here, sit on this bench and put on these headphones to follow the conversation," she said.

As his eyes became accustomed to the dark, he saw the screen was about the size of a normal cinema screen and curved. He was looking at a quadrant of the United Kingdom that included southern Scotland, Borders, Yorkshire, and about halfway down the coastline to the

Wash. The entire area of the screen was covered in a grid that was moving. It was then that he noticed a series of blips at the top of the screen that were moving down from the right. The targets were quickly labelled, like a typical radar screen where blips designate aircraft, but were all labelled ASC on the screen. James listened with interest to the words of the air traffic commentary.

"Attention, London. You have ASC coming in from the north. Five Alternative Space craft – two now leaving to the northwest and one coming down into England."

He saw the craft was following the coastline. This ASC continued south towards the centre of England, made two jumps and then stopped. A red glow came off the blip, but that wasn't explained by the commentator. After another few minutes or so the officers stood up and Ruth nudged James that it was time to leave. They filed out and back into the airlock, where they asked James what he thought.

"Yes, it's most impressive. Manned 24/7 I take it. These Alternative Space craft are UFOs, right?" James asked.

"Yes, there aren't many other planes flying about today, except for Ruth, of course," came the reply and everyone laughed.

"The Norad reporting system records all unknown air traffic in North America, and as you saw all around the United Kingdom, which interests us more," the colonel explained.

"So why the red glow on the screen?" he asked.

"That happens when the ASC land. What you saw today was a landing at the headquarters of GCHQ in Gloucestershire," the colonel replied.

"You mean these aliens have taken over our communications centre in England?" he asked.

"Yes, not only taken it over, but are using it for their own surface-based communications on the planet."

"How did you get the screen down here and link it into the NORAD transmissions?" James asked.

"We got lucky and did that before the CME hit. We had been advised by US Space Surveillance to move it to an alternative location. An Army signals unit was using this building, so the infrastructure for covert monitoring was already in place. Basically, we didn't want to alert the aliens that we were watching them," he was told.

"Thank you, gentlemen. I think it's better if we continue this conversation upstairs, don't you," Ruth London suggested and they all filed out back to the lift.

Once upstairs, the group reconvened in a conference room and were joined by two young communication engineers, who specialized in electronic warfare and had more questions than answers from James.

"These men here have read the Royal Engineers report from the incident on the beach in Montserrat. We know it's over ten years ago, but would you be willing to take some questions," the colonel asked.

"I'm not sure if I have answers, but go ahead," James replied.

"This cylinder on the beach was moved by its own power, do you know how that was done?"

"I assume that it was the same or a similar anti-gravity system to the hover plane we have been testing at the 22 Airbase. The scientists tell me that within the lower part of the craft is a gravity propulsion system that uses power from an anti-matter reactor. Remember that anti-matter was first made by Manchester University at a research centre in Switzerland in the nineties. Small quantities of anti-matter have been used in MRI scanners in hospitals for years, so that's nothing new. What's new is how to generate and contain sufficient energy to travel and jump through time, which is beyond us at present," James replied and turned to the second engineer who was eager to ask his question.

"You mentioned jumping through time, can you explain how that might be done, please?"

"Yes, manipulation of space and time is possible with the propulsion system I mentioned. One of the boffins at the airbase tried to explain how it might work, but I'm not sure I understand it fully." The man looked so disappointed, James continued, "Okay, you want me to try. Remember that gravity distorts time and space, so if you are in a spacecraft that can generate a huge gravitational field, by turning on your gravity generator it may be possible to warp space and time by folding it. Then when the pilot turns the generator off, the craft will have moved a huge distance through space, but time won't have changed. That's why the UFOs you track here, sorry what they call Alternative Space Craft, appear to jump on the screen. What the Americans call tic-tacs in the US Air force," James replied.

"So the ASCs are not really jumping at all?"

"I'm not a scientist, but to me it appears like gravitational distortion. It's like looking at a mirage in space. The only time you really know what the craft is doing is when the power is shut off and it's sitting on the ground. The short answer is, we don't know," James replied to a round of applause.

"Thank you for that. I'm sorry, that's all the time we have for questions from our Royal Signals men, doing a great job stuck underground for hours on end," the colonel announced and went to shake the hands of his two engineers who were escorted out of the room, and everyone relaxed.

"Thanks, James, that was most helpful," said Ruth smiling.

"Yes, although I didn't understand a lot, it was just what the men needed. Rumors that we have a spacecraft have been circulating for weeks, so confirmation that we have people doing something about these bloody aliens is most useful," replied the junior officer.

The colonel came back and sat down next to James. "Well done, James, do you really understand any of what you said?" he asked and turning to his junior, told him to break out the scotch.

"Ruth told me you have met and worked with an alien woman when you went back to that island. What was she like?" he asked.

"You want the scientific or a man's view?" James replied, laughing as whisky glasses were passed around the table. "We found her on Montserrat beach where the cylinder crashed, inside a life support pod, and took her up to a house with a female RN officer. She was revived in some oxygenated water. When I went back more recently, she had not only recovered but had moved the cylinder up onto the access road to the beach. I only worked with her over one night as she left on the spacecraft the next morning."

"What was she trying to do?"

"If you've read the reports, some eight hundred persons were recovered alive from that cylinder and she wanted to take them back to her planet, wherever that is. Sorry, but I don't know," James explained.

A bottle of ten-year-old scotch was passed around the table with Ruth listening to their conversation.

"Look, she was like any other woman on this planet. Not tall, but slim with blue eyes and blonde hair, and she spoke good English. Yes, I thought that was impossible, but I was told that she had been rescued by an exo-planet team that was put together with the ESA and France back in 2020. Does that make any sense to you?" James asked.

"Yes, do you know the name Captain Claude Duquette?"

"Sorry, no, never heard of him," James replied.

"Then you might want to look at the names on this mission list because I think you must know the RN officer who was involved," the colonel replied while the junior officer handed out faded copies of a paper to James and Ruth with a list of names.

"My, my, you have been busy," said James seeing the logo of Kings College, London at the top and the date July 2020.

"Right then, if you're ready can we go through the list of names together," the colonel said and James nodded his agreement.

"First name on the list is Claude Duquette. He was a lieutenant on the French aircraft carrier that stopped off on a humanitarian mission to Lebanon. The carrier went on to fight ISIS in Iraq. Later we believe he became the project leader for the team to the exo-planet. Can you remember the date?" he asked.

"Yes, it was January or February 2015, I remember because I was there," James replied.

"You were in Iraq at that time?"

"No, I was in Lebanon at a place where the first survivors returned. Then a replacement team was sent, but I knew nothing about that."

"So contact with aliens on other planets was being made as long as fifteen years ago."

"Yes, it was being done on a covert basis by the ESA, although I expect the training was done by NASA while the US Government continued to deny all knowledge of aliens. Special investigations in the US were trying to reverse-engineer the alien space craft they had in Nevada, at that time."

"Right, that's our understanding as well. So let's move on to Anita, it says US Special Forces – did you ever meet her?"

"No, never met her. I saw her just once. It was at a conference at a hotel in Bosnia, where the survivors of the last mission agreed to return to rescue two of the team that were left behind."

"And all three returned again?"

"No, just the captain and Anita. Elizabeth K must have stayed behind as she turned up on Montserrat when the cylinder landed."

"Of the two left behind, Susan and Bee. We know Bee was a microbiologist who worked at Kings College in London as this list was found in her file. Susan was an astrophysicist who had worked at CERN, did you ever meet either of them?" he asked.

"Sorry, no. The person you should be investigating was Elizabeth K. She tried to have me shot at Janet's house and went over to join the US army," James replied.

"In fact, James, she's been most helpful to us. That move wasn't exactly pre-arranged, but her presence in the US helped persuade the CIA to support leasing the alien plane to Janet. If it wasn't for Elizabeth, you might not be here today," Ruth interrupted.

"So, James, that just leaves one nigger in the woodpile, doesn't it? Nathalie Boyana, head of the Core Facility at the National Laboratories in Albuquerque, New Mexico, close to Kirkland Air Force Base. That's not so far from the Nellis Military Operations area in Nevada. Do you know Nathalie?" asked the colonel. Everyone in the room stared at James.

"Yes, of course I do, she's my daughter," he said and everyone gasped.

"Good, we seem to be getting somewhere at last. Does she have the same time travel abilities you do?" he asked.

"I think that's something you have to ask her," replied James.

"But you've been to the Papoose Mountain range at the Nevada Test site, haven't you James? Because after a lot of delay, we received a copy of a security pass issued by the Department of Energy, Naval Intelligence, in the name of James Pollack, in 2010," the colonel stated.

"Yes, but when you travel through time, well I pick up security passes from all over the place. Look, here's one from the base in High Wycombe from 2030. It was given to me by the RAF after I met with Ruth London," James replied, placing his UK pass on the table.

"Okay, point taken. Can you tell us what you or your daughter were doing at the Nevada test site, because we really are a bit desperate here to understand more," he finally admitted.

"Yes, she was testing one of the alien craft that had been repaired. Can we just back up a minute and take a break. Perhaps go somewhere more comfortable to complete this discussion?" James asked.

"Of course, James, would you like some tea or coffee?"

"I think coffee and more sandwiches would be good."

Everyone stood up to allow James and the colonel to leave the conference room. The junior officer and Ruth then returned to the table to look at her notes.

"My God, Ruth, this man has been working with alien craft for the last twenty-five years, while all we ever thought about was the threat from Russia or China," he said.

"No, I think he's only ever time travelled around our planet. It's his daughter, by the sound of it, who may have travelled from our world to another exo-planet," Ruth replied, and continued, "Look at what he said about space time distortion – you don't get that from talking to the boffins at the airbase for ten minutes. Then he told us that watching spacecraft was like a mirage. He must have been on the ground in the past watching flying saucers in the sky above him. Remember, he was only ever a passenger on the craft at High Wycombe, and never watched it fly."

"But you still think he's a candidate for "Operation Mongoose.""

"He sounds like the best person we've got," she replied.

They looked at the bottle of scotch on the table and nodded.

Twenty minutes later the colonel returned to the conference room sweating and looking concerned and holding a plate of half-eaten sandwiches.

"This is madness, he said he had to leave and, in a flash, he was gone," he said.

"Yes, Colonel, that's what time travellers do. Did he agree to help us with Project Mongoose?" Ruth asked.

"Yes, well. He said he would take a look. I gave him the co-ordinates and the location of the last time he was seen in Canada, but the dates are impossible. To go back to June 2030 before the cataclysm," he said, taking the whisky bottle and pouring himself a generous shot.

"No, Colonel, that's an easy day's work if you're a time traveller like James. Now what else did he ask for?" Ruth replied.

"He wants to meet us at Ben's house up at the High Wycombe airbase at ten tomorrow morning, for a final decision on Ben using the craft. You need to prepare your transport for early in the morning," he ordered.

"Right, noted, wilco," Ruth replied.

"In the meantime, he asked if the screen downstairs could be set to monitor the Canadian east coast for the next twenty-four hours. Something about wanting to keep an eye out for ASCs coming down from the north," he said.

Draining his glass, he stood up to leave the room. "I'm going to text NORAD to satisfy this latest request, as now he's worried about being tracked. You two had better come with me back to the basement to see if we have any ASCs around here," he said.

Ruth and the officer looked at each other and got up.

"Oh, and don't forget to bring the sandwiches, Junior," he shouted on his way out.

31 – MONT ROYAL

James jumped back from the Army Barracks to the old London City airport to try and leave little trace of where he had been. The airport was a deserted site, where no one worked or lived anymore, so this was his neutral base. He also needed time to think of how to meet two of the most important people to the UK, who had been sent to live in Canada months before the flood.

It was then he realised he was standing close to the runway and knew he had better move. The sun was setting in the west over what once had been the City, and with the windows of the only building shining orange he had a sudden impulse to walk over there. He climbed up onto the road, crossed the Connaught Bridge and reached the building just before it got dark. The entrance door wasn't locked and with no one at the old hotel reception desk, he quickly took the back stairs to the first floor where he knew Ruth had her office.

James had already searched her office and found nothing, so this time he wanted to check out her bedroom next door. It was just a feeling, nothing more than that, but from the discussion earlier it was clear she had been in touch with Elizabeth more recently. Reaching the door, he activated his medallion and walked inside, to find the body of a man on the floor. He was dressed in blue overalls and wearing black boots that looked the same as on the man he had seen in the control room.

His gaze was brought back to the body again – had he been attacked in the room or met by someone he knew? There was a long smear of blood on the tiled floor, as if he had tried to crawl towards the connecting door to the office next door.

James knelt down to feel the man's pulse, but there was nothing, except a note in his hand and he saw the name Jessica. Prising his fingers open he retrieved the note and put it in the top pocket of his jacket. It was only then that he saw the man had been aiming for something near a low bedside table on the side of the double bed. The side table was not fixed to the wall but fitted neatly against the skirting board. James pulled the unit away from the wall to look behind. He saw a small metal ring that stuck out from a joint. When he pulled on the ring, a small section of the skirting came away from the wall and fell into his hands.

When he felt inside, he found a long black box and pulled it out to see what was inside. The box wasn't locked, and when opened he found a leather bag. Inside was a device about the size of a large mobile phone, but with an octagonal shaped crystal at the top. He remembered hearing about such things being found on alien craft but had never seen one before. He knew that the crystal, when held in the hands of a person, could display pictures from the past. These pictures were recordings of events on planet Earth, from the present to many years ago. James pushed the bedside table back and sat on the bed to see if he could input the date and place he had been given for the mission in Canada. After a few tries of seeing only black and white images of poor quality he gave up.

The question was how and when Ruth London had obtained this device. He could imagine Ruth lying in bed in this room watching past images from the planet for hours at night. Perhaps she or Elizabeth had obtained the crystal as part of a trade in the past. Perhaps this had come with the hovercraft, although that was over fifty years ago. Then he wondered why the man from the control room wanted to access the past, and why was he was attacked? The only way to find out was to see who was in the control room now. Replacing the furniture in the room, he placed the device in the pocket of his jacket, tip toed around the body, and quietly left.

James walked down the corridor to the control room door and listened. He could hear the high-pitched voice of the girl from reception shouting at someone inside.

"I don't care what the problem is, our friends will be landing on the roof shortly and we need to show them we're ready," she demanded, after which he heard a man's voice mumble some excuses.

James decided it was time to leave. If it was true that people from the Home Office were actively talking to other people or aliens, he thought he should let his friends up at the airbase know. He walked to the stairwell at the end of the corridor, reset his medallion to 6 pm in the bedroom at Janet's house and pushed the button. He woke up to find he was lying on a bed again, with Jana helping him drink from a glass of water.

"James, where have you been all day? You left a note about London and the Home Office, so what's been happening?" she asked.

"Yes well, bit of a long story. I want you to look at this," he replied, pulling the leather bag out from his jacket and handing it to Jana. She opened the bag, and when the device fell onto her lap she looked at the images in amazement.

"James, have you already activated this device, because everything you have done today is recorded on this thing!" Jana exclaimed.

"Yes, I tried to, but couldn't get it to work," he replied.

"That's easy. It works by messages you send from your brain. Look, there are no controls or anything, but here you are at some deserted airport in London. Then you walked over to a hotel, looks like a Hilton from the design. Odd, but the whole area looks to have been flattened by water. Is it?"

"Yes, that's the damaged London City airport, where Ruth London flies to when she leaves on her plane from here."

"Who's Ruth London," Jana asked.

"She's someone Ben and I met when I first arrived here and said she was from the Home Office. I've discovered something really dangerous and important. Can you run over to the gate-house and call Justin at his office? Ask him to come over and meet us here at the house, with Janet and Ben as well."

"Yes, of course, if you say it's really important," she replied.

"Don't let the guard hear you say anything about this device or that I just returned. You just say you have a code red at the house and he should come immediately," James explained, and Jana nodded.

She put on a cardigan and went downstairs to leave the house, while James went to shower. Jana must have run quickly, because by the time James had changed and went downstairs with the leather bag she was back with him in the sitting room.

"I'm going to make some tea for everyone," she said.

There was a knock on the front door and Justin entered the house, smiling when he saw James sitting in an armchair.

"James, you're back with some important news, I take it," he said, walking over to shake his hand.

"Yes, you remember that difficult person, Ruth London? I can tell you that she has little to do with the Home Office, and from what I found may be working with some aliens," James replied.

"All right, James, calm down. Let's wait for Janet and Ben to arrive and you can tell your story," Justin insisted.

Jana handed out mugs of hot tea.

"I can do better than that, watch these images of my movements today," James replied and passed the device to Jana who sat on the sofa next to Justin.

The images unfolded on the screen until he saw James and Ruth London board an army amphibious craft and set off across the Thames river.

"James, it looks from this as if she's working with the British Army, somewhere near Woolwich, isn't it, from the pictures," he asked.

"Yes, at this stage I was quite impressed with her close relationship to the military, but see what happens next," James replied.

They watched the group descend to a basement and Justin saw a screen with UFOs moving across the UK. Janet and Ben entered the house and Jana stood up to let Janet sit next to Justin.

"Can you stop the screen right there, James, so Janet can see the images, because this is important," Justin said.

Janet took one look and almost shouted at James. "Where did you get this device, James? It was stolen from the hovercraft years ago."

"I found it in Ruth London's bedroom. It was hidden under a skirting board with the dead body of a computer engineer in the room," he replied.

Everyone gasped at images of James in the hotel bedroom and the video came to an end.

"James, you most certainly have been busy today. I don't know what to think," said Justin, reaching for a rather cold mug of tea.

"None of this is new to me. I had been invited to watch a similar screen in Texas monitoring those spacecraft, but had no idea that the UK still had access after the cataclysm – that is a surprise," Janet said.

"Okay, James, let's try to get to the bottom of all this. I assume this army group up at the old barracks in Woolwich were asking you for some kind of help. Can you tell us what they want you to do?" Justin asked.

"Yes, they want me to jump to these co-ordinates in Canada on this specific time and date to meet and return this family back to England. Using Janet's plane, obviously," James replied.

Everyone in the room looked confused until Ben started to make sense of the plan. "If this couple have three teenagers then the parents would be William and Kate. They were sent to Canada some months before the cataclysm hit. Do you know the location, James?"

"Yes, it's here on this paper, with the date, but I couldn't find it on that device," he replied, at which point Jana took the device, thought hard for a moment and handed it back to Ben.

"Wow, that's the Mont Royal Cross above Montreal. That would be a good pick-up spot if the family are still there," Ben replied, looking at the image of open space below the Cross.

"Wait a minute, Ben, you're not taking my plane anywhere until we have carefully thought this through. How do we know this couple still want to come back to England after the CME? We're not even sure where they are now," Janet insisted.

"At the time, he wanted to help the army. They really do want to place a King on the throne again. Now I'm not so sure after finding that body in her bedroom, with the image device. With other spacecraft around the UK, I would be concerned about their safety. Listen up, everybody. Ruth London wants to meet at Ben's house tomorrow morning, so we have until then to make our decision," James explained.

"As a military man, I don't think we could offer good security even if they lived on the airbase. We just don't have enough Marines. Windsor Castle is out of the question as the land around still floods at high tide. Frankly, James, I'm sorry but this plan looks like a nonstarter to me, even if the couple wanted to return," Justin said.

Jana went to find more refreshments for the guests and taking the device with her, started to look for images of the couple when they first moved to Canada. Using her mind she quickly found what she was looking for and returned to the discussion.

"Look, everyone, I found that after they moved to Montreal in June 2030, the couple went for a picnic at Mont Royal Park. They sat on the grass below the Cross, as if they were waiting to meet someone, or get picked up. It's all here on these images if you take a look at the dates," Jana explained.

Ben snatched the device away from her to check, nodded and passed it on to James.

"I know it means the plane has to go back in time but you've done that before, haven't you, Ben. So, I think Ben and James should at least take a look at this park at end of June 2030," Jana explained and taking a deep breath went on. "James can ask Kate if she is willing to take the risk to return to England with her children. Tell them the truth, the country is badly damaged, with no government, little electricity or food, and limited resources for the children, but let them decide," she said.

"And if they find no one there, what happens?" asked Justin.

"Then the craft returns empty with Ben and James, and we can call Ruth London's bluff tomorrow morning," replied Janet.

"I can see that Ben is ready to give it a try, but what about you, James? Are you up to it after everything today?" asked Jana.

"Yes, it sounds okay, as long as I only time travel on the craft as a passenger, and we do it tonight," James replied.

Justin put his hands to his face and thought carefully about where to house the family. "All right, I can go along with the plan provided the family stays at Janet's house down in Windsor and not at the base."

"Yes, I think I can agree to that. It's time I did something for King and country. But can Ben and James sneak into the hangar and steal my plane tonight?" Janet asked.

"Consider it done, Mother," Ben replied.

"Right then, let's get the show on the road. I'll go back and send a jeep of marines to take Ben and James to the hangar, to make it look official. Meanwhile, Janet, you come with me. We need to load a truck with the supplies and you will need a generator. Then you take the truck back down to the house to prepare for visitors," Justin said smiling.

After that everyone got up to leave and plan what they were going to do next.

32 - LATER

James was travelling in a bus along a dirt road with nothing to look at but tracts of desert, crags and hills and a lot of brush, with dried up lakes and river beds. The time must have been years after the departure of Jessica from that railway station near London. Now he was on a journey to an area he guessed was somewhere miles south of a dry lake, and north of Las Vegas. When they arrived, he was allowed to leave the bus but was surprised by what appeared to be huge aircraft hangers built into the base of a range of mountains. The doors sloped at an angle and were covered with paint to make them look like sand. Two security guards watched them leave the bus and one shepherded the group of scientists away while James was left on his own with the other guard.

After a short wait, he was told to board the bus again and was driven straight into an open hangar. He walked towards a row of offices next to a saucer shaped disc that he thought must be an actual alien spacecraft. When James turned to look closer, he saw a poster on the wall warning of test activities for the detonations of A-Bombs – by order of the US. Atomic Energy Commission. Looking outside again, he saw in the distance a large mushroom cloud rising into the sky and thought he could feel the heat emanating from the blast.

Then everything stopped, and he woke from his dream.

"James, what's been happening, you look dreadful," Jana said, feeling his head. James looked around the room, but only saw Ben standing in the bay window waiting for Justin to return.

"Sorry, I must have dozed off for a minute."

"That looked more like a bad dream. Do you remember meeting someone called Jessica Loeza? I found her name written on some paper you'd put in the top pocket of your jacket."

"Yes, I remember from my time working in London. It must have been in the nineties. She taught me how to jump through time before I was given the medallion."

"Did you ever travel to the States, or were at a base in Nevada? When I read your mind I saw you there, looking at a flying saucer."

"No, I don't remember that. I went to Dallas once to meet up with my daughter Nathalie. Then there was some mix up with her army pass, but I don't remember all the details."

"That's the problem with these people, they can make you forget. They can remove events from your memory, where you went, what you did and who you were with. Remember that when you need to travel through time, and be careful for your next trip," Jana warned.

Ben appeared from the window, yawning and looking bored. "Can you make us something to eat, I'm starving."

"I don't know about you two. Never eat a proper meal and so tired that you fall asleep. Would you like the full English breakfast to keep you awake during the night?" Jana asked the two men.

"Absolutely, that would be great," Ben replied smiling and James nodded in agreement.

Jana left the men chatting on the sofa and went into the kitchen to start preparing the food.

"James, do you have the coordinates of where we are going in Canada?" Ben asked.

"Yes, of course. This was what I was given by the Army Colonel, together with the dates and time," he replied handing the note over to Ben.

"What about coming back? Remember we agreed to return to Janet's house down by the river. Do you have the coordinates for that and a time of arrival?"

"Yes, let me add that to the paper. We should make the arrival time at eleven tonight. That should give Justin time to set up the electric lighting and for Janet to prepare in the house," James replied, handing the note paper back to him. "Oh, one last thing, Ben. I don't think you should get out of the plane when we land, as it may be dangerous. Let me get out and do the talking in case I get apprehended. Should that happen, you must take off with the plane and leave me behind, is that clear?"

"Yes of course, I understand. I'll try to land to keep my eyes on you all the time," replied Ben.

Jana announced the meal was ready.

Shortly after they finished eating, Justin arrived with a marine driving an army jeep and they were ready to leave. After saying goodbye to Jana, James and Ben were driven down to the hanger with the hover plane and taken to the changing room for pilots. Once they were both dressed in the light blue jump suits, they took their flying helmets and went to find Justin.

"Your plane is all prepared out on the landing pad if you really want to do this," he said.

"From our last flight to Montserrat Island it shouldn't be a problem, should it, James," Ben replied sounding nervous.

"No, a piece of cake. I have given Ben the coordinates to arrive back at Janet's house around 11:00 tonight. Can you prepare some lights for us to land in the front driveway?" James asked.

"Okay, eleven tonight should be possible, once we get a generator connected down at the house," Justin replied and led them out to the plane sitting in the last of the evening sunshine on the launch pad. Standing at the hanger doors were both Janet and Michelle, nervously watching the departure scene.

"Gentlemen, this is as far as I can go. From here on the launch team have control, and the maintenance men have the ladders ready for you to board. Wishing you both a safe return," Justin said.

Shaking them both by the hand, he left them to board and went back to stand and watch with the women. Ben boarded first in the front cockpit, then James climbed the ladder at the rear and took his seat at the back of the passenger compartment. Connecting his headphones, he made contact with Ben to check the correct coordinates had been entered into the plane's computer and they were given permission to launch.

"You still want to do this, James?" Ben asked as the plane lifted off the launch pad and hovered three hundred feet above the airfield.

"Engaging the hyper-drive now," he said, and without waiting for a reply he pushed on the lever. Making no noise, the craft disappeared and jumped back in time to Montreal in 2030.

****

It was later that evening. Justin was standing in the drive of Janet's house down by the river in Old Windsor. Everything had been prepared by the Marines during the evening. An aging electric generator was running beside the garage, providing power to the house with an arc light illuminating the drive. Justin looked at his watch, becoming concerned when he noted it was just after eleven. Then one of his men ran across and pointed up at the night sky and he saw that the craft was hovering over the house, descending onto the driveway fast.

"Shall I tell the medics to prepare?" one of the marines asked.

"Yes, and bring the fire truck around here," Justin replied.

The plane descended in a blue haze with sparks of electricity falling off around the fuselage. Everyone could feel that the air was filled with static electricity. Justin withdrew to the steps of the house where Janet and Jana were watching the landing.

"My god, Justin, how can anyone have survived inside that plane?" Janet asked.

"Don't worry, James will come out of there alive. The only question is, will he be with the others?" Jana replied.

The plane finally touched down and the power was switched off. Immediately the men in the fire tender started to hose down the plane with water and clouds of steam were released into the night sky.

"So far, so good," murmured Justin to the others and they watched as the medics positioned a slide against the passenger entry and waited for the door to open. A person appeared at the entrance and went down the slide into the arms of the medics. The person was unable to stand and was quickly carried to a gurney nearby.

"That's James," exclaimed Jana and ran down the steps towards the man on the wheeled stretcher, where she was stopped by one of the medics in a white protective suit.

"Let me through," Jana shouted at the medic who removed her helmet, revealing herself to be Michelle.

"I only need to touch his head to find out what happened," Jana said.

Justin came down onto the drive to try to restrain her. Jana pushed Michelle aside and on touching James, saw everything that happened on the plane.

"James has come back alone with Ben as the others wouldn't leave. They have brought back lots of papers and some cargo on the plane," Janna explained to both Justin and Michelle. Meanwhile, the other two medics wheeled James away towards the steps of the house.

"Frankly, that's a relief, "Justin replied and helped to remove the slide to allow the plane to leave again. Almost immediately, the door closed and Justin ran back to the steps as the plane started to power up again.

Without making any sound the plane lifted off and rose into the sky above the house. Justin watched in the moonlight as the dark shadow from the plane moved across the fields, heading north towards the airbase in High Wickham.

33 - HYBRIDS

It was early morning when Justin drove three of his marines in his jeep to Ben's house at the end of the runway. The Chiltern hills rose above them as the first rays of sunshine shone onto the tarmac. On hearing the noise Ben came outside to greet them.

"Morning, Ben, you are up early, how do you feel after that flight," Justin asked.

"Feeling fine, and no I haven't seen any UFOs down here all night," he replied, shaking Justin's hand.

"I had a call early this morning from the Air Field Marshal. He wants your sitting room torn apart for the meeting at ten. I've brought some men with me to help replace most of the furniture with chairs and a table for the top brass," he explained.

"I thought this was going to be an informal gathering?"

"Yes, very informal, and confidential, but with RAF flags since he's invited Colonel Harris to attend with Ms. London," Justin explained. "You, of course, will be the top gun pilot for this inquiry," he continued.

Ben ignored the comment. "Do you have any news of James? I'm more worried about Michelle, she's still with the medics down at Janet's house," Ben said.

"Sorry, no, I'll ask later. Let the men get on with moving the furniture, and if you have some coffee we can discuss what to expect with this inquiry."

Before they could leave an open military truck arrived with four men dressed in battle fatigues. They were soon joined by the marines who started to unload the table and chairs for the meeting, now less than an hour away.

"Are we expecting an alien invasion to occur here, Justin?

"I have no idea, but it looks unusual," Justin replied. "Come on, let's go inside and watch from the back of your house to see what's going on," he continued.

Ben agreed and led the way inside the house. They sat on the terrace at the back, drinking coffee as the men in uniform started to set up equipment at the two rear corners of the house.

"Any idea where these squaddies came from, Justin?"

"By the patches on the uniform the insignia looks like part of the old NATO forces we had before the cataclysm, but I have no idea what they are doing here," Justin replied, finishing his coffee and standing up to leave.

"I have to pick up Janet at the side gate at quarter to ten, if you want to come along," Justin offered.

"Yes, that would be good. I don't want to be left alone with all these goons at the house," Ben replied, and the two left the house for Justin's jeep still parked outside on the runway.

As they drove back towards the main airbase buildings, they saw an open RAF military car with the Field Marshal and what appeared to be all the top brass, driving towards the house. Ben noticed that driving the car in the opposite direction was a young woman in a light blue dress uniform wearing a RAF cap and medal to match.

"Wow, James, it looks like we need to drop by the hangar to find you some RAF pilot's kit," Justin remarked as he saluted the senior officers in the car. When they arrived at the side gate, Janet and Jana were already waiting and after a short embrace, Janet climbed into the back of the jeep with Jana. In her hand was the leather pouch that everyone had seen the previous evening.

"I don't think we want to put all our cards on the table, Jana. Now we've seen this meeting has become a high-ranking military inquiry, we need to get Ben some RAF uniform before we return to the house," Justin explained.

He started the engine and turned off to the launch pad hangar where Ben ran inside to find his pilot's outfit. When he came back dressed in his flying kit, Justin drove back onto the runway to find the single engine Lysander plane coming into land. He slowed down to let it pass to taxi to the end of the runway. By the time they reached the house, both Ms. London and the colonel had gone inside after being welcomed by the Field Marshal and the other RAF officers. Justin turned his jeep outside the house and waited for them to be called, adding a few words of advice before they got out.

"Is everyone ready for this? Don't be intimidated by the military set up. From what we saw, there will be a table at the far end of the room where the RAF top brass will sit. On one side will be the chairs for the Army and the Home Office with chairs for us on the other side facing the window. What we don't understand is why this equipment has been installed outside the house, unless one of you has some ideas.

"Yes, I've seen this on the viewer James found, or something similar. Those two pods are to stop any magnetic waves from being detected from outside. I would expect there are two more pods at the back to cover the whole building," Jana explained, taking the device out of the leather pouch and activating it.

"Look, this was set up in Nevada… oh, years ago, but I don't know if they worked or not," she continued.

"Looks like some high up are now worried about a UFO attack on the base if they need these measures," Janet replied.

A marine approached the jeep to say they were ready to start the meeting and they all got out and followed Justin into the house.

Once inside, they found the living room had been transformed with a long table facing the entrance and four distinguished persons seated with the Air Field Marshal in the centre. On his left was a man in a white coat, probably a scientist, thought Janet. An Air Vice Marshal officer was seated next to him. On his right was the Chief Medical officer, who she recognized from the base. The airwoman they had seen in the car sat at a small desk by the window to record the discussion.

"Welcome, welcome," boomed the Air Field Marshal standing up and coming to shake them all by the hand. After that introductions were made to the colonel and Ms. London, who like Justin, Ben and Janet, they had already met on several occasions. Then they were led to the chairs facing the window and the proceedings started.

"I understand that Mr. James Pollack is in quarantine at your house down in Windsor, so he won't be joining us," the Air Chief Marshal stated, to which Janet nodded her agreement.

"Well then, before we start, let me first explain why we have convened this meeting in a small house at the end of a runway and not in the conference centre at the airfield. Today we're going to discuss matters that only five years ago would never have been discussed openly before. We know from the work Colonel Harris and his team do down in Woolwich that alien craft frequent our skies most days, while our own planes are forced to sit on the ground," he reported and explained more.

"Ever since the US Director of National Intelligence assessment of the threat posed by unidentified aerial phenomena, or UFOs, changed in June 2021 to clearly pose a threat to national security, we have been following this closely here. We now know that the people who fly these craft, better known to you as aliens, can control our emotions and have the ability to bury our memories of them. Accordingly, we have taken special measures today to protect these discussions, so that none of this can reach any of these persons outside," he said and asked the man in a white coat to turn on the equipment. When nothing untoward happened, he sat down to look at his notes and started the proceedings, with a nod to the woman taking the notes.

"Perhaps I can start with you, Mrs. Romford. Can you stand up and explain how you came to have leased the plane from the American authorities. Let me see, before the comet impact," he asked.

"Yes, my private jet had certain time travelling abilities that interested the authorities. When I returned to the US the plane was impounded by NASA, so I've had a business relationship with the Americans for over ten years," she replied confidently.

"At what point did you learn that the US authorities might have UFO crash retrievals in their possession?" he asked.

"Oh! you mean at what point did I recognise that the US government stopped explaining away UFO sightings as hoaxes, delusions and witnesses labeled as drunks or mentally defective?"

"Please, Mrs. Romford, answer the question."

"My discussions with the US government are confidential. During my eight years in the US, I was invited by NASA to look at the UFO remains in Nevada on several occasions to comment on the propulsion, lift and anti-gravity capabilities they were trying to reverse engineer," she replied, the discussion getting off to a rocky start.

"Yes, I understand you had a frustrating few years there, but how did you learn of the craft we have here?"

"You have to understand that there are some aliens who have been trying to help us. Once the New York Times broke the story at the end of 2017 and leaked the AAWSAP report, I was told by someone in Washington that they had another alien craft that had been moth balled in a hangar for years and never been flown."

"That was the Ariel Phenomena Task Force report, for our minutes, was it," he asked, nodding to the secretary.

"Correct. When I made more inquires I hit a brick wall, but then I got lucky, as on my next invitation to Nevada I met someone who confirmed that this craft not only existed, but with all the hype about UFOs they didn't want to test it in the US and I saw my chance to lease it for testing in the UK. That was agreed at the beginning of 2030 and a US cargo plane brought it over to the airbase here in June 2030. I'm sure you have a record of that in your files," she explained.

"Who was this person you met in Nevada, an investigator, a top scientist, or someone quite different?"

"No, someone quite different, as I'm sure she was an alien, or at least a time traveller. She took me to see the plane and I photographed it and showed the pictures to NASA, who then agreed to negotiate. Her name was Jessica Loeza and she had worked with James Pollack some fifty years ago in London. You see, not all aliens are dangerous like you said, there are several types of aliens that have several different agendas," she replied and sat down looking indignant.

"Very well. Thank you, Mrs. Romford, and now can we hear from Ben Romford who was the pilot of the plane last night. Whose idea was it to fly to Canada, and who authorized the mission?" he asked.

"The mission was authorized, or at least requested by Colonel Harris as explained to me by James Pollack, after his visit to the Army headquarters in Woolwich. I think the co-ordinates for the target in Montreal may have been provided by Ms. London, but she can confirm that to you shortly," he replied.

"You think that you really did fly back in time almost a year to June 2030 to meet members of the British Royal Family, because some of the discussions here today sound quite bizarre to me."

"Yes, sir, we did. That's quite clear from the cargo we brought back in the plane. Royal papers from years ago and a red dispatch box with the initials of E.R, our last queen," he replied.

"I understand that you stayed in the cockpit seat the whole time, so you never heard any of the conversations, but what did you see?"

"Yes, sir, that's correct. I landed the plane on an incline sideways on to the Royal family so I could watch Mr. Pollack all the time. He was concerned that persons there might try to abduct him."

"And did that happen?"

"No, sir, but they did have bodyguards with them who looked like 'Men in Black' if you know what I mean. I saw him shake hands and then sat down on the grass to talk to the couple. From his body language, he explained who he was and where he had come from. They didn't seem surprised to see him at all, as if they were waiting for someone to come. There was a bit of shaking of heads and then the bodyguards came forward carrying the cargo and papers. James stood up and followed them back to the plane. I opened the passenger door and the cargo was loaded onboard. I watched as James walked around to the other access door, waved goodbye and climbed aboard the plane again."

"How long do you estimate the plane was on the land in this past dimension, as you call it?"

"Probably not more than ten minutes, and I kept my flying mask on all the time. The boffins here installed more than thirty minutes of oxygen on the plane for the pilot," Ben explained.

"Can you explain how you can fly around in this plane with only thirty minutes of oxygen to Canada and back?"

"Yes, because the plane doesn't fly around in space like you think. It uses something called a *Flex Transfer Event*, that opens a wormhole. It's something that's been funded by the US for over thirty years, trying to replicate it."

The man in a white coat nodded in agreement and Ben continued, "As soon as I input the coordinates we jump back through time and space. It's instantaneous, one micro second in Canada and the next landing at my mother's house in Windsor. It's something difficult to understand, but I have done the same with jumps back in time to Portugal, and even back to the island of Montserrat and it worked every time." Ben sat down to applause from his mother and some of the others.

"From the discussion we have heard, I think we need some more explanations from Colonel Harris," the Air Marshal requested.

"Thank you, Air Marshal, for giving us the opportunity to discuss these matters in an open forum. My command is a large area south of London from Kent across to Salisbury Plain, where most of our pre-cataclysm regiments are still based. In the past this region was the bread basket of England, but not anymore. Most of our military patrols are helping farmers find tractors and agricultural machinery that can be operated after the CME, distributing food and fertilizer to try and restart agriculture again."

He paused for breath and continued, "The one factor missing, and a factor that has held our country together for centuries, has been our Royal family, a figurehead who can lead the military and our people. So when Ms. London proposed the possibility of returning a member of the family I was interested in the idea and we started "Project Mongoose," he explained.

"That's a curious name, but we've had worse in the RAF. But how did you know where in Canada this family would be, after they left in June 2030? I'm starting to find this all difficult to understand." He looked across to his personal assistant taking the notes.

"Let me explain as a military man. If an alien force wants to invade and control another planet, there are only a couple of options. Number one is to attack and destroy the whole planet's population to take control by force, but leaving the aliens with no workforce to control. The second option is to covertly infiltrate over a long period of time using abductees, both male and female, to create a new breed of humanoid hybrids that look like us, slowly integrated into our society but still under the control of the aliens."

"Yes, that's almost certainly the way it's been done using telepathic control of the human population. Go on," the scientist said.

"To put it in simple terms, after the cataclysm there was no human society to integrate into our planet anymore. With the population of the UK reduced by fifty million or more and the world's population estimated to have been reduced by billions, these hybrid people are left without support from their creators. Our patrols often find many of these people wandering around on the roads looking lost. No one will take them in with the shortage of food, so our patrols take them to what were hospitals or abandoned open prisons to live together," the colonel explained.

"And then what happens?" he asked, but the airwoman taking the notes jumped up.

Pulling open her dress uniform she lunged at the colonel, and looked him in the eyes, whereupon he collapsed on the floor.

Immediately, Jana stood up and shouted to all at the meeting, "Don't look at her eyes, she's a hybrid."

Justin launched himself at the woman, but she avoided him and ran towards the outside door, followed by Justin. When she got outside the house there was a soldier with a rifle on her right who she immobilized, but the other soldier on her left fired a round that hit her in the head. Justin watched as she fell to the ground. After taking a closer look at the body, he went back to the meeting inside where everyone was helping the colonel to his feet.

"You need to know that this person was shot outside and is now dead," Justin announced.

People went back to their seats and the medical officer helped the Colonel resume his place.

"What happened? I don't remember anything. What are we doing in this place, Ms. London?" he asked looking around.

"I'm sorry, but my assistant assaulted you and Justin here probably stopped the worst of the attack, you don't remember that?" replied the Air Marshal.

"Hold on. Yes, I can remember events from the past quite clearly, but little since being here," the colonel said.

"If you are able to continue, Colonel, how do you rate our planet's survival now," the Field Marshal asked.

"We are finding that these bigger tic-tac machines are landing and taking their hybrid people back to their mother ships. Same with the recent landings at GCHQ – they appear to be taking all hybrids back from there as well," he replied.

"Do you think that the invasion from these aliens is over or just delayed?" the Chief Field Marshal asked.

"No, most certainly not over, but delayed as they realise our planet is not quite as easy as they expected. Now that these hybrids have been exposed it will be more difficult for them in the future."

"I must apologise for the interruptions. I've had my suspicions about my PA for a while but didn't realise she had infiltrated our high command so well," he said.

"Dangerous, if you ask me. If she had made it any further outside it would have alerted the aliens for certain and we would have had flying saucers on the runway before long," the colonel replied standing up.

"Thank you, Colonel, for your analysis of our current situation. Now can I call on Ms. London for her opinion on the recent events," he asked.

She stood up and spoke to the meeting. "Some of you have met me before, as in my present role I work closely with Colonel Harris on security in and around London. My other job after the flood has been to transfer all Home Office electronic data onto a new data base close to London City airport. It has not been easy to find technical people with most of London still flooded at high tide, but I have been able to make contact with someone you would call a time traveller."

"You don't mean to say that you're now working with aliens?" Colonel Harris interrupted.

No, no. I had a visit from Nathalie Boyana, who some may remember as the daughter of James Pollack."

"Yes, I remember. Wasn't she someone high up at the National Laboratories in Albuquerque, New Mexico," the colonel replied, but Janet interrupted the conversation.

"That's impossible. Nathalie Boyana left on a mission to an exo-planet ten years ago. How's it possible that you met her in London so recently?" Janet asked.

The scientist at the table spoke. "There are many ways to time travel, some using portals from another planet in our galaxy. NASA had a propulsion unit to warp space-time, using negative energy to produce a stable wormhole passage and that was back in the 1990s."

The Air Chief interrupted. "Yes, I remember, the European Space Agency's spacecraft flew together with NASA around a wormhole that opens and closes on an eight-minute cycle. This may not be all science fiction after all, and explains why so many UFOs find it easy to visit our planet. But please continue, Ms. London," he said.

"Janet, I can understand your doubts. But remember, that was a covert European space project that went badly wrong. After some recent difficult events, she wanted permission to return with the survivors to our planet now," she explained.

"That's not going to happen, the ESA is no longer active here in Europe. What did you tell her?" The Air Marshal demanded.

"I explained that our planet's badly damaged and gave her the co-ordinates of Janet's house in Portugal. From what I understand there's no one living on the island of Culatra anymore. That should be a safe place to land to return the survivors."

"Colonel Harris, what do you think of this development?" the Air Marshal asked.

"Not sure, but I think we should consider a plan with NATO to get down there to meet them," he replied.

"Yes, there's an old Douglas C-47 plane in a museum close by. Remember, it was used during the last war, no electronic equipment so it might just fly today. That carried thirty of our troops, so we could take it down to Portugal and bring the whole team back here. The only question is will it still fly?" the Chief Marshal said.

"You're the only people who can get down there with your vintage plane. But do we know how they will travel back, and when we can expect them?" the Colonel asked Ms. London.

"No, not a precise date. With time travel, dates are changing all the time, but they appear to have access to some small time travelling machine that can bring them all back together," she replied.

"You mean something like that 'tic-tac' device that landed on the island of Montserrat," he asked.

They were interrupted by a knock on the door. One of the marines entered and spoke to Justin.

"Excuse me, Captain, but there's a nurse outside who wants to speak to you," he said.

Justin got up to leave with the Head of Medical behind him, and saw Michelle outside the house, looking distraught.

"Something happened down at Janet's house?" he asked.

Janet, Ben and Jana stood in the hallway with the colonel in the doorway.

"Yes, it's James. I came as fast I could on the back of that motorbike," she said, pointing to the bike with the postman on the runway. "James got up this morning, feeling better. Then he told me he needed to go back to the house and just disappeared. Is that normal?" she asked.

"Yes, it is for James, but where's he gone to?" Janet replied.

"Could be back to Portugal, as I also think he's taken your plane, Janet," Ben replied pointing to the craft hovering above the airfield.

"Oh, no! Looks what's happening now, his plane is being surrounded by blue orbs of light," Janet said in a low voice.

"Yes, I think they have found this location. Everyone back inside the house, including you, marine. Come on inside, quickly now and let the soldiers outside shelter inside too," shouted the colonel.

Everyone returned to the meeting room and shut the door.

"What am I going to do about all my people and staff at the airbase?" the Air Marshal asked.

"There is nothing we can do. If those orbs see us outside driving down the runway, they'll alert alien craft to come and intervene. Our patrols have seen them close to the GCHQ. When we tried to launch missiles they all failed and only attracted these orbs to come and investigate. We can only hope that James has managed to draw them away and we might be safe again," the colonel told everyone.

"What exactly are these orb things anyway?" Justin asked.

"They're some form of surveillance device controlled by these intelligent beings, a bit like the helicopter drones we use. But they have a high energy, so if they touch you it has caused cancer in my men and death in few months," the colonel explained.

"Right then, if the cloaking device is still operative outside, we stay here and hope we're hidden from them," the Air Marshal said.

"Yes, sir, it's working at full power," the scientist reported.

"Then, Captain, tell the men to keep a watch on events at the back of the house and perhaps the ladies could make us all some coffee," the Air Marshal asked politely, smiling at everyone again.

"Yes, I'll go and show them the kitchen," replied Ben. He turned to give Michelle a big hug and slowly people started talking together and to relax.

Justin went to check the windows at the front of the house, where everything looked quiet and he thought they had been very lucky.

PART SEVEN
JUNE 2061

34 - PYRAMID

The sea washed over the body of Nathalie as she sank further down from the surface and the submarine left her behind. Far off in the distance, she heard a voice calling out to her. At first, she ignored it, let it just wash her away, but it was insistent, shouting at her.

At the edge of her awareness, she opened her eyes to see a row of lights deep in the water below her. Someone, or something, was following her downward path, so she was not alone in her dream. Concentrating all her mental powers she decided to jump through time and space to see where she landed. Finally, as she started to breathe again, she felt hands dragging her across a solid deck and she was placed in a sleep pod, until everything went black.

Tia, the pilot of the tic-tac, closed the lid of the pod, turned on the power, checked that enough oxygen was being supplied for a recovery and set the temperature to a normal level for an advanced humanoid hybrid. Knowing that any recovery would take at least six to twelve hours, she walked back across the passenger deck and climbed the stairs to the control room, shaking her head.

The last message that she had received from Nathalie was a cry for help and she was thinking – over and over again.

Yes, I'll help you, do whatever I can do… for Nathalie. Something must have gone very badly wrong to have been thrown off her own ship. A mutiny, by the humans, it could never have been her Amarna crew after all these years. She would only find out if and when Nathalie recovered. In the meantime, there was no choice but to keep following the submarine from a safe distance and see if others would be tossed into the sea.

As soon as the ship had left the island Tia had followed behind it, underwater and unseen. She had tried to repair some of the damage to the tic-tac that Kiya brought back, but it needed a major overhaul to put it back into working order again. Then on the first night, running short of food and water, she decided to act. Rising to the surface she set new co-ordinates to her home planet where she knew the old craft could be repaired.

Arriving back less than a day later, Tia continued to follow the submarine in a new craft that came with executive seats in the main passenger compartment, the latest cryogenic sleep chambers, and a week's supply of her favourite food and drink. The control room was also the latest design with a row of ports to help with landing and take-off and sofa beds at the back for sleep and relaxing. Having found the submarine again, she set her new tic-tac (mk 4) on auto pilot and waited. In fact, she didn't have to wait long when an alarm sounded that something was in the water close by. It had a sort of a human form but when she looked outside, she could make out the shape of a woman, someone she knew only too well.

Nathalie hugged the blanket tight around herself. She had been woken up by the sleep chamber that automatically opened when she had recovered consciousness. Looking around the chamber, she thought she must be in the passenger compartment of some large transport craft with all the rows of seats in front of her.

She kept replaying the moment that she had hit the sea and plummeted down into the depths below. The water that slammed into her body felt solid, not liquid at all and after that she must have blacked out for a few moments, until she saw the lights.

From high above her on a platform she saw a familiar face. It was Tia looking down at her who waved with joy and ran down the stairs of the compartment to greet her.

"Nats, Nathalie! You're alive and woken up at last. I thought that was the last we would see of you," she exclaimed.

Nathalie shook her head in amazement at her recovery.

"Come on, let me help you stand up and move you to somewhere more comfortable," Tia said and they started to climb to the top of the stairs where the control room was situated. "Slowly now, it's in here," she said as the door hissed open and they entered a circular room with four small windows above a control panel of switches and dials, and two bunk beds at the back.

"What is this place, and where are we? Under the sea?" Nathalie asked.

"Yes, this is the latest tic-tac craft that I traded in for the old one Kiya brought back. I've been following your ship on the surface for days, but it's so slow and almost driving me mad. That was until you suddenly appeared. Tell me what happened, a mutiny, or is the ship damaged?" Tia asked, sitting her down on one of the beds and giving her a big hug.

"I don't know, except it was Kiya. Did you know she's pregnant?" Nathalie exclaimed.

"Really, expecting a baby, our first in over twenty years, I can't believe it," Tia replied smiling. "The father must be Captain Claude?"

"Most likely, and the baby has been playing havoc with her mind and her hormones," Nathalie added.

"You realise the child will be a humanoid in every way with both telepathic and verbal speech, but very independent," Tia replied.

"Yes, I think it tried to kill me already," she said.

"Really, whatever did you do?"

"Remember when I sent Kiya back to our planet Earth on the old tic-tac craft? I think it must have upset the child, as Kiya drugged me and put me in the cold chamber on the ship," she said.

"But how did you end up in the sea?"

"I don't know. Things had gotten out of control just before we left the island. Claude was running around with a pistol, saying he was leaving me behind. Anita and most of the crew were terrified of him," said Nathalie. "Anyhow, someone must have dumped me overboard, but you saved my life, Tia, by following the ship."

"It was complete luck that I saw you out of the windows. But what do we do now?" she asked.

"We've no time to waste on these past events. We need to concentrate on what to do with the whole exo-planet team. Basically, their job is done. They are all desperate to return home and we need to protect the Amarna crew from any more fighting onboard," Nathalie explained.

"But the ship still has two more days before it reaches our destination, assuming that the captain doesn't make any course changes. What do you need to do?"

"I need to get back onboard the ship again, talk to the exo-team to calm them all down and explain how they will return to Earth. We already have possible co-ordinates for a landing site, so can you plot us a date to return two days from now?"

"Yes, that's all possible. Getting you back onboard will not be so easy without exposing our presence to all the crew."

"But you have been in contact with Scota, haven't you?"

"Yes, of course. She knows you are alive and onboard here. If we do it at night and land you on the after deck only Scota and her crew will know what's happening."

"All right, let's plan for that to happen at three tomorrow morning assuming the weather is still calm on the surface. If you can drop me off in a sleep pod, none of the crew will be certain who's coming on board. Then I can make my presence known to Claude and his team in the morning."

"That's going to be quite tricky, maneuvering this tic-tac alongside a moving submarine and holding it steady for long enough for a pod to be carried onboard, but I can try my best."

"Good, let me get some rest until then. Please, can you tell Scota what we plan to do in the morning?" Nathalie asked smiling and fell back onto the bed from exhaustion.

Early next morning, Tia woke Nathalie with some herb tea and they went over the plan again.

"I looked at more details of this new craft and there's a lock-on device that might help to keep us alongside the ship," explained Tia.

"You mean something like a tractor beam to attract the ship and lock it onto the tic-tac?"

"Yes, maybe, but I've never tried that before, so I don't know how powerful it is, or if it really works."

"Let's try it. Now, can you move the tic-tac up behind the ship and slowly rise to the surface to see what the state of the sea is outside? Looking at the time on the ship it must be almost 3 am, so how do we know if Scota is ready in her place?"

"She said she will shine an orange light on the rear deck to let us know. If you come and look out of the windows you can see we are coming up on the ship now. Let's turn on the tractor beam and see if we can get alongside to slow her down," said Tia, who activated the beam to pull them alongside the ship.

"Yes, I can see an orange light on the deck. Come on, it's time, I get into the sleep pod below," Nathalie shouted.

She ran out of the control room, down the stairs and placed a pod on the floor close to the entrance door. Tia helped her inside, then went back upstairs to open the outer door to allow the transfer to the ship.

Everything looked to be going to plan. The door of the tic-tac opened just as two of Scota's women ran across the deck, took hold

249

of the pod and dragged it down onto the deck, where they attached it to a line of rope. Tia watched as Scota pulled on the rope and the pod was moved to the after-entrance door and the crew returned close behind. Then the whole ship was bathed in a green light from above. Tia closed the outer door, cut the tractor beam and slowly the tic-tac disappeared below the waves.

"What in our maker's name is that thing?" Scota shouted at her crew members above the wind and the sea spray. Looking up they could see something in the sky as big as a building, with four flashing red lights on each corner of a huge craft following the ship, just a few hundred feet above them.

"Come on, let's get inside quickly," Scota ordered, closing the outer door.

Her two crew members carried the sleep pod down the stairs to the galley and placed it on the bed in the makeshift hospital. Closing the door behind them, Scota opened the lid of the pod and helped a very relieved Nathalie sit up.

"Thanks, Scota, for rescuing me, but what was that green light I saw once you got me onboard?"

"That, Nathalie, is who we are going to have to meet when we reach our destination. You don't think they gave Tia the latest craft without an agreement, some sort of pay back. Now one of us is going to have to convince the Galactic Federation to continue with the Amarna project in order to let the Earth people return home," she explained, but Nathalie could only look at her, confused.

****

Meanwhile, up on the bridge of the ship, Claude watched the lights above him in amazement as one red light turned into three in a triangular formation. Then more red lights emerged on the leading right-hand edge, six more bright red lights with a green glow on the water below. When more lights appeared on the left side, he could see it had the shape of a pyramid. This was a full-sized pyramid, magnificent and majestic like a giant building appearing from out of the sky.

Claude grabbed his binoculars and looked closer, realising there were others on the bridge now. The pyramid was turning very slowly anti clockwise and swung down almost to the sea in front of the ship, until it righted itself.

"Has anyone ever seen anything like this before?" he shouted at the group of people watching from the windows.

"Yes, Claude. South Wales in 2016, a similar pyramid craft was seen one night and chased away by planes and helicopters. That convinced the ESA to start this project to an exo-planet, in case you don't remember," replied Susan, as the pyramid fired a bright green object out of the top that hovered above it.

"Look, I think it's going to crash into the sea," Anita said, but then it ejected a band of lightning and the lights changed colour from red to bright white. The brightest lights illuminated part of the sides of the pyramid to reveal that it was a solid craft, as if it was made of stone. Slowly, the pyramid moved away from the ship, leaving behind the green light hovering in front of them. There was no noise, nothing from the pyramid craft as it moved away and Claude turned on the lights on the bridge to see who had come up to watch.

"Anyone see anything down below, before the light show started outside?" Claude asked.

"Yes, I heard a huge noise in my cabin as if we had hit some object in the sea, and came up to see what was happening," replied Bee, but then everyone turned around and gasped when they saw Nathalie standing at the door to the bridge.

"Nathalie, I don't believe it. We all thought you were dead," Susan exclaimed and rushed across to hug her.

Claude and all the others hung back and looked at her in disbelief.

"Well, well, Nathalie, I must say you have done well to remain hidden onboard all this time, so why make an appearance now?" Claude asked.

"Why now? Because I have found a way to transport you all back to our planet Earth, for those who want to return. But you will need to justify your reasons to that higher intelligence you just saw outside. If you don't believe me, try to turn the ship, Claude. Try to stop the engines, flood the ballast tanks or open the outer doors, because your ship has been taken over by that green light hovering outside," she said.

Everyone could see that not only was Nathalie back, but in charge once again. Claude was glaring at her, his eyes bright with rage.

"We will continue this discussion in the morning at ten, when you will have had time to think and I will explain how and when you can return," Nathalie said and turning she went below to her cabin.

"How did it go with the team, were they shocked?" Scota asked, sitting at the desk in Nathalie's cabin.

"Half-half. Claude thinks I've been hiding onboard all this time, the others not so sure," she replied and sat down on her bunk to rest.

"I've been talking to Tia on your communicator machine. She's plotted a course for the tic-tac that can take you back to planet Earth on the first of July 2031, if that means anything to you," Scota said.

"Wait, that's after the cataclysm when the planet will still be badly damaged. No NASA, and no governments to protect our people. Is that what the team gets after ten years on another planet?" she replied, and then continued, "Please can you ask Tia to find something about this space rock that hit planet Earth. I have to give the team some news."

"All right, but if they go back before, no one will believe them anyway. Look, Nathalie, don't be so hard on yourself. The project has been a success. You proved that humans can live on another planet with us hybrids and survive despite everything that was thrown at us," Scota added.

Nathalie burst into tears. "All right, I know stay positive, but what are we going to do about Kiya?" she asked.

"We can't hide her away. Why don't you confront the problem head on and go and meet her? She will be on duty in the galley from six and should be alone until the crew eat breakfast at seven." Smiling, Scota covered Nathalie with a blanket and left her to sleep.

When Nathalie awoke, she saw the time was past seven on the ship's clock in her cabin. She remembered she should have met with Kiya but couldn't face talking to her so early in the morning.

On a side table was a paper that she hoped would provide her with the information she had requested and she eagerly read the report.

*Scientists announced in April 2022 the largest comet yet discovered, about 75 miles wide and travelling at 22,000 miles per hour from the Ort Cloud. NASA's official announcement confirmed it would miss the Earth and safely pass by in the year 2031. The comet impacted on the Earth's surface in summer of 2030…*the report ended.

'What, what! No, that can't be true, there must be some mistake,' she said. She stood up, shaking at the news, and threw the paper on the floor.

She felt dirty after all the time she had spent in the sleep pod with Tia. She tore off her navy shirt and pants, removed her underwear and went for a shower, washing her hair several times to remove all the grime. Returning to her bunk, she dressed in clean clothes and had sat down to think when there came a knock at the door and Scota entered with two mugs of steaming drinks and a plate of bread and jam.

"Good morning, Nathalie, good to see you are up and about already," Scota said smiling, then seeing the paper on the floor, she sat down beside her.

"Scota, I can't give the team that news if they are going to return after the impact. Susan will see that the flight path of the comet must have been changed by what, more intelligent aliens?"

"You don't know that. That comet might have glanced off a planet or a moon on its flight into the inner solar system, we don't know," Scota replied.

"No, and we can't change events that happened thirty years ago. Did you tell your crew about the lights last night?" she asked.

"Yes, but they already knew – word travels fast amongst the Amarna women, as two crew members saw the lights of the Pyramid. I confirmed that we would reach our destination tomorrow where the humans, sorry your earth-team, would leave to return home, that's all," Scota explained.

"And Kiya, was she there?"

"Yes, and looking radiant with her pregnancy. Why don't you come down to the galley and talk to all the crew before your meeting at ten? You can give thanks to Tia and confirm that she now has a tic-tac that will be a great help for us all in the future," Scota said.

"All right, let me drink this tea first. It would be good to get out of the cabin and walk around again," she agreed.

"Keep it informal and thank each of the crew for their work on the ship if you're thinking of returning as well."

"I don't know where any of us will be going back to after last night," she replied and they both stood up to walk down to the galley.

After talking to the Amarna crew for almost an hour, Nathalie finally came face to face with Kiya.

"Kiya, I know what you did, what do you have to say?" she asked.

"I was worried that you would try to separate me from Claude again as he must be the father... I'm sorry, I shouldn't have done that," Kiya replied with tears running down her cheeks.

"Apology accepted, but can we make a truce and stay out of each other's way from now on?" Nathalie replied and giving her a big hug, she stood up to leave.

Feeling much more positive, Nathalie was ready to face her own team on the bridge of the ship. Some minutes before, Scota had asked Toby to join them and they had both made their way upstairs. When they entered the bridge, the whole team were already assembled, looking at the green light in front of the ship. Nathalie made her way to her chair on one side and sat down.

"Thank you for coming to discuss what I hope will be the final phase of this project, your return to planet Earth," she said opening the discussion and then continued, "Since I left the ship two days ago, I was onboard a new and more advanced tic-tac that's piloted by an experienced captain, who some of you know as Tia. Based on her calculations it will be possible to return to an agreed co-ordinate on the planet on the first of July 2031, for those of you who want to return tomorrow," she explained, as she looked at all the eyes staring at her.

"That, ladies and gentlemen, is the good news. I regret to tell you that since you have been away, your planet was hit by a comet with a core some 75 miles wide. It was forecast by NASA to never get closer than a billion miles away from the sun. We believe that this comet impacted our planet in the summer of 2030, causing massive damage to coastal areas and the loss of a way of life that has changed everything you knew before you left," she said pulling a folded paper out of her pocket and smoothing it out on her knee.

"Do any of you have any questions, because I'm here to help and will try to answer them," she said, passing the paper to Susan.

"Well, yes, is there not any update to this report, and do we know the extent of the damage?" Susan asked.

"Yes, Tia has been looking, but since the date of the impact there have been no further human transmissions detected from the planet.

255

The report we have was sent out in 2022, forty years ago, and nothing since," Nathalie replied.

"You said a co-ordinate had been agreed, do you know where and by who it was agreed?" Claude asked.

Nathalie looked flustered. "Roughly, yes, although I'm not familiar with it. The proposed landing site is an uninhabited island off the coast of southern Europe. I'm afraid I don't know with whom it was agreed," she replied.

"Wait, I have a question," asked Anita, looking at the others. "You said you found no further human transmissions since the impact, but have there been other transmissions from the planet?"

Nathalie's face screwed up as she put her hands to her face and her face crumpled with tears. She finally answered just with just one word, "Yes," and then she composed herself and tried to continue. "We have only found traffic that's coming from unidentified aerial phenomena," she said to all on the bridge.

"You mean UFOs, don't you," Susan asked and Nathalie nodded.

"That would make perfect sense, to have a landing site away from possible interference from these UFOs. Sounds to me that our return from this exo-planet has just become a lot more covert. Someone, somewhere on the planet is being very careful to keep our return a secret from people who might want to do us harm," Claude advised, smiling at everyone. He went on, laughing, "Come on, everyone, let's return. Let's do it. It can't be any worse than the past year here," he said.

Nathalie saw a hand go up at the back of the group to ask a question.

"I've never been to your planet, but I know my brother went there, so can I go to see if I can find him?" Toby asked.

"Yes, of course you can go, Toby, and any of the Amarna women would also be welcome to leave," replied Nathalie, looking around for any more questions.

"Nats, it's clear you don't know what to expect, so why don't we just take a chance. We travel back in time and see what kind of reception awaits us. If we find no one on this deserted island, we can always come back here, but at least we will have tried," Claude said.

"Yes, Claude, you are right, I don't have all the facts. But I think I've given you enough information to help you make a decision, so let's close this meeting for now and let you go away and think about the choice," Nathalie said.

Climbing down from her chair and walking towards the door, she left the bridge to the others. Once back in her cabin she found Scota sitting inside, waiting for her.

"So, how'd it go?" Scota asked.

"About as bad as I expected. Claude thinks he can leave and if it doesn't look good, he can come back here again. He has no idea about time travel. This is a one-way trip back to 2031 with no return, it's not like a ferry service," Nathalie said.

"Did you tell them that?"

"No, of course not, but I told them about the alien craft on the planet."

"Nothing new about that, we've had these people visiting us all my life," replied Scota, giving her a big hug. "Come on, let's go down to galley and see what's for lunch. The important thing is to appear to be calm, even if inside your life is going to hell in a handcart!"

"Wherever did you learn that expression? You know it's a very human phrase," Nathalie replied laughing, and they went down below to find something to eat.

But life onboard didn't continue as before. A much-reduced lunch and dinners were served at the usual times and the watch keepers kept a lookout on the bridge, but saw no other ships or any land. Most of the Amarna crew kept to themselves in their cabins or in small groups, discussing the uncertain future as no one knew what to expect.

After lunch, Susan went to speak to Nathalie in her cabin for more details.

"Have any conditions been set to allow us to return to our planet?" she asked.

"Not yet, any conditions will be given when Tia meets with members of the Sky Council tomorrow," Nathalie replied.

"Is that something we can talk to them about?"

"No, you can't talk to them. They only communicate telepathically and will tell us what we must do."

"Have you ever seen these people; do they look human?"

"No, they are not human, Susan."

"Are they Reptilian hybrids, who can shape shift as well?"

"Yes, they are dangerous, but have been fair with us so far. You must tell your team to respect whatever they ask," Nathalie replied and said she had no more answers until they arrived.

It was early the next morning that land was sighted right ahead of the ship. At first, all they could see were high mountains covered in green vegetation, but slowly a coastline appeared and a town of stone houses with a harbour. All of the exo-team gathered on the bridge to watch their arrival, while Scota detailed two of her crew to go forward and aft to secure the ship with ropes. As they entered the harbour the ship's engines stopped and Claude realised, he had control of the ship again.

"Slow astern both engines," he ordered as their ship gently came to rest against the quay. Scota and her team went ashore to secure the mooring ropes. Nathalie, up on the bridge with the others, looked at the port. The place appeared to be deserted with not a person in sight. Then she saw the pyramid high up on the top of a hill, its stone work glinting in the sunshine.

So, you're still keeping an eye on us, she thought.

Anita shouted to everyone and pointed to the quay opposite their ship. Sitting on a jetty was a small tic-tac with its outer door open and a collection of empty chairs arranged in a circle. Sitting on a chair in the centre was Tia, who looked to be reading a book.

"What the hell is Tia doing here already?" Anita asked.

"I think she's come to take you back home. Come on, Claude, Anita, let's walk over and ask her," Nathalie replied, and the three of them made their way down to the cargo deck to go ashore. When they reached the deck, Toby had already lowered the ramp to let them walk onto the quay.

"Wow, it's good to be back on dry land again," Anita said as they walked along the quay.

"Anita, if we do get back home, I'm thinking I might date you again," Claude said smiling at her.

"No, Claws. What about your girlfriend with a bun in the oven?" she replied.

That amused Nathalie walking behind them.

"Kiya, that's pure speculation," Claude said, and she smiled, thinking perhaps things were getting back to normal between them.

When they arrived at the tic-tac, they both waved but Nathalie ran on ahead to greet Tia and sat down on a chair next to her.

"How did it go? Did you meet the intelligent beings from the pyramid?" Nathalie asked.

"Let's wait until your friends arrive and I will tell you everything," Tia replied as Claude and Anita took seats in the chairs.

"In all my hundreds of your earth years, I have never been so honored to meet with them as today," she exclaimed beaming at them.

"You mean they came down here to talk to you?" Anita asked.

"Yes, Anita, the Sky Council came down here and sat in these chairs. But you don't talk to these people, it's done with telepathic communication. We are a hybrid people who can speak and talk telepathy," she replied.

"Yes, yes, but what about us? Will they let us leave to go back home?" Claude almost demanded.

"They told me they have been following our ship for the past year and insist that both Claude and Anita must return to help rebuild the damage to your planet. The rest of us are free to choose. They are giving the Amarna women the right to live in this deserted port and make it their home with a safe place for the ship," Tia explained.

"How much time do we have to decide?" Nathalie asked.

"Not a lot. As the pilot of this craft, I need to leave at twelve noon in your time to make the connections in the time continuum. It's not that simple to travel back to 2031. So please, return to your ship, gather your personal belongings and come back here before noon. You should tell your team members to hurry if they want to leave as well," Tia insisted, and they looked at each other in surprise.

"Well, Claude, it looks like you got your wish to leave," Anita said.

"And you too, Anita," Claude replied, laughing in fear, as he knew he was staring down the barrel of a gun.

"Right then, come along. Claude, can you help me carry these chairs back on board the craft? The rest of you might like to see how you will be travelling. You can bring something to eat and drink. You won't need it for the time jump, but to refresh you when you arrive. Remember, no weapons are allowed onboard, warm clothing and a blanket to travel is all you will need," Tia explained, and they all went inside to look at the accommodation.

There were four rows of seats for as many as twenty passengers and more sleep pods on the rows behind. When Claude touched the metal construction it felt so smooth, like nothing like he had ever touched before and he realised this craft was from another world.

"Tell me, Tia, have you done this before?" Claude asked.

"Why, are you getting nervous, Captain? While you were sailing in your ship at what, fifteen units of speed, I took the old tic-tac back to our home planet in the constellation of Arcturus. There I exchanged it for a smaller model, returned and followed you underwater for days. So yes, I have done this before," Tia said smiling and led them back out onto the quay.

"You have one hour and thirty minutes to return here if you want to leave," she shouted at them as they walked back towards their ship.

When they reached the ramp, Scota had all the female crew lined up and saluted him. "I'm sorry, Captain, but we can't allow you to come back on board," she said.

"Ah yes! It's that telepathy thing, isn't it? So, you're staying here with the Armana women," he replied.

"Yes, of course, all of us except Kiya, Toby, and Nathalie, who has other duties to perform on your planet," Scota replied.

When they saw Susan and Bee coming down the ramp with their two children Nathalie ran forward to help them. Both of them were holding just one bag each and a blanket, and as Susan approached them, she had tears in her eyes.

"It's hopeless to argue, Claude. They won't let us take any of the scientific data on this planet I have saved for months. Anything electronic cannot travel and none of my notebooks will survive the time difference," she explained.

"Don't worry, you can always write it down again when we get back," Claude replied, trying to put a positive note on the situation.

He turned to face Scota again, but she had read his mind.

"Captain, it has been our pleasure to serve with you on our ship *The Destroyer*. You have taught us many things from your planet, how to sew our shirts and pants, how to tell the time on your strange clocks, but most of all you have taught us how to smile and laugh. It is with some sadness that you leave us today, so we want to give you, Anita and of course Nathalie some small gifts to remind you of the time you have spent with us."

261

A crew member came forward and gave each of them a bag and a blanket.

Both Claude and Anita turned and saluted Scota and went to shake the hands of each crew member, while Nathalie went to give Scota a big hug. After that they each picked up their bags and started to walk back to the tic-tac, ready to return home.

"Christ, Claws, what do you make of that? We came here to rescue Susan and Bee with nothing and are now leaving with a bag and a blanket," Anita complained as they walked back along the quay.

"Don't think like that, you know they can read our minds. I'm no longer worried about the time travel, even if we survive that. I'm more worried about what happens when we arrive. You heard, a drink to refresh you when you arrive on a deserted island – that perhaps has no water. We have women and children to care for and it sounded as if we are being thrown out of the place here," Claude replied.

"Look, Claws, I know we've had our differences in the past, but can we sit in the back row of the seats for this return journey?" Anita asked.

"Yes, no problem. I just want to look in my bag to see how much water we have been given," he said as they arrived back at the tic-tac to meet Tia again.

"Wonderful, back already, that's really good. Now your baggage has already been approved so I can lead you to your seats in the front row, if you come with me," Tia requested leading them onboard.

"Now Claude, according to my onboard computer that takes into account your size and weight, you have been assigned this seat here," she said, pointing to a front row seat at the end of the aisle.

"But Claude and I were hoping to sit together," said Anita.

"No, I'm afraid that's not possible. You are also in the front row at the other end," said Tia, looking sympathetically at her.

Reluctantly, Claude took his seat and placed his bag on the floor between his legs, while Anita went to take her place. Meanwhile,

Susan and Bee came onboard with their children and occupied the row between Claude and Anita. Susan was sitting next to Claude, Bee next to Anita, with the two children in the middle.

"Claude, I see we have all got front row seats for this journey. Do you have confidence that it can travel through time?" Susan asked.

"We checked the craft out earlier, and I'm sure we can all survive, I'm just not sure what happens when we arrive," he replied.

"Did you see that Kiya and Toby were on the boarding list, but have still not arrived," Susan replied.

"Yes, and neither has Nathalie. Apparently, she has other duties on our planet, which leaves me in some doubt of what's really happening," he replied.

"Yes, I heard that as well. The people in that pyramid appear to be helping the Amarna women, but do we know if they will help us on our planet?" she replied

Toby appeared wheeling a metal hand barrow with a sleep-pod that he took to the seats behind the back row.

"Do you think that's Kiya inside the pod? But why send her back? It's as if wonders will never cease," Susan said smiling at Claude.

Finally, Nathalie appeared and went straight to the children to check they were all right. Then, waving at Claude and Anita, she went up a staircase Claude hadn't noticed before.

"Looks like Nathalie is travelling first class up in the control room. Do you get the feeling that our project has been stage managed since we left Amarna, or am I missing something?" Claude asked.

"But then, why send us back to a damaged planet? Is it to get us to do the fighting against aliens that the pyramid powers can't be seen to be opposed to in their galactic world?" Susan asked.

The outer doors closed and lighting in the passenger compartment was reduced to just strip lights on the floor.

"I would really love to know the science behind a time jump," Susan said, and after a short wait the craft started to vibrate with more and more energy and then lifted into the sky.

"Looks like we're leaving," Claude replied, and everything went blank.

PART EIGHT
JULY 2031

35 - RETURN

Perhaps, James thought, this was always how it was meant to end. Most towns and cities had fallen apart, people had moved back to the country to survive and grow their own food. Only the military had access to the dwindling stocks of fuel and supplies.

James looked out at the coast line as his craft hovered over a huge pile of debris just outside the town Olhoa on the coast of the Algarve. He needed to land in the sea if he was to shake off what looked like blue orbs of energy around his plane just before he jumped. Pushing his craft forward, he moved further offshore to some blue water close to the island of Calutra and let the plane slowly descend into the water. There he sat on the sandy seabed, put on his oxygen mask and watched as the bubbles of energy rose off the hull of his craft.

So far so good, it didn't look as if he had been followed, and he finally relaxed and let his mind wander. A voice in his head kept repeating a message of the first of July, the first of July. He knew that must be coming from his mind reading partner Jana, but what was so special about the date? He couldn't understand her message until an image of a tic-tac flashed into his mind and he knew what was going to happen.

First of July, the island of Calutra, that's where they were going to land, he not only thought but knew, and that was only in two days.

Did Janet and Ben know of the date? Did the army know of the location and were they going to prepare for this event? Seeing that his oxygen was being used up fast, James decided to do a quick jump over to the remains of Janet's house on the island to see for himself.

Resetting the location and the date to the morning of the first of July, he pressed the button and waited, to find his plane hovering directly over Janet's house where one side of the house was now covered with green vegetation.

This looks much more promising, he thought and let the plane slowly descend and land beside the trees. It was only when he switched off the power that he saw two men dressed in white suits come forward with a ladder to help him climb out of the craft.

"Good morning, sir. You must be James Pollack; we were told to expect you. We urgently need your advice on the preparations we have made for the landing site. If you can come with us, please," James was told to his relief.

"Yes, of course, but how long have you been here?" he asked.

"Only a couple of days, we came over on a boat from Faro with two water bowsers as there's no drinking water on the island," he said, pointing to a small camp site they had made in front of the damaged house. "You've been here before, have you? It was quite a popular place before the tidal waves destroyed all the houses," he went on.

James looked out across the island beneath the bright sun, still covered in flat sand with a few tufts of grass growing in places. "But who are you? Who gave you the orders to come on down here?" he asked.

"We're part of the local NATO force. We got our orders direct from the HQ in Brussels," the man explained, and walking out onto the sand he pointed to the preparations they had made.

"We have painted white markers on the sand for about half a mile and built this landing pad all painted white as well. What do you think – will that be enough to land one of these UFOs?" he asked from where they stood in the middle of the white landing pad.

"It's absolutely brilliant, but do you know when this space craft is expected to land?" James asked.

"No, we thought you would have more details. We were told you have been on one of these things in the past. Will it make a lot of noise and dust when it lands?"

"No noise, maybe some dust with all the sand here. Once it touches down the craft will need spraying with something liquid. Sea water will do if your fresh water is limited," James replied.

"Right, we already have that in hand. Come on, let me take you over to see our field hospital where new arrivals will be screened for onward transportation," he advised.

"You mean there're more people coming here?"

"Yes, of course, they already landed at Faro airport and are on the way here as we talk," he said.

They entered a hospital tent where coffee and refreshments were laid out on a folding table.

"Let me sit down and think about this more clearly," James said sitting down in a canvas chair and accepting a cup of coffee.

All he needed now was for the tic-tac to actually arrive. It doesn't matter how hard nature pushes the human race down, someone, somewhere, will always survive to create a way of life again.

The tent was baking hot, but their wait was broken by a man running in and shouting that an orange flare had been seen from the airport.

"Excuse me, sir, but that means an unidentified flying object has been spotted over our coastline and is heading this way. We should all take to our posts outside. Please, can you talk to the people on the alien ship when it touches down?" he asked.

Everyone finished their drinks and filed outside in their white suits and helmets to watch the arrival. James walked back out to the landing pad and waited to see if he could spot the craft coming in from the west.

He was still wearing his pilot's jump suit and thought he would look ridiculous to anyone piloting the tic-tac, but that was better than having an army by his side. When he spotted the craft, it was already at 300 feet and slowing down fast, following the white markers, before it came to a stop and landed right in front of him. He noticed that once again the air was filled with static electricity and his hair was standing on end as he took a few more paces back.

This was not the huge tic-tac he had been on in Montserrat; this craft was much smaller with four window ports at the top, above the entrance door. Feeling relieved, he waved at the pilot, smiled and gave a thumbs up sign in a gesture of friendship. Meanwhile, the ground crew were busy with the water bowsers, spraying jets of water onto the cylinder. James moved back even more to avoid the spray. Then he patiently waited for the outer door to open.

When nothing happened for another ten minutes, he walked back and stood right in front of the door, hoping someone would come out to talk to him. When a small door opened, a person he had known in the past appeared.

"James Pollack, whatever are you doing here all alone?" she asked.

"Same as you, waiting to greet your exo-team after what, ten years, so why don't you open the door?" he replied.

"But where are all your people, the army with all their weapons, or don't you have that anymore?" she asked tauntingly.

"We mainly have a lot of alien visitors who drop in to steal our water, mutilate our cattle and abduct our people, is that why you're here?" James replied sarcastically.

"No, so who are all the people in white suits, what's their purpose?" she asked.

"Medical staff for the field hospital they set up to check on who you're bringing here, humans or hybrids. We see a lot of greys on our planet now. Small greys, tall greys, Reptilians and hybrids, can't be too careful after the cataclysm we had," he replied.

"Come on, James, I'm only bringing back the four humans who were on the exo-team, and their two children," Nathalie said, but James was getting messages from Jana that there were more.

"Really, so what about the one at the back in a sleep pod?" he replied, guessing from the messages he saw in his mind.

"Ah, so now you're reading my mind," she shouted at him.

"Please, Nathalie, open the door, there are young children inside and we need to take care of them," James asked again.

"What if I refuse, and we leave again for another location where you can't stop me from letting these people go?" she threatened.

"Of course, that's your decision, but I think you have left it too late for that now." James pointed across the island to where four open jeeps were racing across the sand with their blue NATO flags flying at the back, followed by an old army truck.

Nathalie turned and raced to the door, but James tackled her to the ground to stop her getting back onboard. The door opened again and Claude appeared, closely followed by Anita. Claude pinned her to the ground while Anita tried to bind her hands with some rope. Finally, the outer door opened and the rest of the team appeared at the entrance, looking on in fear. Two of the men in white suits ran forward and took the hands of Susan and Bee holding their girls and ran back to the safety of the hospital, when James thought to introduce himself.

"Hello, my name is James. I don't think we have met before, but welcome back to planet Earth," he said, to which they both just laughed.

Meanwhile, Janet and Ben appeared at the side of the cylinder to see what the delay was and came forward to talk to James and Nathalie.

"Nathalie, why were you fighting with James? What's the meaning of the delay to open the entrance door?" Janet asked.

"I think I can explain. Nathalie's got more than humans onboard her craft and may be trying to infiltrate some kind of hybrid onto this planet," James explained.

"We've seen that before at my airbase," exclaimed the Air Marshal, who now appeared with Justin and Colonel Harris at his side.

"Is anyone willing to go inside and see who else is onboard?" he asked the crowd of people.

"Yes, I'll go and have a look," said James.

"No, I think we know the people onboard. Let Anita and me go and bring them out," Claude said and they walked towards the entrance again.

After a short wait, Claude appeared with an old man pushing a hand cart with a sleep pod.

"This is Toby, our ship's cook, quite harmless, and in the sleep pod is a pregnant woman who is probably carrying my child," Claude admitted.

Anita appeared with another older woman. "And this is the pilot of the tic-tac who has flown us halfway across the galaxy. Perhaps she should be allowed to stay if she wants to," Anita announced to a round of applause.

"Come on then, let's go and celebrate your return," said the Air Marshal pointing the way to the field hospital, where water and refreshments had been moved onto a table outside the tent. There were chairs for the travellers to sit in and admire a view of the blue waters of the Atlantic Ocean.

At the same time, unseen to all who had returned including Nathalie, the army truck had pulled up behind the cylinder. Soldiers from NATO jumped out and started to erect transponders on the four corners of the cylinder that would provide cloaking from any alien craft. The same scientist from before opened a pack of cigarettes, took one out and quietly started to smoke. Shortly after, an engineer started an electric generator at the back of the army truck, connected the cables and the transponders went live.

While all of the humans passed the medical examination in a matter of an hour, it still left the medics with the sleep pod and the other hybrids to consider. Nathalie had been sedated and remained unconscious on a table inside the field hospital. Outside, sitting at the table with Claude and Anita, was the Air Marshal and the colonel who explained the difficulties of flying an aging museum plane down to Portugal.

Meanwhile, the scientist from Harlow walked down to the group sitting outside the hospital and, catching the eye of the Field Marshal, gave him a thumbs up sign that he acknowledged.

"What was that all about?" Anita asked.

"Aliens, short or tall greys, whatever you want to call them, they destroyed the remains of our government and took over our security centre," he said, reaching for a beer.

"But you have counter measures, surely," Claude said.

"Some, it's a cloaking device. We just installed it around that craft out there. Whether it works is another matter," he replied.

Outside the hospital, Justin approached James and asked him where he had parked his plane.

"It's beside Janet's old house. Why, do you think there are others on the island?" James asked.

"I don't know, but there are too many people here we don't know anything about, and I don't think the children should spend the night on the island."

"Okay, can you go and talk to Susan and Bee and tell them of your concerns, please? Explain that I can fly them back with their children to a secure airbase in England before it gets dark tonight. I agree after what happened today that we should get them off this island on Janet's plane as soon as possible," James said.

"Right, I'll go and talk to them now," he replied and walked off to find them, while James went to wait beside the plane. After ten minutes, Justin returned with Susan, Bee, the children and Ben.

"James, we all think it's a good idea, but would you mind if I flew them back to the airbase? It's Michelle, you know she's pregnant and may be worried about me," Ben said.

"No, not at all. Probably better if I keep an eye on things here anyway," James replied and bent down to talk to the girls.

"I'm going to help you get on board this plane with your mums and this man here is going to fly you at a very fast speed back to England in time for a cup of tea. Is that okay?" he asked, to which they both nodded.

"Right, Ben. If you can open the passenger compartment, I'll place the ladder for them to climb on board," he said.

Ben hoisted himself into the cockpit and the two women climbed up the ladder to board. Then James passed the two girls up to their mothers inside. Once all were onboard, James stood back as the engine started and the plane rose in the evening sunshine and disappeared.

James turned to find Justin standing beside him. "It's that woman you call Nathalie, she's disappeared from the hospital," he said.

"Of course, she's disappeared, Justin. She's a time traveller, as soon as she regained consciousness she jumped. The question is where?" James asked and continued, "Come on, let's check out the tic-tac as the most likely place. Maybe she wants to leave the party early."

As they ran back towards the landing pad one of the medics came out of his tent and confirmed that the other old hybrid man and the old woman had gone and the sleep pod was empty. When James and Justin looked at the landing pad it was also empty. The tic-tac was gone.

"We need to tell the Air Marshal right now," exclaimed Justin, and they ran back to find him.

On hearing the news Colonel Harris went to see the evidence in the field hospital with Justin, closely followed by James, Claude and the medic.

"Looks like that old man opened the sleep pod," said the medic.

"Yes, but look at these tracks in the sand. Those are the prints of a three footed reptilian, definitely not a female hybrid," said Justin.

"If that's the case, we have one of the most intelligent aliens loose on the island. Remember, this alien can shape-shift into a tall humanoid and pass undetected to most humans," replied James.

When the Air Marshal heard the news, he ordered the field hospital and the camp to be shut down before dusk.

"I don't want any of my men to be left on the island during the night. We must take full security measures to ensure that alien doesn't infiltrate any of our vehicles or the landing craft when we leave," he ordered, looking at the faces of Claude and Anita in the fading light.

"Where exactly are we going?" asked Claude.

"And what about Susan, Bee and the children?" asked Anita.

"Don't worry, Anita. They have already left the island on a sonic plane that was hidden behind the house. It has room for two adults and the children and should be back in England by now," James replied.

"As to your question, Claude, first we return by boat to the airport at Faro. It was badly damaged by the flood, but the runway has been cleared and we can fly out of here on an old Douglas airplane we told you about," Colonel Harris said.

"Justin, how long will it take to pack up all the tents and leave? I want us all back at the landing site by sunset," the Air Marshal said.

"Not more than half an hour, sir, but we need to pack up your table and chairs now."

"Very well, we all need to move, ladies and gentlemen," Colonel Harris said.

"Might I suggest that you all make your way to the Land Rovers and I will stay to load the last of the tents onto the army truck," Justin said.

"Very well, be as fast as you can," replied the colonel and waved at the army truck to come down to the house. When it reversed to load the tents and equipment, he saw it was already fully loaded with the transponders and the generator and shouted at the men to off load them.

"We're going to have to leave this equipment behind. With the extra passengers it will be too heavy to fly back to the UK. Anyone got any ideas what to do with it?" he asked.

James raised his hand. "Yes, can we install it inside the old house here? It might even trap that reptilian after we leave," he said.

"Very well, you have precisely five minutes to get that set up again," replied the colonel. Justin could see what James was thinking and helped carry two of the transponders inside the house, while James sought out the scientist.

"Can you come and manually set the equipment at maximum force?" he asked.

"Yes, that's possible, but that will kill anything that enters."

"That's exactly what we want to do," James replied.

Another two transponders were placed against the rear walls and the wiring was connected again to the generator placed just outside the entrance.

"Wait a minute, I have another deterrent," shouted Justin. He ran inside with two land mines and carefully placed them at the entrance under the sand on the floor. Running back outside again, Justin shouted it was all clear to start the generator. Now the colonel smiled at what he saw was a deadly booby trap.

"Do you think the noise of the generator may attract the alien? There's only enough fuel for another couple of hours," the scientist explained, climbing into the front of the truck with Justin.

"Maybe, but we hope to be far away from here by then," the colonel replied as the last of the soldiers piled into the back of the truck. Justin started the engine to leave but saw James toss the two halves of the sleep pod inside the house and run back towards the truck.

"James, whatever were you thinking, you might have set off the explosives. Come on, climb aboard now," Justin ordered. The truck started to move forward and James jumped onboard.

"Yes, but if that reptilian came out of the pod it would have its scent all over the casing and might attract him back inside," James explained.

The truck bounced over the uneven sand towards the landing beach by the sea. When they arrived, the first landing craft was just leaving the shore with the sun setting in the west. The men in the back piled out and the colonel went to talk to the leader of the local force. They could see the second landing craft was almost aground with a falling tide.

When the colonel returned, he explained the situation. "We're going to have to leave the truck here and wade out to the landing craft, or we'll be stuck here until tomorrow's tide," he reported.

The men started to wade out into the shallow sea. The scientist looked at Justin and realizing he couldn't swim; Justin gave him a piggy back before they went into the water.

James made a short jump through time and was the first back on the craft. He started the engine to make sure it was not fully aground, then put the landing craft into full reverse and coaxed it back into deeper water. Turning the craft, he lowered the front door and went back to pick up all the men. When all were onboard, he handed over to a local man to steer the craft back to Faro.

About halfway back across the channel, or the Ria Formosa as it's known locally, they saw an orange flare in the sky above them to indicate another UFO had been spotted. All eyes were trained on the western sky, but this time the flying object was very large. It was like a giant building that had flown into their space. As it got closer, it became clear it was a full-sized pyramid almost as big as Calutra island itself, now receding in the distance.

In the twilight they could see red lights all along its perimeter as it hovered above the island near Janet's house. It swayed in the air as it came in to land and remained stationary for a few minutes. Then a bright light was seen over the island and a few seconds later they heard a tremendous explosion as something was detonated on the island.

"My god, Justin, was that the land mines that exploded?" the colonel asked.

"Could be. I think it's taken a direct hit to its hull," he replied.

The huge UFO ejected two hands of lightning and the pyramid became brighter as one side crashed into the ground. Twenty orbs came out of the top and exploded all across the island. Watching with binoculars, Justin saw that some fell into the sea on the other side of the island. Looking up behind him, Justin saw the scientist was taking pictures with an old movie camera.

"Hey, my friend, do you understand what's happening?" he asked.

"Yes, the transponders have injected too much energy into the craft, now it will either crash into the sea or explode," he replied.

As they watched, the pyramid slowly turned and dipped down on one edge, and all they could see was one side high up in the air above the island. The rest of the pyramid was out of their sight and must have fallen into the sea on the ocean side of the island. Clouds of steam filled the air all along the coastline and travelled towards them.

"Captain, can you fire a red distress flare towards the airport at Faro?" Colonel Harris asked, but the chief of the local forces had already opened a rocket and fired it towards the mainland.

Smiling, he came over to talk to them. "Congratulations to you both, it looks as if your small booby trap may have damaged that huge alien craft. Do you know where it came from or which intelligent beings were piloting it?" he asked.

"No idea, but I read recently that there are four hostile civilizations in the Milky Way that are ready to invade Earth. I think we have now identified two of them, the Greys and the Reptilians. You should be very careful about going back to that island for some time," Colonel Harris replied, shaking the hand of his local partner.

"Don't worry, we are not normally active along this coastline and spend more of our time at a base up in the hills over there." He pointed inshore and they saw it was snowing from the clouds.

"What the hell is this stuff, snow?" he asked, turning to his scientist.

"No, it's not snow or even made of ice," he replied, rolling some of the stuff in his fingers and watching it crumble away. "It's been seen before from encounters with these large pyramid craft in South Wales. Not dangerous, but most likely it has come from that alien craft that's been damaged." Everyone stared back at the island, now completely covered in cloud.

As their craft neared land, a lookout was posted on the door at the front to warn the helmsman of debris floating in the sea. They reached the landing place on the mainland in another half an hour and found two of the jeeps empty and waiting for them. Justin drove to the airport and without any perimeter fence, continued straight onto the runway, also covered in the white 'snow.'

Waiting on the tarmac next to the aging plane was the Air Marshal, with his RAF team and Claude and Anita.

"Did you see that huge pyramid UFO over the island?" Colonel Harris shouted, jumping down from the jeep.

"Yes, we saw it and our two travellers here say they saw the same pyramid craft on the planet they just returned from," the Air Marshal replied.

"What about the explosion, did you see that as well?"

"No, the two here wanted us to drive as far away as possible. They think these people are very dangerous."

"We set a booby trap with the transponders and landmines and our man here thinks the craft was badly damaged. It was lying on its side and half in the sea the last we saw," the colonel explained.

"My god, you did that! Now we really do have to leave tonight. Come on, let's get all your equipment loaded and get onboard for the flight back to our airbase," the Air Marshal announced.

"Do you really think that's a good idea to leave tonight? We have no Satnav or directional beacons anywhere across Europe, unless you let me help fly the plane," James said.

"All right, Mr. Pollack, you appear to be able to fly your hover plane all over the planet, but what makes you think you can navigate this old lady back to England?" the Air Marshal asked.

James just pointed to the sky, and laughing, ran up the boarding stairs to the plane where he sat down in the cockpit next to a much older RAF pilot.

"There you are, ladies and gentlemen, a true pilot if ever I saw one," the Air Marshal said and they followed James up the stairs.

Claude and Anita sat alone at the back of the plane while the front rows were filled up with the RAF team, NATO soldiers and Justin's marines. The Air Marshal and Colonel Harris sat in the front row next to the cockpit.

"I don't know about you, but I never went on a transport plane as old as this," Anita remarked.

"The French military had some pretty bad army planes that often crashed," Claude replied giggling.

"Stop it, Claws. So, what did you think of your first day back on planet Earth?" she asked.

"I'm not sure what was the best part. The fighting with Nathalie was good. Was it you who pushed her overboard?"

"Yes, Claws, it was me. The only question is, how did she get back on board again?"

"Back to our arrival – it looked quite well organized until the cavalry arrived and we lost the tic-tac people. After that it was pure chaos, just like on the ship."

"At least we know that Kiya never came with us, or her baby," she said smiling.

"Yes, and to think that Nathalie was made to bring a Reptilian onto our planet. Do you think the pyramid ship came back to pick up the alien? Is that possible?" Claude asked.

"But to have damaged something as big as that flying pyramid, we all saw. That's not likely, is it."

"I'm not so sure. That science boffin was playing around with some kind of transponder force field over the tic-tac. If they left it active and anything landed close by, it might have caused a big explosion."

"You mean like a booby trap or something?"

"Yes, maybe something like that. Listen, the engines are starting. Have you ever been on a twin engine prop plane before? It's quite an experience," he said as the noise at the back increased to stop most conversations.

The aging transport plane taxied to the end of the runway. The pilot opened the throttle and it raced down the runway. The plane lifted into the air and quickly turned north. When Anita looked out of the window it was already dark outside and she had no idea where they going, except what she had been told, somewhere in the south of England.

THE END

ONE MONTH LATER

Susan was sitting in the front garden of the little house at the end of the runway. The August sunset cast a golden light across the fields below her and she caught the scent of the wild grass growing in them. White clouds billowed across the Thames valley. She could still not believe how lucky they had been to have returned to this airfield on the Chiltern hills, surrounded by English countryside. After a while Bee came out into the garden to sit beside her.

"I've put the girls to bed and they're asleep at last," she said passing her companion a glass of cold tea.

"Thanks, I'm really enjoying life here," she replied.

Everything had worked out for the best. Ben and his partner Michelle had decided to move into married quarters close to the airfield hospital, as her baby was due in another month. When their house became vacant, they had wanted to move in straight away. Although the house was a bit small for a family with two children, they were still not ready to integrate back into human society. Susan needed somewhere quiet to write a report on the exo-mission.

At first, the authorities were not happy with the idea, but Justin could see that the house was just the place for them to adjust to life back on the planet. After some deliberation, Susan announced that she and Bee could not write a report living in the glare of service personnel and they accepted their request to move to the house a month ago. What she didn't tell them was that she had brought back her notebooks, together with Nathalie's logbook, smuggled in the bags they had been given.

Not all her notebooks had survived the time transfer, but the logbook and photos were good enough to start work on the report. Justin had provided her with an old laptop that included a word processor and she had started writing with haste. There was no internet or WIFI, but she found working offline with an English keyboard easy.

Justin came in person most mornings, bringing food and supplies, and sometimes two takeaway meals from the NAAFI. It was no surprise when he appeared one morning with a black cotton cover over what appeared to be a briefcase. They sat together in the sitting room as he placed it on the table. Removing the cover, they saw it was a battered red dispatch box with the initials E:R embossed in gold on the front.

"Wherever did you get that from?" Susan asked.

"It was given to Ben and James on a flight they made to Canada," he replied, but gave no further details.

"But the initials E:R? That box belonged to Elizabeth Regina, the last Queen of England, yes?" Bee asked.

"Yes, and it's been opened and studied by the scientists here who think you should consider the papers for your report," he replied.

"No! No way, this is going back way too far," said Susan.

"Susan, trust me, I have looked inside. There are no confidential documents of State inside, just scientific papers on that comet that hit us," he replied, opening the box and handing the top document to her.

Susan's eyes opened wide as she read the report that stated astronomers had confirmed the biggest comet yet discovered was headed to the inner solar system, from images taken by the Hubble Space Telescope. When she searched for the date, it was confirmed on January 8, 2022.

"The Heads of State knew about this ten years ago?" Susan exclaimed, handing the document to Bee.

"Not only that, but NASA's official announcement said that it will never get closer than a billion miles from the sun," said Bee.

"Something must have gone seriously wrong. Let me study the papers, maybe there is something more I can find," Susan replied, closing the box again.

"Oh, a couple more things. The Air Marshal is asking if your presentation will be ready by the end of the month," Justin said.

"Yes, Justin, tell him it will be ready. Anything else?" she asked.

"Both Claude and Anita are asking if they can come and visit you here," Justin said.

"And what has Claude been doing for these past weeks?"

"He wants to transfer to NATO in Brussels. I think he's only waiting to hear your presentation before he leaves."

"And Anita?"

"She's been working with me on security for the base and training some of the Air Force regulars. Why don't you see her?"

"All right, but just Anita. Wait, why don't I meet her in that canteen place of yours? I can give her an advance copy of my report at the same time and get to be seen by some of the air force people," Susan replied, standing up to thank him for his visit.

"Are the girls doing all right down here?" Justin asked as he was leaving to which both of them answered that they were fine, and he left.

Susan sat down and looked at the red box again before turning to Bee. "Coffee, Bee? Can you bring me a strong cup, it looks like a long morning of reading."

"Why the sudden interest to meet with Anita at that canteen?" Bee asked, bringing two mugs of coffee.

"You realise that once I present my report we will probably be forced to leave here? I want you to come with me, and the children, to go and check out that kids' creche close by," she replied.

"Okay, but what's the rush with that, we've seen it already."

"I want you to contact that woman who lives with James, to see if we can meet him here alone," Susan explained.

"Yes, I remember how he stood up to Nathalie, as if he had known her for years. And then he offered to bring us back here on that plane so maybe he knew the pyramid UFO would appear. Do you think he knows a lot more about what's been going on in the past, and perhaps in the future?"

"The best way to contact him may be through his partner at that kiddie's playgroup where she takes her daughter. I think her name's Jana. We need to find out where James has been for these last weeks," Susan replied.

Two days later Susan and Bee, with their two girls, sat in the back of Justin's open jeep and drove down the runway towards the centre of the airbase. The sun was shining, and although not the end of August, Susan couldn't remember the south of England being as hot as this before. Justin pulled up outside the NAAFI social club and they all made their way inside to find Anita.

She was wearing her army fatigues and sitting at a large empty table at the back and waved at them as they entered a largely empty hall.

"Hi, you guys, you've missed the morning rush so we can sit here without being disturbed. Now, let me look at you two girls. Wow, looks like you're grown since I last saw you," Anita said, giving each a kiss, while Susan and Bee sat down opposite her.

"My mummy's taking us to play with some other children so we can't stay for long," said Bee's daughter.

"Yes, I thought to take them over to the creche, and let you two talk together," explained Bee.

"Right then, off you go. You remember where it is, right?" Anita asked and Bee smiled and nodded at her.

"Everything all right, Susan? You two look worried," she said.

"Yes, well, I brought a first draft of the report I've been writing. I thought I should let you see it before I hand in a final version," Susan said, handing her the document.

"Wow, the title *Life on Earth 2.0* is pretty bold, isn't it. I don't remember it being anything like that," Anita said smiling.

"The title is what the scientific community were searching for with SETI, before we left."

"Oh, you have a copy of those photos you took on the island. How did you manage to smuggle those out?" Anita asked, opening the report.

"Yes, I took Nathalie's camera and the images were still intact."

"Let me get us both a cup of coffee and you can explain," Anita said, getting up from her chair.

When she returned, she could see that Susan had been crying. "All right, Susan. I could see that both of you look worried and I know that when you are worried, I should be too. Come on, spill the beans," Anita insisted.

"No, no really, it's just all been too much, coming back here with the girls and seeing you again," she explained.

"So why the sudden interest in the kiddies' play group, are you hiding something?"

"No, not really. Well, there are so many things that don't fit together since we got back. I mean, I want to meet that pilot we met when we first landed. You know the man; I think he's called James. Do you know where I can find him?"

"Maybe you are right to be concerned. I have seen him before, and he always appears to be around when Nathalie comes on the scene. All I know is that he's working with that army Colonel down in London but have no idea when he may be back. Let me ask Justin and I will let you know when I have some news. Now then, take me through this report of yours line by line, as I want to understand your thinking, of why you sound so worried," Anita said.

****

When Bee entered the creche the two girls whooped with joy at all the children and the activities.

"Hello, I'm Bee and these are our two girls. Can I let them play with the other children here?" she asked one of the assistants.

"Yes, of course, you're most welcome to stay for the morning if you want," she replied.

"Thanks, that's most kind. Also, I was hoping to meet another of the mothers by the name of Jana, if she's here."

"No problem, she's right over there," she replied pointing to a woman looking out of a window.

Bee walked over to introduce herself but before the woman turned, she spoke to her first.

"I know who you are, Bee, I can read your mind. Don't go looking for James, you should be looking for Nathalie," Jana said abruptly.

"You know all about us already?" Bee asked.

"Yes, but we can't talk here. You have to follow me outside," she replied and started to walk towards the door.

Bee ran over to the assistant to say she would leave the girls for the morning and ran outside after Jana to follow her. When she got to a side gate of the base, the guard asked her name and looking at a list gave her a salute. Once outside she found she was on a leafy road with townhouses on one side. Standing at the entrance of one of the houses was Jana, so she continued walking. When she reached the house, the front door was open so she peered in and found Jana sitting inside.

"Come on in, my dear. Come and sit with me on the sofa. This is Janet's house; you may remember her from when you landed. I live here with James," she explained and continued as Bee started to panic, "No no, don't be afraid, I'm going to help you. Perhaps a glass of white wine might help calm you."

She stood up to fetch a bottle from the kitchen, pouring them both a glass and drinking hers down in one gulp.

"What I'm going to show you is something that came with the plane you flew on back here with Ben. Do you remember?" Jana asked.

Bee nodded and drank her wine more slowly.

"While you have been away, was it really ten earth years, some people here like Janet have been busy. She acquired a plane that was given to us by some friendly aliens, to put it simply," Jana explained, helping herself to another glass of wine.

"You don't mean those people on that huge pyramid craft we saw on another planet?" Bee asked.

"No, not them, they are most dangerous. But let me show you what happened after you landed again," Jana said opening a black tablet that was sitting on a low table in front of them. "Now then, cast your mind back to when you landed on the island, as this device only works with your brain memories."

Bee thought of the past event but nothing happened until she remembered the screams from her daughter, and the screen lit up. At first it was just a flicker of light, then when the entrance of the cylinder opened, she saw Nathalie and James fighting on the sand.

"Good, good, now focus on Nathalie," Jana said, but Bee said she couldn't do it any more, it was too frightening.

"Don't worry, now I have the image and the time, I can help you find where she went after they left the island," said Jana, playing with the controls and thinking deeply as the screen lit up again.

Bee watched in amazement as first Nathalie ran back to the tic-tac craft. Nathalie was closely followed by Tia the pilot, and lastly, hobbling behind the two was Toby, the ship's cook.

"That's amazing, but do you know where they went?" Bee asked.

"Patience, my friend, let's see if I can find that for you," she replied as the screen lit up again.

This time it showed an image above a city as the craft descended onto what at first looked like wasteland with stretches of water, and then a runway where the craft was landing.

"Wait, I have to see where Nathalie is going," Bee said.

The entrance door opened and Nathalie was welcoming onboard an older woman. When the door closed and the screen went blank, Bee drank the rest of her glass of wine and collapsed back on the sofa.

"Jana, do you know who that person was?" she asked.

"Yes, of course, that was someone called Ms. London, a representative of the British Home Office and held in high regard by the Air Force base here," she replied.

"Is that known to James? That she's an infiltrator? Is that what James has been working on in London?" Bee asked.

"Exactly, my dear. Another glass of wine might help you now," she said, refilling her glass.

"What do we do now? Where I came from, we spent most of our time fighting off people and now it looks no different here," said Bee.

"Where do you want to go?" Jana asked.

"I don't know, somewhere off the grid where I can bring up my daughter without all this fear."

"I'll tell James. He will contact you and Susan when he's ready, so don't try to contact him again. Now, I think you should be getting back to your children, don't you?" Jana said making her feel guilty. "Wait, here, let me give you a new bottle of wine to take back with you to drink with Susan," Jana added, placing a fresh bottle in a bag and giving her a big hug.

Bee left the house and walked back to the airbase to find the children, who said they had the best morning ever. Making their way back to the social centre they found Susan waiting outside the canteen.

"My goodness, Bee, how did it go? You look a bit tipsy. Are the girls all right?" she asked.

"Yes, I had a few glasses of wine with Jana and found out things you would never believe," replied Bee.

Susan looked at the bag she was holding with interest. "What's inside the bag?" she asked.

"Present from Jana, a bottle of wine for us to drink tonight. How was your meeting with Anita?" Bee asked.

"Ugh, worse than I expected, let's talk about it when we get back. I asked Justin to meet us here ages ago, and look, he's arrived at last," she replied, waving at him.

Later that evening, once the girls had been put to bed, Susan and Bee sat outside in the front garden at their house watching the sunset.

"Tell me all about Jana, you must have made quite an impression to be given a bottle of wine," Susan said.

The bottle was open on a small garden table and they were enjoying the taste of chilled white wine on a summer evening.

"I don't know, she's not an easy person to believe. First, she could read my mind before we even met, so that was quite off putting. But I went to her house, well Janet's house, where she's living with James. It's very close to a side gate into the base that we've never seen before."

"Was James there?"

"No of course not. He's working down in London with that army Colonel we saw. But she explained that the plane we flew back on is another time travelling craft given to them by some helpful aliens. Do you believe that?"

"Yes, I knew they had that technology because we arrived here at the base almost before we left. What else did she say?" Susan asked, taking a taste of the wine.

"She had a device, about as big as a tablet, that showed me the past and the future. I saw us when we landed back on Earth. Remember James and Anita were fighting with Nathalie on the landing pad…"

"Bee, maybe you were drinking a lot of wine," Susan said.

"No, not at all, just one glass. I was very stressed, Susan."

"Very well, what happened next, you saw a future event?"

"Yes, I saw that tic-tac craft we flew on descend over a city and land. It must have been somewhere outside London, and Nathalie welcomed a woman onboard who is high up in the Government," Bee said, looking at Susan again.

"Calm down, Bee. I don't think we should be surprised if these aliens have tried to infiltrate the government and I'm sure James and the colonel are aware of it."

"You really think so? But I don't want our children to grow up with these aliens on this planet. Where else can we go?"

"That's a very good question, now listen to what Anita had to tell me about this comet that hit Earth. It seems everyone has read the papers in the red box and the BB comet," Susan said.

"Why's the comet named BB?"

"That's just the names of the two scientists who first saw the object coming out of the Ort cloud. Berardinelli and Bernstein if I remember from the reports, and it became known as the BB comet."

"So how did it change course and hit our planet? Bounce off one of Saturn's moons, made a glancing pass by Jupiter? Something must have altered its path to the inner solar system, Susan."

"That's what Anita and I were arguing about."

"Does she think it was done by the Pyramid people on that UFO we saw?" Bee asked.

"Not exactly, because it was reported to be moving at 22,000 miles per hour and I don't see why any aliens would want to destroy a planet as rich in water and minerals as ours."

"So, what then?" Bee asked.

"Really, I don't know. Anita's ideas about science are not the same as mine. She thinks that time is an illusion. From the science we've seen with these space craft we have little understanding of this or how people like James can move through time."

"Yes, that's what I told Jana and she told me to wait for James. He's going to come and take me and my daughter somewhere safe. If you don't want to join us that's up to you," Bee replied and got up to take the empty bottle inside.

Susan stayed to look at the stars as dusk fell, and thought of what Anita had told her from a discussion with Kiya. The question of how anyone could travel through time was difficult to understand, unless time was an endless feedback loop of some kind. *But in that case, the future would influence the past and the past influence the future*, she thought, *but that's too weird to grasp. So was our time spent on the other planet like a dream, a shared dream in a shared reality, where we created every moment of our time? No, that's ridiculous. But if our reality is made of information that's created by our own consciousness, did we ever really leave this planet?* she asked herself.

She was brought back to her place in the garden when she heard Bee calling her to come inside. When she looked up, she saw the planet Venus was following the sun down into the growing darkness in the west until it finally disappeared from her view.

****

A week later, Susan was sitting in the front row of the conference centre at the airbase, waiting to deliver her report to the assembled panel of dignitaries who would be sitting on a low platform. They were wearing some of Michelle's old clothes she had left behind at the house. With little choice of what to wear for the meeting she had gone with something more formal, white shirt and dark trousers. Bee was dressed in a cobalt blue kaftan that Susan thought was inappropriate, but Bee insisted she was not in the military.

Susan smoothed down her white shirt and squeezed the hand of Bee sitting beside her, as the Air Marshal arrived with Colonel Harris and four persons in dark suits. Susan didn't recognise any of them except the small man who was on the island when they arrived. The rest she guessed were probably scientists from the Harlow laboratories close by.

The presentation had been opened to only a few officer ranks at the airbase so the rows behind Susan were hardy full, including the front row where the chairs were labelled 'reserved' but empty of either Claude or Anita. Standing at the entrance to the hall was Justin in full uniform, and outside were two marines doing an identity check.

The Air Marshal stood up and made a short welcome to everybody, with a brief introduction of Susan's career with speculative science at CERN in Switzerland, without any mention of her exo-mission.

"We are delighted to welcome today one of Britain's leading Astro Physicists who has recently returned and is going to present her scientific paper entitled *Life on Earth 2.0*," he said.

Some in the audience clapped briefly and he sat down. It looked as if everything was going to plan as Susan stood up and went to the lectern at one side of the platform. But before she had a chance to speak, she heard a commotion at the back of the hall and saw James and Ben arguing with Justin, just before the lights were dimmed. A few moments later the General Alarm at the base sounded and everyone stood up to leave.

Bee immediately grabbed Susan's hand and pulled her towards the entrance. "I told you James would come for us," she shouted above the noise.

Everyone filed out of the room and they walked across towards the exit to join James and Ben.

****

Meanwhile. back in the conference room, the Air Marshal stood up and seeing that the room was now empty shouted at the marines to close the doors, leaving Justin inside.

"I want the airbase locked down until that hovercraft leaves with its passengers. No one is to come in here during our discussion, do you understand," he ordered.

"Yes, sir," Justin replied and saluted.

The people at the table looked at their copies of the report until the Air Marshal sat down again.

"Now then, where were we before that necessary interruption," he asked.

The leading scientist opened the discussions. "Thank you, Air Marshal, for the advance copies of this report that has been studied by my colleagues here…"

"Yes, yes, get on with it, man," replied the Air Marshal.

"Looking at the fifty odd pages of her report, there is no mention of any aliens. The author explains how they escaped on a ship, or a submarine I should say, with the survivors after an attack on their home base, by what sounds like a strong military force," he explained.

"What do you think, Colonel Harris?" the Air Marshal asked.

"That's true. It sounds similar to our situation here today, but where is your line of thinking taking us?" he replied.

"I know some of this may be hard to grasp, but from the description of the ship, although it may sound advanced, it's most certainly not an alien craft," he replied.

"Why is that so important?" the Air Marshal demanded.

"From what's stated in the report, there is a description of the ship's clock, exactly the same as the clock we have in this room. A time system based on twelve numbers and two equal periods of time. These events were recorded to have happened in the year 2062, and that made us start thinking," he replied pointing at the clock on the wall behind them.

"So, you're saying it's impossible that people living on Earth 2.0 would have the same time device as we have here in 2031? Did you reach a conclusion?" the colonel asked.

"Yes sir, a possibility, but not a conclusion. You see, it's not just the ship's clock, but many things in the report. The description of a star globe is similar to what we had on ships here fifty years ago. The images and the numbers she claims to have brought back have all been found on this planet. All of this leads us to think that this team of explorers may not have been on another planet at all. I know it may sound impossible, but it's more likely they were on our planet, perhaps even further in the future than they could understand."

"But that would make these people like time travellers. What about the moon that appeared on their planet every ten years that caused a cataclysm?" the colonel asked.

"Yes, a very good question. As you must know, our planet has similar cycles. Our planet has a cycle of extinction events that repeat approximately every thirteen thousand years. NASA did a lot of research back in the 1990s and found that this was caused when a dead binary star approaches on a distant orbit around the sun. The huge mass of this star heats up the sun and causes more volcanoes and earthquakes to occur on Earth. As we have all seen, if a CME is then released, it has a disastrous effect on the life on the whole planet."

"Do you think that this massive object, which I assume must orbit far outside our solar system, might have attracted the BB comet and caused it to collide with our planet?" asked the Air Marshal.

"Yes, that was exactly what NASA were tracking before the impact on their eastern seaboard, and sadly they have been offline ever since," he replied.

"But that's amazing, and we were never told." The Air Marshal looked upset but continued, "I remember now, confidentially, there were some top-secret reports from long ago by Admiral Hoover. He said that the 'biggest secret' was to do with the abilities and the power of the consciousness of these time travellers. He thought that many of the people on these UAPs were humans from the future and not extraterrestrials," he explained.

The lead scientist nodded in agreement.

"So, when the military found out these people were from the future, and they knew what these humans were capable of, everything had to be covered up," Colonel Harris added.

"Yes, if these people could rearrange the reality around us, as future humans appear to have done, that would give them the ability for time travelling and cause chaos around us."

The door opened and Justin approached the platform.

"Lieutenant Benbow, have they all left?" the Air Marshal asked.

"Not quite, sir, but they're all onboard. We're just waiting for your permission to let them leave," Justin replied.

"Permission granted. Once the craft is gone you can sound the all clear for the airbase," the Air Marshal replied smiling, knowing that the first part of his cover up would now succeed. The two remaining officers were military personnel, who he knew would be returned to their respective units in due course and cause him no further problems.

****

Once outside, Ben led the way across the base to the hangar where the hover plane was stored, but standing on the launch pad they saw the plane was ready to leave.

"Bee, tell me what's happening? I'm not going to leave without our children," Susan cried out loud. But the two big arms of Claude lifted her off the ground and carried her to the steps at the rear of the plane, where Anita was waiting.

"Your two girls are quite safe and onboard already," Anita explained as two smiling faces appeared at the passenger entrance.

"So, they're throwing us off the airbase like this, but where are we going?" demanded Susan.

"James is taking you to Janet's house on a tropical island where you and the girls will be safe. Janet and Jana have been there for a few days and will welcome you on arrival," explained Claude.

"This is goodbye forever?" Susan asked.

"No, not all. We will come and join you once things have settled down here. Then Ben and Michelle will come, as soon as her baby has arrived," Anita replied, and gave Susan a big hug. Bee had already started to climb the stairs to enter the craft and join her daughter. Susan climbed onboard.

Claude and Anita waved goodbye and went back to the hangar to find James, the pilot.

"You planned this all along, did you Bee? No wonder you're wearing a kaftan for the tropics," Susan said.

"Not really, it just happened. James only found out last week that the blast from the pyramid craft had moved the house back to Montserrat and he took Janet and Jana to see. They found it was just the same as ten years ago and they decided to move us there first," Bee replied.

"But what about language, food and schooling?" Susan asked.

"You said yourself, we can never stay here. Think about our two girls. They saw most of what happened on the ship and already entertained other children at the creche. Kids talk and tell parents who would then only gossip about us," Bee replied.

"And what about my research paper, what will happen to that?"

"Most certainly it will be studied, but then covered up. Your report cannot be admitted by any government and never on a military base. Perhaps parts of it will be released in ten years."

"What did I do wrong?"

"Nothing, it's what we all did wrong by coming back here," Bee replied.

They watched James walk out towards the plane. Behind him were Anita and Claude, carrying the two bags that had been given to them before. Anita climbed the steps to the entrance and spoke to Susan.

"Sorry about the delay, but we thought you should have the evidence you brought back last time, and we included the laptop," Anita said passing the bag to Susan, before turning to Claude to pass up a second bag.

"Bee, we collected some of the toys for the girls to play with from the creche," Anita said with tears in her eyes, and quickly ran down the stairs which Claude moved for James to climb into the cockpit.

"Tell me, Bee, what happens to this plane now?" Susan asked, placing her bag on the floor of the compartment.

"It's become an embarrassment at the RAF airbase, even before that incident in Portugal. The Americans want it back, but few here really want to hand it over. The best solution is to hide it on a British Overseas territory, far off the grid, for the time being."

"Sounds like there's been a lot of discussions going on behind my back."

"True, but you were so busy writing. I only heard bits and pieces recently and you should be pleased that Claude will take a copy of your report to NATO, when he goes to take up his duties there," she replied.

Postlude

Meanwhile, the two girls sitting on the floor opened the bag with the toys and laughed with glee. "Look, Mummy, I've got a submarine, just like we lived on that other planet," Susan's daughter exclaimed and they all laughed, until the entrance door hissed shut and they felt the engine start.

Slowly, the plane hovered up into the sky and they looked down on the base for the last time, until it disappeared in a flash.

ACKNOWLEDGEMENTS

Compared to anything else I've written; this book goes into a more speculative direction than before. I hope this story has answered some of the questions that were difficult to understand from the previous five books. I didn't consider linking UFOs to the characters until late 2021, when I started some UFO research. What I found was a much bigger story to tell you here.

Below are just a few of the sources I found helpful.

With thanks to the following for the inspiration.
- Richard Dolan – *Alien Agendas*, 2020.
- Ingo Swan – *Penetration*, 2020
- James Lacatski – *Skinwalkers at the Pentagon*, 2021.
- Paul Wallis – *Echoes of Eden*, 2021
- Caz Clarke – *The Pentyrch Incident*, 2021
- Andrew H. Murray – *The Last Day*, 2020.
- Freddy Silva – *The Missing Lands*, 2020.
- Ben Mezrich – *The 37ᵗʰ Parallel*, 2017
- Anthony Peake – *The Hidden Universe*, 2019
- Nick Pope – *Encounter in Rendlesham Forest*, 2014
- David M. Jacobs – *Walking among Us*, 2015
- Jenny Randles – *Breaking the Time barrier*, 2005.
- Zecharia Sitchin – *The Lost Book of Enki*, 2002.
- Timothy Good – *Alien Contact*, 1991.
- Michael Talbot – *The Holographic Universe*, 1996.